D1555256

Flawed Scales

Also by Freda Davies

A Fine and Private Place 2001
Bound in Shallows 2003

FLAWED SCALES

Freda Davies

CARROLL & GRAF PUBLISHERS
New York

Carroll & Graf Publishers
An imprint of Avalon Publishing Group, Inc.
245 W. 17th Street
New York
NY 10011-5300
www.carrollandgraf.com

AVALON
publishing group incorporated

First published in the UK by Constable,
an imprint of Constable & Robinson Ltd 2005

First Carroll & Graf edition 2005

ISBN-13 978-0-78671-672-2
ISBN-10 0-7867-1672-X

Printed and bound in the EU

For Petra

Chapter One

In the car was endless silence.

Above, autumn sunlight filtered through the branches of an ancient oak and a breeze disturbed the leaves. The driest fell, dappling the sleek lines of the car with motes of glorious colour.

Noise from the nearby road increased as the day warmed. With the advantage of a high seat in a lorry, its driver saw the car and a man able to sit in peace. Envy suffused the workman as he faced the hard work and hassles of a long day with heavy boxes and annoying shopgirls.

Hours passed. The delivery man returned in his empty vehicle and glanced at the oak, surprised to see the same car, its occupant still resting under the tree. Puzzled, he pulled into a lay-by, taking time to make up his mind before reaching for his mobile phone.

The road was like many in that part of the Forest of Dean, narrow and winding, arched green distances between houses. There had been occasional flurries of traffic during the day, a school bus morning and evening, cars with parents and children, workers taking a short cut between home and office. Late in the afternoon a patrol car eased its way slowly along a quiet stretch, the constable at the wheel inspecting every location where a car could be hidden under a spreading oak tree. Once, twice, he got out of the vehicle and walked into the undergrowth, returning quickly. The third time he used his radio to give the site, confirm there was a car, a dead body, and ask for the necessary services as back-up. After that all he could do was wait.

It was not long before a large green Rover pulled in and walking towards him were two big men, unmistakably police officers in suits. The dark one he remembered from rugby matches but it was the younger man who led the way, walking over the uneven roadside with the enviably athletic swing of a fit body. The patrolman saw the cut of his dark grey suit and the quality of the cloth, wondering how long he would have to save to pay for one like it and aware he had to look up at the tall, good-looking newcomer. He saw smooth light brown hair topping regular features and a pair of keen hazel eyes which missed nothing.

'I am Detective Inspector Tyrell and this is my colleague, Detective Sergeant Clarke. You are?' he asked, his voice deep, unaccented.

'Pelham, sir.' The PC pulled his hands from his pockets and shook his luminous yellow jacket into tidiness.

'The car was as reported?' Tyrell asked.

'Yes, sir. Dead man at the wheel.' Surprised, PC Pelham realized he was standing to attention. 'The old boy must have felt rough, pulled over for a spell and – well, he died.'

'Thank you, Pelham. Did you notice anything on your way in?'

'Sir?'

'Tyre marks?' DS Clarke asked. The sergeant was big, dark as were many Foresters, his size of muscle and bone and nothing to do with excess fat. A normally calm expression covered a sharp mind and shrewdness, while a thick cap of black curls emphasized the strength of features pulled into a frown.

'Oh, yes. One set only going in. Crushed grass, sir,' he explained to the DI.

'Good, well spotted.' Tyrell looked at the ground around them. 'A bit hard for footprints. I can't even see yours, Pelham,' came with a smile. 'Let's get to the car.'

Pelham led the way and was about to open the driver's door of the gleaming black car when Tyrell stopped him.

'Debris on the roof. As you first saw it?'

The sturdy young policeman frowned, trying to remember. 'I think so, sir.'

'We need a chat with the van driver. He might remember enough to give us an idea how long the car's been here.' As he spoke the DI began pulling on a pair of thin latex gloves. 'When you opened the door were you wearing gloves?'

Pelham shook his head. 'No, sir. I needed to check he was dead.'

'What did you touch?'

'His neck, sir, looking for a pulse – oh, and I lifted the hand nearest me and put it back on the wheel. It had dropped down as I leaned near him.'

'Arm loose and easily lifted?'

'Yes, sir.'

'Anything else you touched?'

'Buttons, sir. I had to undo them when I looked in his jacket for some ID and got his wallet. That's how I know his details.'

'They are?'

'He's Francis John Harding of Droitwich. There's a photo of a wife and a couple of teenagers.'

'Cash? Credit cards?'

'Plenty of both. The car's registered to him and not a company freebie, so he's not short a bob or two if he can afford a motor like that. It's only a year old.'

Tyrell smiled at Pelham's enthusiasm for a good motor. 'You'd better get your notebook up to date and enter a list of everything you've touched.'

'Everything, sir?'

'Oh yes, Pelham,' Tyrell said softly. 'It's always possible in a case like this the death is suspicious.'

DS Clarke flexed his fingers in their latex covering. 'You'd be surprised how many undertakers have taken delivery of a body dead of natural causes, only to turn it over when they get home and find a stab wound or a bullet.'

'Nothing like that here!'

'Perhaps not, Pelham, but we'll still take precautions,' the DI assured him. 'Ready?'

Clarke nodded, going to the passenger door and waiting for Tyrell to reach the one by the driver's body. The DI nodded and they opened the doors simultaneously, leaning into the car from each side.

Clarke sniffed. 'Something's wrong.'

'Agreed, Brian, and rigor's long gone but we'll have to wait for Chris Collier before we call in the troops. In the meantime, what do you make of the hands?'

Clarke scrutinized the driver's left hand and peered at what he could see of the right one, lying limply on the steering wheel. 'I see what you mean.'

Without disturbing the body Tyrell examined all he could of Francis John Harding, registering the man's approximate age, his dark brown hair greying at the temples, cheeks plump with good living. The suit the body wore was of fine grey herringbone tweed and the DI could see it was tailored to minimize the chunkiness of a solid torso. He bent to see the expensive striped poplin of the shirt and the careful knotting of a maroon silk tie.

A car door slammed shut and Clarke went to meet its driver, a man over six feet in height but slightly built, his thinning fair hair streaked with white. Bowed with tiredness and the weight of a medical bag, he smiled at DS Clarke and the lines of his face lifted.

'You and Tyrell, you drag me to some pretty weird deathbeds. Who've you got this time?'

'Mr Harding, a businessman from the Midlands, Dr Collier. Seems he fancied a snooze while he was driving along the A48, so pulled off to find a quiet spot. At least that's what we're supposed to assume. It just doesn't smell right.'

Chris Collier put down his bag and squatted as he opened it and took out a pair of rubber gloves. The DI and his sergeant watched Dr Collier examine the body, walk round the car and inspect the corpse from the passenger side. With the doors closed he stripped off his gloves, completed his notes and picked up his bag.

'If you hadn't been here already, I'd have sent for you myself,' he told them.

'Death might be from natural causes but the disposal of the body's suspect?' Tyrell asked.

'That's my guess but the PM will sort it out for you.' Dr Collier glanced at his watch. 'As for me, I certify life extinct at 17.37. He's all yours. By the way, Sergeant Clarke, there was no smell.'

The DS grinned. 'I just said it didn't smell right. Sitting there all day after he'd died, it should have hit you. I'll bet you a tenner when he's lifted out, that car seat'll be clean and dry.'

'No takers – I need my cash. I'm taking my wife out to dinner,' Chris Collier said, his smile lopsided with exhaustion. 'If you two have any such plans, forget 'em, you'll be busy.'

They did not watch him go, Tyrell checking the ground around the car and towards the road as Clarke used his mobile phone. In minutes the sergeant had notified the station, called in SOCO and arranged with the appropriate department to have the car sealed and transported to the forensic labs as soon as possible. Later, once the necessary photos had been taken, the ambulance called by PC Pelham carried away all that was left of Francis John Harding.

'Not my imagination, then?' Clarke said as they waited.

'No, Brian, you were right. You noticed his hands?'

'The lividity along the edges and upper surfaces?'

Keith Tyrell nodded. 'It would have been on the underneath of both wrists if he'd died with his hands still grasping the wheel – and why didn't he undo his jacket buttons when he started feeling odd? Pull loose his shirt collar at the very least? It would have been the natural thing to do.'

They watched increasing activity under the trees as uniformed officers and the white-overalled scene of crime experts went to work. Striped plastic tape shaped an arena of death, screens hiding the car from any prying eyes and cameras on the roadway. A reporter screeched a question at the DI from across the bushes but he turned away, raising a hand in negation. He was listening only to the echoing murmur of quiet voices under the trees and hearing the sound of work progressing steadily. There would be time later for public announcements.

Ignoring the press, both detectives scrutinized the grass and bushes in the clearing, Tyrell pointing out areas to be charted and photographed, although there were no indentations worthy of being recorded as casts. By the time the SOCO team had finished it was late and the DI was relieved to see Harding's car lifted on to the back of a transporter.

'Shall I pick you up in the morning?' Clarke asked.

'Thanks, Brian, I'd be grateful. The fewer cars the better since the hospital car park's usually full. I'll check with Dr McBride first thing – she can give us some idea when she'll do the PM.'

Moroccan lamb.

Keith caught the fragrance as he turned his key in the front door and his expression softened as he remembered a special holiday. His spirits lifted as he heard cadences of Chopin and he became convinced the meal cooking was a sign of progress. For so long Jenny had devoted every possible moment to cleaning and painting the house, laundering anything worn once as she struggled to exorcize her demons. Hard as it had been to stand by and watch, Keith had been patient with his wife's choice of therapies. Tonight he was relieved she could relax enough to play her favourite CD as she spent time blending spices she knew he enjoyed.

'Hard day, darling?' she asked as she stood by the stove, turning chopped coriander into steaming couscous. Her smile for him was happy, untainted, her eyes free of shadows under winged brows.

Keith bent and kissed the top of her head, glad there was no longer panic in Jenny when she was touched. She leaned against him as he said, 'Not bad.'

'Hungry?'

'Ravenous. Can I do anything?' He glanced at the table, already laid and with Jenny's touches of candles and a nosegay of flowers.

She was lifting dishes from the oven and there was a burst of tempting aromas.

'I posted off the parcel for Imogen today,' Jenny said when they had begun to satisfy their hunger. 'She still hasn't decided on a name for the baby.'

'Knowing my sister, it will have to be just right – as long as she has it ready in time for the registrar,' he added as he helped himself to more vegetables.

Keith had almost finished his meal and was ready to enjoy the rest of the evening when the phone rang. Even that could not dispel his euphoria until he heard Sergeant Willis's apologetic tone. Keith stifled a sigh as he heard, 'Sorry, Mr Tyrell, but it's urgent and technically your case.'

'What's happened?'

'That body in the car. Harding. His wife and son turned up at the station, wanting to know where he was. I had to tell 'em – still at the hospital. They've gone off at the speed of light. Can you get there?'

'How long ago did they leave?'

'Two, three minutes.'

'Then I've got a head start. I'd be grateful if you could ring the hospital and alert them. Tell whoever can get things done I'll need an attendant to prepare Harding's body for viewing and identification.'

'There'll be a bit of resistance at that end, this time of night.'

'And you're just the man to deal with such a problem. I can add my persuasion when I get to Gloucester.'

Keith turned to Jenny as he switched off the phone. 'Sorry, darling, you know how it is.'

*   *   *

A sudden squall sped storm water across the hospital entrance. The automatic door opened and DI Tyrell stood to one side, allowing a young couple into the foyer. He could see the girl was heavily pregnant, her features a mask of pain. Beside her, an anguished boy held her. She raised her head to smile at him as agony eased for a moment. 'We made it,' she said and the very young man pulled her to him and kissed her gently.

As a porter pushed a wheelchair towards the expectant parents, Tyrell took out his warrant card and offered it to the receptionist on duty. She gazed at it briefly and he had a chance to look at her, storing the image away in his memory of a tired woman in her late forties, with very dark lipstick and a rigid hairdo.

'Oh, yes,' she said dismissively, 'we got the message.' Her tone implied all the inconvenience it had caused. 'One of the pathology staff has had to stay on.'

It had been a long day but the DI thanked her with his normal courtesy and the hushed atmosphere in the foyer lifted a little. It was only momentary, the smooth rustle of the main door making him turn. He expected to see Mrs Harding but an elderly man was limping into the hospital helped by a woman, clearly his daughter. The glimpse of a pyjama jacket beneath the old man's coat had Tyrell guessing the reason for their haste and he hoped they were in time to say their goodbyes. It was a need denied Mrs Harding and her children.

Dry and patient, Keith Tyrell waited behind the door, watching scudding rain drive leaves along the ground and relieved the day's possible crime scene had been dealt with before the onset of bad weather. He remembered too many other situations when heavy downpours had ruined evidence which could have been useful. There was no time to tire of his thoughts as minutes later he saw a sturdy woman of middle height and middle age being hurried into shelter by a young man who shared some of her features.

'Mrs Harding?'

Barbara Harding raised her gaze to him. Despite her

hasty journey south she was stylish in a dark suit, her grey hair dampened but barely disturbed in the gusts of wind scurrying litter. The DI recognized a woman who was carrying on as normally as possible while in the first stages of shock. She had reached anger.

'I want to see my husband. Now!'

This was a woman used to her orders being carried out without hesitation, Tyrell thought, whether in a golf club committee or an Inner Wheel meeting. 'It's being arranged,' he assured her, 'and we'll be called when everything's ready for us.'

'Why Gloucester? My husband left here days ago.'

'As yet, we have no idea, Mrs Harding. Our enquiries have only just begun.'

'And why should I have to wait to see him?' she demanded to know. 'Matthew brought me as soon as we were told and he's driven hard to get here. Are you trying to hide Frank from me?' she asked, going on to berate the DI for all the difficulties she had encountered.

Tyrell was calm, attentive, waiting until her torrent of words slowed, then stopped. 'I'm grateful you came as soon as you could – both of you. We were able to name Mr Harding from his belongings but we do need an official identification by his next of kin.' His deep, even voice began to control the situation.

'But why here?' Barbara Harding asked again, fury holding her tears in check as she pleaded.

The DI explained exactly where the car had been found, that the hospital in which they stood was the nearest and most suitable facility. As he spoke he could see that the passion which had sustained her through the first terrible hours was abating and she was an exhausted, unhappy woman who was suddenly a widow and bereft. If anyone had speeded Frank Harding's death they had claimed more than one victim.

'My mother's right, Inspector Tyrell. We just don't understand why we've had to come to Gloucester.' Matthew Harding was in his early twenties, one of the teenagers in Harding's wallet grown to manhood. The

DI could see the resemblance to the father in a young man devastated by his loss yet trying desperately hard to be the strong support his mother needed.

'It's not yet clear to us, Mr Harding. Later, I would like to talk to you and your mother at length. Perhaps in the morning when you've both had some rest?'

A man in hospital greens walked into the foyer and Tyrell went to greet him with a warm smile and a handshake. 'Thank you for waiting.'

Pete Coombs was almost as tall as Tyrell but dark, with craggy features. He nodded to the Hardings. 'Holding up?'

'Pretty well, considering.'

'The chapel's empty so I put him in there – going through our labs can be a bit scary this time of night if you're not used to 'em.' Pete waited while Tyrell approached mother and son.

'If you are ready, Mrs Harding?'

She sensed his sympathy and that she could trust him. Barbara Harding swallowed nervously before putting out her hand to her son and together they followed Tyrell on the walk to the hospital's chapel, Pete Coombs leading the way. Mrs Harding tried to appear calm and in control of herself but Tyrell could see she grasped her son's hand so tightly her fingers were white with the strain.

The chapel was dim but Pete had positioned the trolley near the simple altar on which stood lighted candles. Frank Harding's body was shrouded in white, the area of the torso and limbs covered by a dark blue velvet cloth. Pete Coombs went to stand beside the dead man's head and waited for Tyrell's signal to lift away the sheet.

Next morning the day had hardly been aired when the pathology department doors swung closed behind them. Clarke shrugged on his raincoat and neatened his tie. 'Dr McBride didn't waste much time.'

'No. I think she's got a full list and wanted us and our

chap dealt with quickly. Even so, she didn't miss a thing.'

'Well-nourished male in his fifties, no external signs of injury, rigor mortis long gone and post-mortem lividity in a pattern which showed positioning for some time in a semi-recumbent posture,' Clarke said.

'Don't forget the query about his kidneys and liver as well as narrowed heart vessels and early calcification of valves.'

'It was Dr McBride's only moment of light relief when you assured her no medication of any kind had been found amongst Harding's belongings.'

Tyrell smile wryly. 'You caught her muttering too? "Must have suffered from angina but liked to pretend he was still too young. The stupidity of men playing the macho game!" came over very clearly.'

'Not in a good mood, our Dr McBride.'

'Understandable in the circumstances. Brian, I'm leaving you to carry on at the station. Get hold of Harding's laptop and ask Mickey Walsh to milk what he can from it. I think the son will insist on taking it home. He'll find it's necessary for the business and they do have government contracts. The boy's trying to fill his father's shoes so he'll need the hard drive in the machine as well as any disks.'

'If anyone can wring data from a computer, Mickey can.' DS Clarke regarded his DI with innocent eyes. 'It's amazing how he's come on in the last few months.'

The Detective Constable Walsh Tyrell had first encountered had been sorely in need of many baths and a barber but the DI had treated him with the same courtesy he extended to all his team. DC Walsh had boundless enthusiasm and in no time Mickey's skill with computers had been harnessed and developed until his understanding of all things electronic was akin to wizardry. As an added bonus, slavish copying of his DI meant the young detective's personal hygiene was no longer a problem for his colleagues.

'I think Rose Walker has a lot to answer for with that young man,' Tyrell said with a smile.

Clarke merely nodded agreement. It had been obvious to everyone but the DI how Mickey Walsh's admiration extended to all things Tyrell.

'You know, someone else might have used that laptop, Brian, and the unknown quantity could have left us a clue.'

'They've certainly not been careless anywhere else,' Clarke said. 'Maybe Mickey can recall discards.'

'It'll be very useful if he can. I'm off to see the Hardings now and I'll do what I can to stall as long as possible.'

'I don't envy you, but Rose'll be a help.'

PC Rose Walker had a quiet strength, a calmness, which made her good at her job. Not strictly pretty, she swept her dark hair away from her face and coiled it smoothly, unafraid of comment and comparisons and always ready to be a very good listener.

The two men had almost reached the outer doors when they were pushed open by a grim-faced porter who was steering a trolley through the aperture. A zipped bag held what was left of a body, its limbs and torso distorted.

'One from early this morning, poor little devils. Bob Vidler's on it – for his sins. He'll have to talk to the families,' Clarke said quietly.

'Four, wasn't it?' Tyrell asked and Clarke nodded.

At 1 a.m. four young joyriders had crashed into the support of a railway bridge in the town. The car had fireballed and taken time to cool, hindering firecrews and police waiting to recover the bodies.

The DI was saddened by the incident, guessing the ripples of shock and bereavement which would spread through Gloucester. 'Little wonder Anita McBride wanted us and our body out of the way.'

'Not surprising, when she has this to face,' Clarke agreed as another twisted corpse was wheeled past them. 'How's she going to manage to prove identity and find a cause of death for each of the poor little souls?'

'If anyone can, she will,' Tyrell assured him.

It was almost time for a lunch break when Tyrell walked into the main CID office.

Clarke looked up from the notes he was making. 'How was Mrs Harding?'

'She's still shocked, of course, and I've left Rose with her in case there are any more snippets of useful information.' The DI sat on the corner of his sergeant's desk. 'It got a bit tricky at one point. I asked her how long her husband had been away. A week. Then I asked her when he was expected home. The lady had an email the night before last, apologizing and telling her he was staying on two or three days longer.'

Clarke reacted more swiftly than his bulk suggested as eyes widened and eyebrows climbed high. 'But by then he was already dead! How did she take that bit of news?'

'I haven't told her – after all, we don't have Anita McBride's official report.'

'And when we do?'

Tyrell sighed. 'I hope we've managed to rustle up some explanation as to who sent her an email from her husband's laptop – and why.'

'So someone else did use it. There's no mistaking it now, Harding's death may have been natural but the aftermath is a thoroughly professional job.'

'Anyone you've encountered in the past who could be this quick-thinking and efficient, Brian?'

'Not to my knowledge. I could give Bob Vidler a ring. He's worked round the county more than I have.'

Tyrell was pleased with the suggestion. 'Good idea. I'll leave that to you. Now, has Mickey been able to resurrect what's been cancelled from Harding's files?'

'Quite a bit but so far it's all to do with business.'

The DI nodded towards Clarke's notes. 'You've been busy. What's new on our Francis John Harding?'

DS Clarke reached for the folder. 'Exterior of car, all fingerprints found matched up with officers present.

19

Interior of car, what prints were found had been left by Dave Pelham.'

'Only those of the Traffic man who was first on the scene?'

'You've got it. Paramedics wore gloves, as did everyone else, but then young Dave had no reason to suspect it was a possible crime scene when he opened the driver's door.'

'Let's face it, Brian, if we ever track down who did get Harding and his vehicle arranged to their satisfaction, we can prove nothing. Not a scrap of evidence was left – and even if Mickey does manage to find it, the email was from Harding's own machine and will be anonymous. None of the victim's own prints turned up where they were entitled to be.'

The sergeant's lips tightened. 'You're right and it makes me wonder why a pen pusher up the line is questioning our "use of resources on what is obviously a natural death".'

'You're joking!'

'I wish! I tried Dr McBride's report on them but was told it was not conclusive and will we desist. I quote. "Desist".'

Tyrell reached for a phone and punched numbers. When he was eventually able to talk to the pathologist she was furious.

'If you wanted to ask questions, you should have done so this morning – at the post-mortem!'

He held the instrument away from his ear and let her rant on at him, understanding her emotion. She had spent all day working on the charred remains of young bodies.

'I'm sorry,' he said when she paused for breath, 'but we do have a problem. If you don't mind, I think it's necessary for me to record our conversation?'

'Get on with it, Tyrell!'

'An admin expert has insisted it's likely Harding's heart attack killed him when he parked up to rest,' Keith told her as he switched the phone to 'record' and smiled at the resultant spluttering.

Anita McBride was a dainty redhead and meticulous but she could snort very effectively. 'For Pete's sake! If Harding died as suggested it was only after he'd been dead for at least two days and lain stretched out in another place with his head elevated, after which his body was cleaned and dressed. Of course, at that point he could have decided to climb into the driving seat, ready to go home. What bloody fool suggested it was possible?'

'Thanks, Anita. With luck you'll convince one of our lords and masters. You'd think anyone reading your report would have had no doubt but not everyone recognizes the importance of absence of rigor, post-mortem lividity sites and no limb damage. All they would have noticed would have been coloration of the skin and lips as well as the state of the heart and its muscles.'

'It's still not necessarily murder, you know!' she informed him.

'I agree – but logic makes me wonder why such a very efficient clean-up job? It rings warning bells.'

'That's your job, Tyrell,' she told him. 'I've got problems of my own.'

'I know – and I'm sorry. It's the stuff of nightmares,' he added, his deep voice gentle.

He heard her sigh as the line went dead and he switched off the recording, wondering if she held back her tears for another time. The DI took a small cassette from the recorder and sealed it in an envelope, Anita McBride's name and the date identifying it. 'That's for the pen pusher, should we need it,' he said as he thrust the envelope in a drawer. 'Now, let's get at it, Brian. Who are we after?'

'Well, there must be two of them.'

'You're right. No person was seen walking along that stretch of road or hitching a lift.' Tyrell gestured to the folder. 'What do we know about this duo – apart from the fact they're darned good cleaners?'

'According to Mrs Harding when she checked her husband's things nothing was missing,' he read from his notes. 'We'd already found plenty of cash in the wallet but every note and coin had been wiped.'

Tyrell was startled. 'Are you sure?'

Clarke nodded. 'Livermore is. Same goes for photographs, receipts, the inside layers of his wallet, his mobile. Double checking was carried out on his briefcase and laptop which were both in the boot with his overnight bag. Eric Livermore says he's never experienced such a sterile crime scene.'

'After all his years in Forensics I'm glad we could provide Dr Livermore with such pleasure. What did you discover about Harding's bank accounts? Credit cards?'

'All stopped as of yesterday but there had been no transaction of any kind in three days. The last was Harding booking out of a hotel in Northampton.'

The DI sat back in his chair, swivelling as he thought, but Sergeant Clarke was restless.

'Why go to all that trouble if the cards and wallet hadn't been handled in order to rob? With no money missing, nothing taken from credit cards, what could anyone be after?'

Tyrell sat up. 'Information, Brian. On the cards, photos, letters – and in the laptop. Get hold of Mickey Walsh and get him to make it a top priority – I'll even take him lunch at his desk. It's imperative we have printouts of everything on that computer before it goes back to Harding's family!'

Sergeant Willis was on his way to the canteen and put his head round the door. 'The DCI's looking for you – and Mr Copeland's with her.'

Tyrell's smile was welcoming for a man he trusted implicitly. 'Am I in trouble?'

'How should I know? I've been running all ends up and you whipped Rose Walker off me today. Still, she's good with the bereaved so I bear you no grudge.' Roly Willis was greying and beginning to show his years but as he stretched tired muscles, Tyrell could see he was one of the few men of his age who did not bulge over the waistband of his uniform trousers. 'Better get on your bike before they start letting the smoke out of their ears,' the sergeant advised.

The DI had folders and envelope ready for his chief inspector and gathered up all she would expect to have handed to her. The new DCI was a distinct improvement on her predecessor, Richard Whittaker, only showing her hang-ups and her temper when faced with laziness or inefficiency. Joan Leggatt was tall for a woman, dark and thin-faced but attractive in a practical, no-nonsense way. Her short hair was seasoned with white and under strong brows were eyes alert to all around her.

Beside her, Detective Superintendent Rod Copeland might be slender but it was the wiriness of tempered steel, allowing him to drive upward through the ranks. He greeted Tyrell and waved him to a chair as Joan Leggatt reflected on the conflicting opinions she had heard expressed on the subject of her young DI. Some said Tyrell was stuck up because of his family's connections, his father being a judge and related to half the county's big-wigs. Then there were others who approved of the young officer fast-tracking his way up the promotion ladder. They insisted he knew his stuff, there was no side to him and he was a damned good detective. On occasion she had over-heard grumbles by the more idle of the station's staff. They were annoyed DI Tyrell expected them to work as con-scientiously as he did but she reflected that in the force there were always those who could only complain.

To her Tyrell had been consistently courteous. The DCI had no doubt he would overtake her one day but there had never been any pushiness on his part, nor had she ever sensed she was being patronized, rare in a service so recently and completely male-dominated.

Rod Copeland was not one to waste time on chit-chat. 'Sit down, Keith. I've had a complaint and as it's to do with proper use of resources I've no alternative but to follow it up. You do have a knack for upsetting admin staff,' he said, his lips twitching as he held a smile at bay.

'I'm sorry, sir. It's not intentional.'

'It may not have been but you were given an order which originated from Detective Chief Superintendent Bayliss's office.' He glanced at a sheet of paper on the desk in front of him. 'You were instructed "to desist from a particular investigation as it was an improper use of resources which could be better utilized in other areas". Is that so?'

'Yes, sir.'

'I find when I get here you still have it active, with DS Clarke on the case as well as DC Walsh and PC Walker – not to mention Dr Livermore and his forensic team as well as Traffic officers checking drivers for what they might have seen. All for a non-suspicious death. Isn't it a slight overkill, Keith?'

'Only if the basic assumption is true, that the man found in the driving seat of his car actually died there.'

'You have proof he didn't?' Joan Leggatt asked.

Tyrell hesitated but only for a second. 'I asked Dr McBride that very question, ma'am.'

He handed the DCI the envelope with the cassette of the pathologist's answer, and with deft movements she set it to play. Fortunately, both Leggatt and Copeland were experienced enough to hide smiles as Anita McBride's voice exploded into the room. When the recording ended there was a silence, the two senior officers waiting for Tyrell's explanation.

'It's possible whoever left him there expected it to be regarded as a natural death and by the time any questions were asked, the crime scene to have been thoroughly contaminated,' he told them.

'It was still a death from natural causes,' the DCI said as she removed the tape and replaced it in its envelope.

'That could be so, ma'am, but it was clear from the beginning great efforts had been made to prepare Harding's body and belongings before he was allowed to be found. From all the reports, even an inexperienced detect-

24

ive would have realized the man's body was found in very weird conditions indeed. DCS Bayliss is not only very experienced, he's also extremely able. I had my doubts he was the one issuing the order.'

There was a moment of tension in the quiet office, Joan Leggatt and Rod Copeland careful not to look at each other. 'Was a crime committed – apart from those involved in not notifying us of the death?' Copeland asked.

'Even if there was, sir, not a scrap of evidence has been left which would link it to anyone.' Tyrell explained the complete lack of prints or any other body traces as the DCI read again the notes on the case.

'This man, Harding. Last seen in Northampton?' She was interrupted by a knock at the door. 'Not now, Clarke,' she said as the sergeant came in.

He held out a sheet of paper. 'Sorry, mam. It could be relevant,' he said and retreated fast.

Annoyed, she read the information he had given her and her expression changed to one of puzzlement. 'Gamma hydroxybutyric acid – that's GHB, the drug used in sex assaults. There were small traces in Harding's blood, along with alcohol and very high blood sugar.'

'There was no insulin, no hypodermics, indeed no medication of any kind. He must have been an undiagnosed diabetic as well as suffering from angina – Dr McBride's opinion after examining the heart,' Tyrell explained. 'If Harding died very soon after ingesting GHB, its metabolism could have been seriously delayed.'

Copeland had no doubts. 'In his condition, drinking and with a date rape drug in him, it's little wonder he keeled over as he did.'

'Maybe so but it still doesn't explain why we should carry the investigation,' Leggatt argued. 'Surely it's Northampton's job? The drugging and death must have happened there.'

'Yes, ma'am,' Tyrell said, 'but he was found here, in our division.'

'Even so, the negative evidence you've amassed could well have originated elsewhere.'

'Could it, ma'am? Check Rose Walker's account of our interview with Mrs Harding. Before her husband went to Northampton he stayed in a hotel just outside Gloucester – the new Pinemount place.'

'I know it,' the super said, 'it's very handy for the M5.'

'Yes, sir,' Tyrell agreed, 'and possibly even handier for the pair who landed us with Harding. They got him right away from Northampton where it was likely he died but they could have moved the body to leave it in a place not so far from their own base.'

Copeland nodded thoughtfully. 'Which would site them in our bailiwick. OK, I can see why DS Clarke and PC Walker, but why DC Walsh?' he asked Tyrell.

'We found out from Harding's son that his father was not only the owner of the firm, he was also its senior engineer, travelling widely and finding out what clients wanted. The business is one of a cartel which numbers arms manufacturing among its products. It could be simple industrial espionage since his laptop was available but it's been a very smooth operation with no panic. Whoever's behind it isn't new to the game – far from it. DC Walsh is checking out any other incidents in which a businessman or woman has had concerns about their property but there's been no apparent theft.'

'You mean, in the county?' Leggatt queried.

'At first, ma'am. With yours and Mr Copeland's permission, I'd like a request for any such cases to go to all forces.'

'Wait a minute, Keith. If it's not to milk bank accounts or get any commercial details, then what other possibility is there?' the superintendent wanted to know.

'By now, whoever was there at his death knows all there is to know of Francis John Harding. Names, dates, family details such as his mother's maiden name. Then there's his passport, sir, it was in his briefcase. No money's gone but they do now have his identity.'

'You think it's part of a scam dealing in false passports – illegal immigrants and so on?'

'No, sir. I spent some time in the Met working on that sort of case. This set-up doesn't fit any of the usual patterns. The biggest share of the trade in illegal immigrants is in creating papers for men and women much younger than Harding who are to be farmed out as slave labour or as prostitutes. Almost always the object of the organizers would seem to be to amass cash as quickly as possible, get it into an overseas account then, when on the verge of being arrested, they head for a safe part of the world and live in luxury. Instinct tells me Harding became targeted in something completely different. The whole operation gives the impression of having been running very smoothly and discreetly for some time, and the ramifications into legitimate businesses are interesting.'

'To what end, Keith?'

'Hard to say, sir, with only one individual to work on – so far.'

Joan Leggatt leaned forward. 'Hence DC Walsh?'

'Yes, ma'am. I think there's a lot more to come and it's all sufficiently covert, needing Walsh's expertise to find links – once we have input from other forces.'

Copeland smiled. 'One man found dead in a car and you're sure we're looking at crime on a grand scale?'

'Not sure, sir, not at all. My guess is they've found a way past the identity checks banks and building societies have recently put in place. Add to that, when any organization goes to such extreme lengths to hide all trace of their existence, it tells me they intend not to be caught so they can go on doing whatever it is that's earning them satisfactory quantities of illicit cash for the foreseeable future.'

'Hm,' the DCI mused, 'you're right. It must be a very efficient organization. Nationwide?' she asked.

'Possibly, ma'am.'

Copeland was restless. 'As you said, you came to us from the Met, so you know full well that if this is a widespread investigation a national squad will take over.'

'In addition, I suppose we're paying the price of being a

county which is very attractive to anyone wanting somewhere pleasant to live,' Joan Leggatt said ruefully. 'It must include anyone moving from major crime areas and bringing their bad habits with them.'

'It is, Joan, and it still means having to hand over to specialized teams from the Yard,' Copeland reminded his listeners.

'All the more reason, sir, to have as much verified data as possible ready for anyone arriving to take over. It's one of the signs it won't be too long before the police will be a national force.'

'Not just yet, and remember, Keith, nowadays it's a police service, not police force,' Copeland reminded him.

'So I've been told, sir, but there're many occasions when local knowledge is absolutely basic to bringing criminals to justice. National squads have their role to play but they shouldn't automatically take the place of a local team.'

'As well as taking any credit going?'

Tyrell smiled. 'Has it ever been any different, sir? There's one thing of which we can be sure.'

'And that is?' Joan Leggatt asked.

'If an investigation gets fouled up at any stage, we'll be the ones getting the blame.'

Chapter Two

Two days later Brian Clarke settled himself in the passenger seat of Tyrell's car. 'How was it in Northampton yesterday?' he asked.

The DI waited for traffic to clear before driving out of the police station yard and turning the car towards Gloucester. 'Very hospitable. The super had made a phone call or two and I had a DI Houghton waiting to show me around.'

Tyrell nodded, overtaking a freight lorry on the steep hill out of Lydney. 'Harding had spent his last night in the Hazelmere hotel just outside the town. It's very popular with the business fraternity and the manager was most co-operative. He had records of the night at his fingertips and after seeing Harding's room we called on the barman who had been on duty that night. The poor devil was asleep when we got there. Joe Brooks.'

'Did this Joe remember Harding?'

'Only after a shower and coffee. He said Harding had been a guest a few times in the past. "Always a very quiet gentleman. Kept himself to himself. Scotch and water. A couple in the evening while he did a crossword, then he'd take a stroll outside and go to bed,"' Tyrell quoted.

'That last night?'

'Now that was different. Harding had a drink or two but this time there was a woman sitting at his table while he finished his crossword. She wasn't "one of those", he said, just a sales rep.'

'After which Harding began to feel confused and had to be helped up to his room?'

29

'Got it in one. Unfortunately, Joe's description of the woman is very vague. "Smelt expensive" was all he could remember.'

Clarke twisted in his seat. 'There's something else, isn't there?'

'You know me too well. We were ready to leave when something in Joe's demeanour made me ask if that sort of situation had happened before – with other customers.'

'Bingo?'

The DI nodded. 'Not often, but enough for Joe to notice. Pressed, he couldn't recall if it was the same woman. He was sure on one occasion it was a man helped the drinker to the lift.'

'Any comeback from others drugged?'

'Twice. A man and a woman. Both went to Joe and asked what had happened the night before.'

'Don't tell me. They were confused and had no memory whatsoever of the last few hours?'

'Spot on. DI Houghton and I spent the rest of the time going through hotel records, trying to unearth any links. We managed to find the woman who'd been drugged and Northampton CID is trying to trace her whereabouts. They'll let us have any data – for Mickey's program.'

'That's coming along nicely. Not a huge response but then most reported incidents are simply to get a police number for insurance in case any accounts are looted. I bet there are a dozen unreported for each case Mickey's entered in his geographical profile.'

'Too many individuals embarrassed to admit being under the weather?'

'Could be.' Brian Clarke looked out at the passing countryside, recognizing the turn to Tyrell's home. 'How's Jenny?'

The answer did not come quickly. 'Good.' The DI was recalling the welcome he had been given on his return from Northampton. 'Yes, I think she's recovered well.'

'I'll tell Brenda if I may?'

'Of course.'

Clarke lay back and closed his eyes until the bridge over the Severn led them towards the city.

'By the way, I meant to ask you, what was all that going on in reception this morning?' Tyrell wanted to know.

'That? Zinna Richards. Said she'd been knocked off her pushbike last night and left for dead,' the DS explained, referring to a noisy argument in reception. It had involved an elderly wild-haired woman who was obviously furious.

'It sounded serious.'

Clarke looked at Tyrell and quirked an eyebrow. 'You've never tangled with her yet, have you? Zinna's spent more years than most of us can remember conjuring up complaints out of thin air. No, Roly Willis saw her off – he's used to her. Next time she's in it'll be for something else and she'll have forgotten whatever she thinks happened this morning.'

'It would be pleasant if all the problems coming our way could be dealt with so easily,' the DI said as he swung the car into a left turn along a curved driveway between smooth lawns and healthy shrubs.

Gloucester's Pinemount hotel was in an excellent setting, far enough from the M5 to be peaceful yet only a few minutes' motoring from the busy artery. The car park was a thieves' paradise with not one old banger in sight but it did have batteries of CCTV cameras to deter the unwise. The building was modern, functional, yet blended well with the countryside, one corner a conservatory protruding artistically into the garden and housing the most expensive of the restaurants. On the roof was another massive glassed-in area.

DS Clarke pointed. 'Swimming pool. Funny having it there but I suppose if the whole place goes up in smoke, all they've got to do is pull the plug and it saves bothering the fire brigade.'

The main door opened automatically and the two detectives walked into the foyer, busy that time in the morning with departing guests. Against the far wall was the curve of a reception desk and behind it two uniformed girls were arguing quietly, forcefully. As the officers made their way through the crowd towards the reception area the taller of the two, a plain girl with heavy glasses, turned away and stalked off. Because of his height the DI could see her brown hair was scraped back and held by a black velvet bow. When they reached the desk the second girl, a pretty brunette, was flushed and breathing hard but she smiled, was pleasant, her expression becoming wary when she saw their identity cards and the county police logo.

'I must call the manager,' she told them when she knew what they wanted.

'Manager' was an imposing title for the very young man who came hurrying in his almost-fitting brown suit. He introduced himself and led them to a nearby office, only relaxing when he realized there was nothing with which his hotel could be blamed.

'No, Mr Booker, we are simply trying to find out all we can about one of your guests who left here almost a week ago,' Tyrell assured him.

Relieved and anxious to be helpful, Booker used his computer to call up the date of the booking. Harding's occupancy became meals eaten, room service, phone calls, payment and time of departure. Tyrell asked for a list of other guests housed during the same period as well as staff on duty. Booker was not happy but the two policemen watched him with pleasant though unwavering gazes until he complied with their requests. Printouts were being tidied into an envelope when the DI leaned forward.

'The credit card counterfoil signed by Mr Harding – may we have it?'

It was a request which resulted in confusion. 'I'm sorry, Inspector, it's against hotel policy – more than my job's worth to hand it over. I wish I could be of help.'

'Never mind, sir.' DS Clarke was at his most comforting. 'How about we settle for a photocopy? You can manage that, can't you, sir – all this equipment you've got at your disposal?'

Booker needed little more persuading, Tyrell and Clarke soon walking out of the careful levels of air, humidity, music, which were the signs of a thoroughly modern establishment.

'I hope to God they never have a real emergency here,' Clarke said as they reached the car. 'Imagine that poor little devil in a proper panic!'

DS Clarke found the CID room unoccupied except for one DC in a corner, intent on the screen of his monitor. The sergeant marvelled anew at the change in Mickey since he began to work with Keith Tyrell. Gone was the officer everyone avoided and in his place was an attractive young man whose cropped brown curls gleamed, cheeks were closely shaved and clothes gave the impression of coming straight from the cleaners. The greatest difference from his old self was that the new Mickey was happy and it showed.

'How's it going?'

Walsh pressed a key and waited for a printout to begin rolling before he looked up with a grin for his sergeant. DI Tyrell came in time to see it and hear his answer.

'I sorted through the reports and checked out the most promising. In each case valuables were out of sight for a while and police contacted to get an incident number but all accounts are intact. I talked to a few and have two possibles.'

'What did they lose?' Tyrell asked.

'Nothing.'

'Was it only cards mislaid?'

Mickey shook his head. 'One said his passport was in his briefcase, the other listed his laptop going walkabout – with no sign of any data being interfered with.'

Brian Clarke leaned on Mickey's monitor. 'Any connection with the Pinemount?'

'I was very tactful about that. Very helpful, they were. One did say he'd stayed at the Gloucester Pinemount before going on to the Midlands and being separated from his goodies. The other guy told the same story but the second hotel that time was a Hawksmere outside Manchester.'

The DI was thoughtful. 'So, no real pattern.'

'Not yet, sir, but it's early days. Once more data comes in I can see what's what and try to improve the program.'

Tyrell smiled at the boyish enthusiasm. 'DCI Leggatt's go-ahead to all forces seems to be bearing fruit. She says the co-ordination's all yours.'

When Sergeant Willis came into the office he saw Mickey's delight and guessed computers must be involved. Normally, it was only those damned machines which got the young blighter going but Rose Walker had a glow about her these days.

'Inspector Tyrell, I've been looking for you. A message from your wife while you were out. Would you ring her? Nothing urgent, she said.'

Keith sought privacy to ring Jenny. 'Darling, are you all right?' With luck he had managed to hide a flare of concern.

'I'm sorry to be a nuisance but I forgot to tell you your mother phoned last night. You were so late coming in and then this morning was a bit of a rush.'

It had been a pleasant start to an unforgiving day. 'What did she want?'

'To remind you about Sunday.'

'Sunday?'

'Aunt Sophie's birthday lunch.'

Keith had forgotten the date and reached for his diary. 'I'll have to see if I'm off shift.'

'How could you! You know your parents wanted us there since your cousins can't make it.'

'I know, darling, I'm sorry. I'll do what I can.'

Jenny chuckled. 'Better than that, Buster. If you don't – you can explain to your mother.'

Small and blonde, Keith's mother could be an angel, as long as nothing was annoying her. Then, she became a very tough lady indeed. Thinking of such an occasion, it was a DI with the remnants of a smile who walked in on Clarke and Walsh.

'This is beginning to look bigger than we imagined,' Clarke said. 'Info's coming in from all over the place.'

'Not all of it useful, sir. Most of it may be relevant but I'm trying to weed out all but what fits the MO of our man's death.'

'Many cases in one locality?'

'That's what's so odd, sir. Looks like the activities've been well spread.'

'Or well organized,' Tyrell said thoughtfully. 'You know, if GHB was used each time it suggests sexual encounters.'

Clarke's heavy brows moved in a frown. 'There was nothing in Dr McBride's notes.'

'I agree, Brian, she was most specific.'

Mickey nodded sagely. 'I guess old boys like Harding, they're not used to it at their age and that's what gives 'em heart attacks.'

'Hey, enough of being old! Harding was only in his fifties,' Clarke insisted.

'Past it, Sarge,' Mickey said and ducked a well-aimed slap with a folder.

'Seriously,' Tyrell said and the mood in the CID office changed, 'I think we've got to be prepared to find mostly women when we eventually catch up with this crew.'

Mickey's eyebrows climbed in astonishment. 'Women, sir? Humping bodies around needs muscle.'

Clarke was in agreement with the DI. 'No, it makes sense,' he said. 'Harding's guard would have been down if he was dealing with a woman.'

'According to the barman, only one person was ever seen chatting up targets but my guess is there was a helper, man or woman, for the very thorough cleaning up afterwards and they stayed out of sight. Harding was handled by a woman and may have been prepared to spend a pleasant evening but being occupied sexually wasn't his intention.'

'Hence the drug. He had to be put out of action, one way or another,' Clarke added.

The DI turned to Mickey. 'Were only men targeted or did any women make a complaint?'

'A few, sir.'

'I wonder. Was that because men are more susceptible? We really need to talk to some of these individuals. Can you set that going, Mickey?'

'Ask 'em if they meant to get on with enjoying themselves and then came over all queer, sir?'

'Tactfully, Mickey,' DS Clarke advised.

Tyrell was silent, reasoning the next step. 'There is another avenue which needs exploring. The ones in the county you discarded, Mickey. Two were separated from their valuables long enough to contact their local police but the items were quickly returned. It would be interesting to find out why they were ignored by these women and apparently not drugged. Who were they?'

Mickey checked a notepad. 'Geoffrey Kernon and Jason Manners, sir.'

'Why did Harding get the full treatment and memory loss – but not them? See what you can unearth.'

'Good idea, sir. Would you mind if I – I got a cup of tea first? I've been sitting here for hours.'

At Tyrell's nod Mickey fled but had barely reached the door when the phone rang. Clarke scooped up the handset, listened, nodded once or twice. 'I'll tell him, Sarge.'

'For me?'

'A prisoner in custody wants to make an official complaint. Bryony Goddard went to a domestic with Sheila Hipwell – a woman beaten unconscious. Bryony saw to the victim and Sheila arrested the man at the scene. He struggled when she tried to cuff him and is claiming assault because of bruises to his wrist. Roly Willis needs a senior officer and the DCI's at a meeting in Gloucester.'

Tyrell picked up his jacket. 'Has Roly called Chris Collier for possible medical evidence?'

'I'll check,' Clarke said and reached for the phone. 'Pity

we couldn't be like the big departments and only have to deal with one crime at a time.'

'That's wishful thinking so get real, Brian. It's not like it is on TV. We're a small team and understaffed.'

'And how! All the troops we have got spend more than half their time on paperwork only needed to keep faceless and useless individuals happy,' he grumbled. 'Sack the empty suits, more than half the paperwork would disappear and we'd have twice as many men and women on the streets and in the schools.' He sighed. 'I know, I know, you've heard the same thing from Roly. Do you want any help downstairs?'

'Thank you – but I'd rather you kept Mickey up to speed.'

'You've got a feeling about these information thefts, haven't you?'

The DI turned at the door. 'Ever had an itch and you don't know where to scratch? Whoever is behind it all is cynically and efficiently using innocent people for a reason we don't yet know. Any damage they cause is irrelevant to them. We get to clear up the mess and the families get to mourn. I want them, Brian. Badly.'

The air in the interview room was stuffy, laden with the smoke of too many cigarettes hastily burned through. The DI glanced at the man arrested for assault before sitting to face him. Beside Tyrell was DC Bryony Goddard, a slim brunette who would have been very pretty were it not for her grim expression. Calmly, the inspector surveyed the bulk of the prisoner and saw arrogance in his eyes and demeanour. The remains of his cigarettes told a different story, of a man afraid and frantic for a way of escape.

The DI checked that the interview tapes were running then introduced himself and DC Goddard. 'Mr Cutler. You wish to make a complaint?' he asked, ensuring his deep voice was as level and measured as possible.

'I know my rights!' The man pushed at the table and

stood, leaning towards Bryony Goddard and glaring at her. 'The other bitch hurt me and I want her sacked!'

Joe Cutler was an inch or two shorter than Tyrell, massive in build and with his dark hair cut short enough to add a sense of menace. Two or three days' growth of beard, bloodshot eyes and foul breath did not make him an appealing character but the DI was as courteous to him as he was to everyone.

'Sit down, please.'

As Cutler took his time he grinned, his smugness irritating the officer who had brought him from the cells and was standing by the door. He had taken one stride towards Cutler when Tyrell lifted a warning hand, then opened a file, waiting until Cutler had sprawled himself into comfort.

'The assault with which you are charged took place in your partner's home in Aylburton?'

'Yeah. I'd gone to see Jackie an' her mum upset me. Jackie pushed at me and 'er old 'ooman called you lot – an' it weren't nothin' to do with 'er, the old mare. Then two coppers come in, two more bloody females. I ask you! Wasn't right. 'Er in uniform shouted at me and pulled me 'ands be'ind me back. Unnecessary force it was – and that's assault.'

'I see, Mr Cutler. You were angered by this?'

'Bloody mad I was – but I know my rights. She can't do that to me and get away wi' it!'

'Of course not, Mr Cutler,' Tyrell said smoothly. 'We take any accusation of assault very seriously indeed. If it's by a member of the police force we are extra stringent so I would ask you to be patient with me while I go through a few details.'

The PC on duty at the door of the interview room had heard about DI Tyrell. When he was being extra polite he was hopping mad and whoever was annoying him had better watch out.

'Now, Mr Cutler, if PC Hipwell was attempting to handcuff you, you must have been arrested. Did she explain your rights to you? Warned you to be careful what you said because it –'

'Yeah, yeah, yeah. So what?'

'PC Hipwell would have begun by giving you a reason for your arrest. What was it?' Tyrell asked pleasantly.

The question hung in the air. It made Cutler restless and he avoided looking at the DI. 'Tha's nothin' to do wi' this,' he said at last. 'It's sep'rate.'

'Of course, Mr Cutler, but when PC Hipwell goes to trial this is exactly the sort of matter about which you will be questioned. At great length.' He inclined his head towards Bryony Goddard. 'Where was DC Goddard while all this was going on?'

Cutler lit another cigarette and drew on it deeply, quickly. 'With Jackie,' he mumbled before glaring at the policewoman. 'You said I 'it Jackie,' he bellowed at her.

'Had you, Mr Cutler?'

The quietly spoken question penetrated, lingered, in a sudden silence. Eventually, Joe Cutler shrugged his massive shoulders. 'Might of.'

'Did PC Hipwell use the words "serious assault" when she was arresting you?'

'Might a done.'

'And you found it necessary to resist arrest on such a charge?'

'You think I'd let some stoopid bitch take me in? No way!' The man sneered at the inspector in a posh suit.

'I see.'

Tyrell kept his expression unchanged as he gazed at the prisoner. It made the man uneasy and he thumped the table, upsetting the ashtray.

'I know what you're doin' – you're tryin' to get 'er off.'

For a moment Tyrell's eyes blazed, then he straightened his shoulders and took a deep breath of the foul air. 'On the contrary, Mr Cutler, I'm trying to see your rights are being upheld – along with those of everyone else present on that occasion. Mrs Nash, for instance. The events we're discussing took place in her home?'

'So?'

All the officers in the room sensed the tension in Cutler as Tyrell checked the notes he had been given. 'She did not want you entering and tried to stop you?'

'Silly cow!'

The DI was finding it hard to remain civil. 'You broke the door in and sent her flying?'

'The old mare shut me out. What did she expect?'

'Then there's Jackie, the girl of whom you profess to be "very fond". There was an argument?'

'She wouldn' come wi' me. All I did was try to persuade 'er.'

'You were very persuasive, Mr Cutler.' The DI lifted a sheet Roly Willis had handed him. 'Miss Nash suffered a fractured cheekbone and left humerus as well as a sprained left wrist, a couple of cracked ribs and severe bruising to the face and body causing her to lose consciousness.'

Tyrell placed the paper in the folder and gazed at Cutler. The would-be hard man no longer saw a 'posh git too soft spoken for his own good' as he would have described him. This was a physically tough individual, staring at him with an intensity which brought a shudder to the podgy bully. He roused himself to bluster. 'You're 'avin a go at me to stop the complaint!'

'Not at all, Mr Cutler. As I said, I am here to protect everyone's rights, yours as well as PC Hipwell's. She had the right to arrest you, the right you fought against, bruising her in the process. Then there is Miss Nash. Did you know she was pregnant?'

Cutler nodded. 'That's why I wanted 'er back – 'er an' my baby.'

'That child also has rights,' the accused man was reminded, 'the right to a healthy life undamaged by your fists at any time in its existence – even before it's born.' Tyrell stood. 'To the present charge against you of grievous bodily harm I am adding further charges of breaking and entering, actual bodily harm on Mrs Nash and PC Hipwell and resisting arrest. It will be up to the CPS whether you should stand trial for those or whether they prefer to charge you with attempted murder in the case of Miss Nash.'

'Murder!'

'Yes. You knew she was pregnant and you still beat her to a pulp. She could easily have died on the spot if the policewomen had not stopped you. As for the baby, if it dies – you killed it.' He glared at Cutler. 'Take him back to the cells,' he ordered the PC at the door.

'Did he have his solicitor with him?' Clarke asked.

'No. He told Roly Willis he didn't need "no useless brief" to make a complaint.'

The sergeant watched his friend tackle paperwork with a rare savagery. 'Was it bad?'

'Making sure an animal like Cutler gets what he demands as his due? Yes, Brian. Very hard.'

'You don't take kindly to bullies, do you?'

Tyrell expelled air in a long, silent sigh. 'No. It's a deeply rooted reaction.'

'Ah well, I don't suppose you hit him?'

'No!' then, 'No,' came more gently. 'I think it must be because I was the eldest and expected to look after those more helpless than myself. My mother encouraged the nurturing part of me while my father –'

'Made sure you didn't thump too many in the process?'

In spite of his mood the DI smiled. 'He was much more keen on me finding a way to get justice without giving or earning black eyes.'

'He was right, wasn't he?' Clarke asked softly.

'Yes – but today was especially difficult.'

'Why today?' the sergeant asked bitterly. 'I know Mrs Nash will take time to recover and as for Jackie . . .'

'Jackie will be in agony for days, maybe weeks,' Tyrell said softly. 'She could lose her baby and be devastated or, in time, she'll give birth and know she has to raise the child of a thug, constantly worrying if her son or daughter will grow to be like its father. She'll have years of it, Brian,

41

but today is the beginning of every one of us ensuring Cutler remains safe, well and happy as long as he's in our custody, either on remand or doing time.'

Clarke smacked the desk. 'And it could all have been avoided!'

Sergeant Willis walked in and heard Clarke's fury. 'Cutler?' he asked.

'Brian thinks it need never have happened,' Tyrell explained as his friend made a supreme effort to control his temper.

'He's right. Cutler's beaten the daylights out of every girlfriend he's ever had but there's nothing on his record.'

'No one willing to press charges?' Tyrell asked. 'Surely some of the girls could have been persuaded?'

'We tried, all of us, but what good did it do? We couldn't provide protection 24/7 so the girls and their families were threatened and bullied until they withdrew charges. Cutler's got no convictions – and nowadays it means no record of any unsuccessful charges for crimes committed.' Clarke was calmer but still seething. 'Even if we do get him over Jackie, it'll qualify as a first offence. Leniency for his lordship, all thanks due to the Data Protection Act. Remember it?'

Tyrell whistled softly and shook his head in despair.

'It's not just that lout,' Sergeant Willis said. 'My wife teaches a Sunday School in our chapel. She was hopping mad having to be put through the wringer to make sure she was the right kind of person to be around kids, then what happens? She's checked out on the database and gets the same result as paedophiles who've had their police records wiped. Go further. Imagine some young mum who can afford a nanny. She queries past history – same thing but she could have a potential child killer under her roof and alone with her baby.' Roly Willis was an angry man. 'We might have recorded something which could have prevented the attacks on Jackie but it couldn't be used.'

'And if things go pear-shaped, we get the blame,' Clarke added.

The two sergeants continued to grumble about the effect well-meaning protesters had had on their workload while Tyrell sat silent, busy with thoughts and possibilities.

'Not everything gets wiped, does it?' he asked quietly and the others stared at him, puzzled. 'There's information tucked away safely. We could use it to see Jackie Nash gets a fair deal,' he explained, a long forefinger tapping his head. 'I'll bet everyone who worked on those cases has a good memory.'

Clarke's angry expression cleared. 'And notebooks!' he said. 'We have to keep those, no matter what!'

'Right, let's get to it. What form did the intimidation take?' Tyrell asked.

'Joe was never part of it. He always had an alibi, usually because he was in custody. His mother and brother got to the girls and threatened them,' Clarke told him.

'When – exactly?'

Roly Willis knew. 'The night after each girl came out of hospital. Day after that – silence all round.'

'But no attempt to harass in hospital?' the DI wanted to know.

Clarke pondered the question. 'Not that I can recall.'

Tyrell smiled slowly. 'Too many CCTV cameras, perhaps?'

The sergeants brightened as they followed his train of thought. 'I see what you're getting at. Will management wash it?' Clarke asked as the DI picked up his jacket and strode towards the door. With his hand on the frame he turned and looked at his co-conspirators.

'Contact the hospital and find out when Jackie Nash is due to be discharged. I'll talk to the DCI.'

'And I'll have a word with Mr Copeland,' Sergeant Willis promised.

It was a busy forty-eight hours, paperwork and plans for some locally organized justice being fitted into a run of burglaries. Those crimes came to an end with the arrest of a pair of eighteen-year-olds from Birmingham.

Opportunist crimes by outsiders were becoming more common in the Forest but an alert pensioner had rung in. Bryony Goddard and Gerry Cross had nabbed the boys and found their haul in a car reported stolen in Handsworth. The DI had been glad to see the boys taken home by officers from Birmingham who were anxious to get the spotty offenders back in custody for breaking bail conditions. The county's turn would come.

Through it all DCI Leggatt had overseen the work to be done on Jackie Nash's behalf. The girl's stay in hospital had been longer than those of Cutler's other victims, Jackie miscarrying her baby. 'Desperately sad for her, Keith,' Joan Leggatt had said, 'but to be realistic, it will solve problems she would have faced with Cutler in the future.'

'Absolutely, ma'am. The man's a walking disaster.'

Her smile was bleak. 'At least with your idea we can try to limit exactly where he can walk.'

It was another forty-eight hours before that had been achieved, and Keith was tired as he drove home longing for sleep. In a dark green housecoat, Jenny was warm, waiting, her hug a benison. 'Pooh! You stink! Where've you been?'

'Interviewing a couple of reluctant transgressors.'

'They kept you late.'

'Mm,' he murmured, 'but not as late as I've kept them.'

Jenny guessed what had happened and chuckled. 'Before you do anything else you'll hang your clothes to air and have a shower.'

Keith did as he was told, the hot water sluicing away tiredness as it cleansed the stench of Ma Cutler and brother, Wes. It had been a busy day, starting with the news that Jackie Nash would be discharged in a few hours.

Joan Leggatt had already shown her worth and an apparent TV man had reached the Nash home in Aylburton the day before an ambulance delivered a shaky

Jackie back to her own bed. She had been left undisturbed, not knowing of the microphones and cameras placed strategically in her home. Neither was she aware of Bryony Goddard and Sheila Hipwell stationed in a neighbour's house, nor of Gerry Cross and Tim Marsden in a car round the corner as back-up. Roly Willis and Rose Walker had already visited Cutler's earlier victims, reassuring the girls of their safety if they were prepared to give evidence in court.

It was a long wait for everyone, Jackie sleeping under careful sedation in her own bed, until it was late evening and the Cutlers arrived. As was their usual practice, they hectored, screamed, bullied, from the second they pushed their way in but this time, and within ten minutes of their arrival, they were under arrest and on their way to custody, together with taped evidence.

From then on the questioning was intensive. Ma Cutler had defied Tyrell as Joe's brother, Wes, sulked his way through interviews with Bryony and Sheila, neither of the girls at all sympathetic. Brian Clarke had spent most of his time with Joe Cutler, going over his past activities and watching the brute disintegrate as he realized at least two of his former conquests were now willing to add to the evidence piling up.

Stepping out of the shower and rubbing himself dry, Keith reflected on how he had felt making the mother realize she had orchestrated her sons' increasing involvement in crime. On the table he had put a photo of a badly bruised girl, her face barely recognizable.

'Had you let your son be dealt with at the time it might have avoided you facing a jail sentence.'

A second girl was named.

'Again, you bullied and terrorized her and her family into withdrawing the charge. Did it make you feel good?' he asked, grateful for a police photographer who kept her negatives safe from all comers. He spread a handful of images in front of Ma Cutler. 'That was the result. You know the girl because you visited her after she came out of hospital and "persuaded" her to drop the ABH charge.

45

Then there's Jackie Nash. This time the damage done to her was even worse – and she lost the baby who was your grandchild,' he said slowly, emphatically. 'So far, it's the first death.'

Smelling of booze, cigarettes and stale chip fat, Ma Cutler was a woman of big build, floppy fat and long hair hanging loose. She pulled out a grubby tissue to hide quivering lips and it was her only response. Without a word Tyrell rearranged the girls' photos, repeating the build-up of injury to flesh and bone over the years, all leading to a dead child. He leaned forward.

'This time Joe will stand trial and all the charges will go ahead. Then there's you, Mrs Cutler, busy perverting the course of justice as you helped your son add to his crimes.'

'You can't prove nothin',' she screamed at him.

He had tried to smile but it was more a rictus of disgust before he listed again all the data on the audio and video-tapes and watched her shrivel. It helped to see her fear as he quoted the stilted words of the charge of intimidation of a witness: '. . . intending thereby to cause the course of justice to be obstructed, perverted or interfered with.'

Getting some balance into the situation had been hard work, draining but satisfying for the team working with him. The 'desist' man would have an apoplexy, Keith decided, tying the belt of his bathrobe as he made his way to the sanity of Jenny and a leaping fire.

Chapter Three

In the early morning, noise from the holding cells could be heard in reception.

'She ran out of cigarettes last night, screaming like a banshee and keeping all the other clients awake,' Sergeant Willis informed the DI, who had just arrived for duty.

'Mrs Cutler not enjoying our hospitality?' Tyrell asked.

Roly Willis's smile flickered. 'Not one bit.'

'And Wes?'

'Spent the night sobbing, apparently.'

'Because of Cutler's counter-charge against Sheila Hipwell we had to fight for his remand,' Tyrell said, 'but with the evidence we've got on the rest of the family, it should be easier.'

The sergeant nodded. 'With luck they'll stay locked up long enough to persuade the other girls who were injured to stick to their stories this time around. If they do, it'll mean the next female Joe fancies might stand a chance of not having her face rearranged – or worse.'

'Joe Cutler and a new girlfriend?'

'I know, the mind boggles. Still, enough coverage of the trial in the papers should work better than a government health warning,' Roly assured him.

'What about the mother when it's her turn to be released?'

Roly looked over the top of his glasses at the DI. 'As a rule of thumb for Foresters, they'd gang up against us any day of the week, but with a dead baby to account for?' The older man shook his head. 'Leave her to her friends and neighbours. They'll sort her out better than we could ever hope to.'

With rain lashing down outside, the CID room was warm, muggy, busy.

'Sir! Another dead one.' Mickey Walsh covered the mouthpiece of his phone as he waited for Tyrell to respond.

'Where?'

'Cheshire – somewhere. I've got a DI Gale on the line. Can you talk to her?'

Clarke and Walsh were attentive as Tyrell sat at Mickey's desk, scrolling details on his monitor and asking questions of DI Gale. It seemed a long wait and the DI was grim when he ended the call and turned to his colleagues.

'Oliver Westmore. Businessman in his fifties, no sign of ill health that his wife knew about. Six weeks ago he woke up fuddled one morning and decided not to drive. Paid his bill at the hotel where he had been staying in Birmingham, got a train, then a taxi but was dead when he reached his front door. His wife determined to find out the reason for his death but it was officially listed as natural causes.'

'Drugs?' Mickey wanted to know.

'Only the usual were looked for but if he had been given GHB he could have lived long enough afterwards for it to be metabolized. As for the car, daughter collected it and there was thought to be no need for fingerprinting. She did comment on how clean it was.'

'Cards and cash?' Clarke asked.

'All accounted for,' Tyrell said. 'Cards were stopped immediately. Laptop was with him, passport left at home. I've asked DI Gale to check if passport details were in the hard drive files.'

'So, these bastards aren't put off by a death. They must have been confident enough to carry on as usual to dispose of Harding. I wonder why they risked this Westmore chap, as well as Harding?'

Mickey had no doubts. 'Didn't think they'd pop off, sir.'

Tyrell let Mickey resume his seat. There was a brief touch on the young man's shoulder. 'You're right. Harding had no medication in his luggage and I wouldn't mind betting neither did Westmore.'

Clarke pulled at his chin. 'Whoever decided they were to be targeted had access to their luggage – toilet bags and so on. Hotel staff?'

'Hey, Sarge, which hotel?' Mickey wanted to know.

'I think that's our next step,' Tyrell said, 'but we still don't know why these men were selected. Both were wealthy, used to dealing in large amounts of cash. Apparently fit and not searching for sex on the side – DI Gale had thought of that. No signs of sexual activity and both wives seemed caring and devoted.'

'Perhaps that's it,' Clarke said slowly. 'No imminent divorce in either family.'

Mickey was puzzled. 'I don't get it, Sarge.'

'You would if your sister-in-law was in the middle of it. Every scrap of paper gone through, every bank or savings book scrutinized like there's no tomorrow.'

'OK, any target must have useful accounts but all the ones we know about have been left untouched.' Tyrell frowned, thoughtful. 'Perhaps the ones that matter exist only in the future,' he said slowly.

Clarke was puzzled by this. 'What are you getting at?'

'From the start it didn't feel like a passport scam. I think passports may be important but not necessarily for getting on a plane or a cruise liner. I don't believe they'd be used for a fake identity – not in the usual way.'

'For Pete's sake, Keith, what for then?'

'Suppose you've managed to get hold of all the essential details, you could open a bank account in Harding's name – or Westmore's.'

'Why, sir? What's the point?'

'Not to rob them, nothing's gone,' Tyrell explained to Mickey.

'Not yet, sir.'

'No, you're right, but I'd guess they've already discarded Harding and Westmore because probate could turn up any funds tucked away in strange places, but what if they'd lived? Someone has the data for an account, or accounts, to be set up in their names and these men actually existed. What about a change of banks, a different town? Should a reasonable look-alike present identity papers made up from the stolen data, credit checks are made and the new account is opened. Why would the bank people argue? They're not Customs and Excise on the hunt for illegals.'

Clarke leaned back in his chair, closed his eyes and sighed. 'Clever stuff, you must admit.'

'But what's it for, Sarge?'

'You tell him,' Clarke said with a grin at Tyrell.

'Dirty money badly in need of a wash. Cash you can't be caught with. Bit by bit into a series of bank accounts until it's a useful pile. After that, transfers here, there and everywhere but who worries? Harding's or Westmore's name on the original account makes it watertight.'

'But they're dead!'

'They are now and with every scrap of finances in their names under the microscope.' Tyrell waited for Mickey to absorb the information. It did not take long. 'What we have to do is find the ones who stayed alive to be used by the scammers.'

'God, sir, there could be hundreds!'

'But can you think of a neater way to launder money long term? Now, DCI Leggatt said co-ordination was up to you, Mickey.' The DI looked happier, more alert. 'Don't forget the negatives –'

'I know, sir. A negative result can be as useful as a positive.'

'Any names that come in as possibles, check their credit ratings. If they're dicey, then I'll bet they've been discarded.'

'Yes, sir!' Mickey said and settled back in front of his computer.

'What do you want me to do?' Clarke asked.

'Liaise with any force which has sent us information. Let Mickey feed it into his system and double-check everything. If this has to go national, we'd better –'

'Dot the i's and cross the t's,' Clarke said cheerfully. 'What are you going to do?'

'Get my desk clear so I can make sure I'm off on Sunday. If I'm not where she expects me to be, my mother's threatened to disown me.'

Rain drizzled as Keith and Jenny drove east and then north across the county. The windscreen wiper was almost hypnotic with its slow rhythm and distant hills, nearby fields even, were shrouded in thick mist.

'This is what my granny would have called a "real haar",' Keith said, lapsing into the haunting accent of Scottish highlands and islands.

'You and your Gaelic.'

'It's not! Haar is an old Viking word.'

They argued amicably until Jenny settled back and daydreamed, content to be enclosed with him in the warm car and be carried towards a pleasant day with people she liked and could trust.

Keith knew the roads well and ignored the major arteries, going through increasingly picturesque villages until all the houses they passed were honey-coloured and the signs pointed to Broadway. Almost a town now with its daily rush of tourists, it was Sunday-busy and Keith drove carefully before he turned in between ancient gateposts. The Lygon was an old coaching inn which featured in so many of Broadway's postcards.

'There's your father's car,' Jenny said. 'We're late.'

'Not really, just last to arrive.'

They went in through the side entrance of the hotel, the foyer gently shrill with a mix of American and Japanese accents. Keith guessed where his family would be and led Jenny to a large room beside the main door, its stonework, fireplace and antique decorations redolent with centuries-old living.

51

'Darlings!' His mother, elegant in her favourite blue, was on her feet in an instant, hugging Jenny and then pulling down her son's head until she could kiss him. 'Have you remembered Sophie's present?' she whispered.

'Jenny has it – and the card.'

His aunt was next for a hug, birthday wishes made with sincerity for the tall, silver-haired woman with a flash of pale cyclamen at the neck of her simply styled grey dress, still beautiful after years as an army wife and now a widow.

'I'm sorry Peter and James couldn't be here,' he said of his cousins.

Sophie Astley's smile warmed him, although there were tears in her eyes. 'Marvels of the modern world, darling. Your father brought over his machine and this morning I saw both my sons and their families as they wished me happy birthday. Digital conferencing, I think your father called it. Marvellous – distances just disappeared. Then I talked to Jeremy. As you know, he's in Brussels, but you'd never guess, the camera shots were so clear. And Imogen – her new baby's delightful. We had a real family morning, your mother and I both blubbing. You know, it's almost worth getting to my great age.'

There was a quick hug for a lady who defied the years before Keith bent to kiss the cheek of a quiet woman standing on the edge of the circle. 'Nanny. It is good to see you.'

Of medium height, Nanny Bowler was ageing but still sturdily built and dressed, as always on a formal occasion, in a navy costume and cream silk shirt, a cameo brooch at the neck. Keith guessed she must have turned eighty but there was no compromise with time. Nanny had not really altered and was still fine-skinned, clear-eyed and shrewd. All that had changed was the colour of her hair and wrinkles increasing in the soft suede of her skin.

'Well, young Keith. I see that pretty wife of yours looks after you. Are you doing the same for her? She looks thinner than I remember.'

'You've a keen eye,' Keith said with a rueful laugh. 'Jenny's had a bad patch but she's on the mend now.'

Nanny Bowler watched Jenny responding to her in-laws and nodded. A gentle hand touched Keith's cheek. 'She'll be fine now – and so will you.'

They were approached by a thin-lipped young woman in a suit who informed them politely their table was ready. As she waited for them to gather their glasses and belongings, she saw a member of staff passing the door. 'Hadley! See to the fire in here,' she snapped.

Keith swung round as he heard the order and a lean young man walked in. Wearing the hotel's uniform, he was almost as tall as Keith and with thick, straight black hair. He had a long narrow face with a strong, determined chin and deep-set eyes.

'Ben!' Keith went towards him, hand outstretched. 'It's so good to see you. I'm sorry about your mother – and that we were in Italy when she died.' The deep voice was quiet, sincere.

'Oh no, Keith. No need to be sorry,' Ben hurried to assure him. 'You and Jenny saw her in hospital before you went away and the flowers for her funeral were great. You remembered how much she liked irises.'

The manageress took a poker to the fire and rattled noisily.

'How's it going here?' Keith asked, ignoring the interruption and Ben gave a slight, philosophical shrug.

'Not too bad. It suited me while Mum needed me at home. And now . . .'

'What would you do if you had the chance?'

Ben was uneasy, shy. 'Mum always kept on about me signing up for the police. She liked the way you got on.'

'Would it be your choice?'

Fire irons were getting a life of their own, the noise designed to break up conversations and get the Tyrell family moving.

'Look, Keith, I'd better go.'

'See you later, Ben? We were going to call before we went home.'

'Hadley!' came with a firmness which could no longer be ignored and Ben lifted a great log from a basket.

With his mother leading Aunt Sophie, the family party crossed the hall and entered the soaring dining room. The table reserved for the Tyrells was central and it took a little while for them all to be seated comfortably.

'You know, I'm sure it was easier to sit down when Don Russell ran this place,' Lady Tyrell decided.

'Of course it was, Cecily. Since it's been taken over there are more tables here – greater demand, I've been told.'

Keith's mother decided to reserve judgement. 'As long as the food's good.'

It was excellent. Discreetly, Keith watched Jenny. As she had fought back towards full health her appetite had been spasmodic. He need not have worried. Seated between his father and Nanny Bowler, Jenny was entertained as she was encouraged. Presentations on plates and in dishes were tempting in themselves and he saw his wife savouring each mouthful.

Keith's attention wandered as his mother and aunt dissected a mutual acquaintance with social ambitions. Another family party arrived for lunch near them and he watched as a baby was eased into a high chair, seeing the tot squirm and beam with delight as it sat on equal terms with the adults around the table. It was all so different from his normal day and he relaxed in the mixture of voices and the muted clatter of a busy dining room where ordinary people of all nationalities enjoyed what they thought of as a traditional British meal.

When a range of enticing puddings had been slowly demolished, Cecily Tyrell suggested coffee in a quieter place. As movement began Keith saw the baby was steadily absorbing milk from a bottle, cradled in its father's arms as one tiny foot kicked gently and rhythmically. For a moment envy surged in Keith as he saw the father's curve of caring and the child content as it trusted completely.

'One day, young Keith. Just be patient – you'll know

when the time's right,' Nanny Bowler said too softly for anyone else to hear.

He smiled at her, pulling her chair away so she could stand easily. 'Sometimes you see too much.'

'Like I did when I saw you with Ben before lunch? I nearly reached in my bag for disinfectant and plasters. You boys wild in the garden! Peter, James, the skin you all broke. Then when your brother, Jeremy, was old enough to play with the big boys, it often seemed wise to bandage you all before you went off in the morning.'

'We mended, Nanny.'

'Yes, you did. All of you.'

Keith waited until Nanny Bowler left the table and was about to follow her when a woman pushed past. He had an impression of a perfume he could not name and a red suit which was probably the most expensive in a room filled with wealthy tourists. He studied the back of the woman as she strode towards the exit. She was quite tall, her height exaggerated by very high heels. A spell spent as a DC in a vice unit had ensured he came into contact with many such women. This was a classy one, the perfume alone pricing her out of the usual run of girls who dressed to attract money.

Ready to rejoin the family Keith suddenly realized where he had seen that walk before. Gloucester's Pinemount. The plain girl marching away from the reception desk. Mentally, he shook his head. It could not be the same one. This was 'high class totty' as she would have been described in the Met's canteens. The girl in Gloucester was a Plain Jane who stumped her way around a steady job.

Leaving the others to arrange for coffee, Keith went in search of the suit and its contents and saw a scarlet flash disappearing upstairs towards rooms in the oldest part of the building. She must be here with a client, he decided, but there had been no sign of a man. He vaguely remembered seeing her on her own in the dining room.

'Ben!' he called as he saw his friend carrying suitcases towards the car park.

Beyond the side door, Ben put down his load. 'What's up? Something wrong?'

'A woman. Brunette, bright red suit, just gone upstairs. Do you know who she is?'

'On her own?'

'That's her.'

'I don't know her name but she comes here occasionally – always alone. Somebody's paying for an expensive wardrobe because we seldom see her in the same outfit twice.'

'Listen, Ben. Can you get hold of her details?'

'Bra size? Shoe size?'

Tyrell grinned. 'No, this is business. Name, address, car registration number – if she has a car here.'

'You bet she does! Dark blue Mercedes sports and not an old reg either.' Ben scowled at him. 'You're not cheating on Jenny, are you? I'd never help you do that.'

'No way! I told you, this is for the job.'

'If you say so. I'll do what I can. Where will you be?'

'In the small coffee room.'

'OK. It might take a while.'

'No problem. My mother, my aunt and my wife will be there – for hours if they get the chance.'

'Come on, Keith, I'm not as useless as all that with a computer.'

As Ben picked up the cases and headed for an impressive Rolls, Keith walked slowly back to his family. He was deep in thought as he made his way across the hall. The big door swung open and there was a gust of cold air ushering in more guests.

'Keith! I don't believe it! It is you – here, of all places.' The accent was American, the hair longer than Keith remembered it, clothes fashionably crumpled. Only the pretty redhead beside the newcomer convinced Keith he was sure who had greeted him.

'Emma! Clay! What on earth are you doing in Broadway?' he asked, kissing Emma's cheek and shaking hands with Clay Gifford.

'Lunch. They tell me it's good and Emma didn't feel like cooking.'

'Where are you staying?'

'Not far,' Emma said, amused by her former DI and his surprise at their arrival and the tourist outfits they wore. 'Clay's taken a six-month sabbatical to write a book.'

Keith's shock was compounded by the idea of Clay, a typical West Pointer, settling in the Cotswolds and becoming artistic. He had always assumed Clay to be army through and through, delighting in his post as a military attaché at the embassy in Grosvenor Square. 'A book? What's it about?' he asked at last.

'Shady dealings in the Pentagon – a five star general with a mistress or two on the side and a daring young captain who sees the old man gets his comeuppance. Emma's helping me with the female bits – it's why there was no time to cook today.'

'That's our reason for this venue, what's yours?' Emma asked with a grin. She had been a promising DC in Tyrell's team until snatched away to marry her American, and it had been hard not to add 'sir'.

Keith took the new arrivals to meet Jenny and the family, and Aunt Sophie was delighted to have more good wishes for her birthday. Only Nanny Bowler was quiet, merely saying, 'I heard you'd taken a cottage in Stanton,' after she had assured Emma and Clay she was pleased to make their acquaintance.

They were surprised by her knowledge of them, leaving Keith to smile at Nanny Bowler's grasp of all happenings in the locality.

'Stanton? That's great. Look, Jenny and I will try to get over soon – and there's no reason why you can't come and see us.'

The manageress had returned to hover, reminding the Giffords of their booking.

'You'd better go,' Keith urged them. 'We don't want you to miss your lunch.'

* * *

After hugs and goodbyes, Keith began the drive home.

'I never thought Clay would take time out – let alone try the fantasy world of imaginary intrigue,' Jenny said when they had crossed the Severn and were nearing the end of their journey. 'Do you have to go into the station now or can you be on call?'

'I'll ring in at eight. The DCI said I could take it easy tonight if it's quiet.'

A few more miles were travelled, the lingering mist making the evening almost mystical.

'What was in the note Nanny Bowler passed on?' Jenny asked.

'Some data from Ben. He doesn't come off shift until late so we couldn't see him as I'd hoped.'

Jenny snuggled down in her seat and prepared to dream away the rest of the journey. 'I like Ben.'

'So do I.'

Ben had been just as efficient as Keith expected. He had written that the brunette was Rosemary Greenwood, address in Cheltenham, and always stayed in the Lygon on her own. Included was the registration number of the car she used as well as that of the credit card with which she paid substantial bills. Ben had added a postscript. 'No sign of naughties. Has a good go at posh British but I once heard her rip into a maid. She's Euro, possibly Romanian. Hungarian. Shall I ring you when she next turns up?'

Monday morning air freshened as a wind stirred and speeded. After a relaxing Sunday and no call-outs, Keith felt ready for anything. Roly Willis nodded a greeting from behind his desk in the foyer and the DI took the stairs two at a time.

As was normal these days, Mickey was showered, shaved and at his desk before most CID staff staggered up the stairs.

'Morning, sir. Anything new for me?' he called to DI Tyrell and was pleased to be handed details of a mysterious woman to check while Tyrell went to knock at the DCI's door.

He sensed tension in her as she waved him to a chair. 'I hope all your records on this man Harding's death are complete, Keith?'

'Of course, ma'am. Is there a reason you need to ask?'

'Our friend in Chief Super Bayliss's office.'

'Not again?'

''Fraid so. We must have annoyed him recently. He's taken it upon himself to bypass HQ and call a friend even further up the line. Mr Copeland called me at home last night. We'll be getting visitors who expect to take over this identity case but he thinks he's managed to delay their arrival until tomorrow. I know you wanted to carry on –'

'But in this day and age we must use modern policing methods?' The whole team, uniformed and CID, had worked so hard and Tyrell strove to keep the bitterness he felt out of his voice.

'Swings and roundabouts, Keith. These national squads do have the cash and the clout.'

'But they lack local expertise!' the DI protested.

'Of course they do – which is where you come in. Work with them.'

'Easier said than done, ma'am. Too often they think of us as useless yokels.'

Joan Leggatt's chuckle was a merry sound on that cool morning. 'You sound just like my old sergeant when I was a probationer. He said the same of Scotland Yard boys called in when a murder case got stuck. Now, is there anything we need to thrash out before they arrive?'

The CID office was quiet, almost empty, only DC Walsh busy at a computer and Brian Clarke in a corner, immersed in a stack of files.

'Nothing!' Mickey sat back in disgust.

'Rosemary Greenwood?' Tyrell asked.

'Like the driven snow, sir. The car's registered to her at

her home address but there's nothing on the PNC – not even a parking ticket. Are you sure she's involved, sir?'

'I can't be positive, no, but the woman I saw yesterday has a record somewhere. That I am sure about.'

'Under an alias?' Clarke guessed.

'No, Brian. I think Rosemary Greenwood is the alias. Do all the details check out, Mickey?'

'Seem to, sir. The address she gave as her home tallies with her driving licence and her bank data.'

'Humour me, Mickey. Run it through again, will you?'

'No problem, sir,' Mickey replied cheerfully, tapping at his keyboard.

Tyrell leaned over the desk, watching the movement of data on the monitor. 'There it is,' he said and read out the postcode.

'Say that again!' Brian Clarke came over to watch the screen. 'I thought it was familiar. Brenda ordered some pine units for the kitchen and the firm had that postcode. It's an industrial area.'

'So, Greenwood has an accommodation address! I knew it,' Tyrell said.

'What now?' Clarke asked.

'Somehow, Brian, we have to tie her to the girl in the Pinemount.'

'You know, that make of car and the newish number, they'd stick out like a sore thumb. This dishy dolly must have a base, somewhere the car's not so noticeable.'

'Spot on, Brian. Logically, the only way we can trace her as Greenwood is to follow her from the Lygon next time she stays there.'

'Get on to Traffic, Mickey. Flag the car's number and ask they only stop and check ownership. We might get a tickle before she next goes on her hols.'

'That's what it was, wasn't it, Brian? Her holiday,' Tyrell said slowly. 'If she is one of the pair we're looking for, her day-to-day job must be very boring, with occasional spurts of hard physical work on the side. This is a lady who needs to dress up in her own clothes and live in style when she gets the chance.'

'We could get try and get hold of the Pinemount rosters and find when her alter ego's working there – and when she's due a break.'

'Sarge, can't we just tail the Pinemount girl?' Mickey wanted to know.

Tyrell and Clarke turned and stared at Mickey who was puzzled by their reaction.

'Out of the mouth of babes,' the sergeant said with a grin.

'Mickey, you're in charge here,' Tyrell decided. 'Come on. Brian, we're for the Pinemount and make sure you've got a camera.'

'I'll get a Polaroid as well as standard issue.'

'Polaroid?'

'Certainly. If we find her you can click away. I'll use the Polaroid and get an instant print, then we can visit that nice Mr Booker and make his day.'

DS Clarke had a long wait after the DI had gone into the Pinemount, screened by a party of earnest tourists talking loudly of Gloucester Cathedral and its surroundings.

'She's there,' Tyrell told his sergeant on his return. 'Don't know for how long.'

'I've been thinking. How can we annoy our Mr Booker and follow this woman at the same time?'

'Snap. I've been wondering the same·thing.'

Within seconds Tyrell was talking to Mickey Walsh, alerting him to the situation. 'See Sergeant Willis and ask him if he'll let us have Rose Walker with you. When you can, drive to the road leading to the hotel and tuck in somewhere discreet where you can see any cars emerging – as if you were going to head for Cheltenham. Tell us where and when you park up and we'll get a photo of her to you, then we can warn you when she leaves the hotel.'

'Know any good stories?' Clarke asked when all was quiet again and there was no sign of any action.

They had swapped many reminiscences before Tyrell

held up a hand. 'Here she comes,' he said and slid down in his seat. 'Damn! She's on foot.'

Clarke was already calling Mickey. When he answered, the handset was handed to the DI.

'Ask Rose to follow – not too closely – and you keep them both in sight,' Tyrell ordered.

'Yes, sir. What if she catches a bus?' Mickey wanted to know.

'Make sure you keep the bus in sight and find out where she ends up!'

Tyrell and Clarke were making their way towards the hotel when Mickey made contact, reporting Rose on the bus.

'Now for Mr Booker,' Clarke said. 'Should be fun.'

With his feet on the desk, collar open and tie awry, the day manager was relaxing at the end of his shift, a tumbler with a few drops of whisky left in the bottom evidence of his preparations for the evening.

The DI greeted him politely, asked for his help and sat as directed by a flustered young man.

'Something wrong, Inspector?'

'No, Mr Booker, not with your hotel, nor with you,' he was assured. The photo was handed to him and he puzzled over it for some time.

'You don't recognize her?' Clarke asked.

'Yes,' he said and nodded. 'Yes, of course I do. It's Janine Nicholls. But why her? She came with an excellent referral from our Dover establishment and I've heard nothing but praise for the way she handles the customers.'

'Is she efficient? With computers and so on?' Clarke wanted to know.

'Very – one of the best girls we've had on the desk. Guests find she can handle any problem and if one of them is having trouble with their own machine, Janine's always more than willing to help sort it out.'

'Laptops?' the sergeant asked.

'Especially those.'

Neither officer showed any reaction to his comment, Tyrell going on to explain the need for Booker's complete discretion. 'We do need the duty rosters for the last couple of months, Mr Booker, as well as the guest lists.'

Booker heard the quiet authority in the inspector's words and almost stopped breathing. 'Head office –'

'Has agreed to let us have what we want.' The DI pulled a card from his pocket and placed it in front of the manager. 'You may recognize this phone number. Ring it now and check the truth of my statement, if you would be so good.'

Numbly, Booker did as he was told, was extremely deferential to the woman who answered, nodded repeatedly and slowly replaced the receiver. He tried to speak, croaked, coughed and at last managed, 'What exactly is it you need?'

'We're anxious not to add to your burdens, Mr Booker,' Tyrell said and Clarke hid a smile as he bent to pick a piece of fluff from his jacket. The DI in this coaxing mood was danger on two legs.

Before he knew what was happening, Booker had agreed to allow an officer to work for one full day in the office, the cover story being that he or she was from head office, checking the computer system presently used in all Pinemount hotels.

'No one must have the slightest idea what is really happening,' Tyrell insisted.

'But Inspector, this officer. Is he – or she – any good with computers?'

'The best, Mr Booker. Now, for the moment we need Janine Nicholls's address and any other details you can find in her personnel file.'

'You can tell me, Inspector. What's she done?'

'To the best of my knowledge, Janine Nicholls has committed no crime of which I am aware.'

Tyrell and Clarke walked back to their car.

'God, you can lie well!'

'Me, Brian? What lie? As far as I know Janine Nicholls has done nothing wrong. Who it is we're chasing and with whom Rose is sharing a bus, I have no idea. I very much doubt her real name's Janine Nicholls.'

*   *   *

63

It had been a long day. The DI went over, again and again, all the arrangements he had to make, wondering if anything had been omitted. Mickey and Rose had been relieved, having spent hours outside a house in Quedgely which had been divided into flats. The one on the ground floor was well lit but not adequately curtained and the silhouette of its owner could be seen moving about as she cooked her meal and ate it in front of a television set. Janine Nicholls was in what the Pinemount thought of as her home.

In Lydney, the DI reviewed information coming in from other forces, leaving the mass of facts to be collated next morning by Mickey. Would the incoming squad expect to take Mickey from them as well as the data? If that happened, Tyrell's team would be reduced and made less effective. 'All for the greater good' perhaps, but at whose expense?

As Keith turned into his drive, fitful moonlight shone on a car at the front door. It was not Jenny's, nor did it belong to anyone he knew. Unease washed through him and he hurried into his home. There were voices, Jenny's and a man's. Jenny laughed, a happy sound holding no fear. The other voice was familiar but he could not identify it with features until he walked into the sitting room.

'Ben! I didn't recognize your car – have you changed it?'

The visitor stood and grinned, the men shaking hands while Jenny laughed again at Keith's puzzlement.

'I borrowed it from a mate at the Lygon. Mine's getting a new starter motor fitted.'

Keith waved his friend back into his seat and reached for the whisky decanter but Ben shook his head.

'No thanks, I'm driving.'

'I'm not and it's been one of those days.'

Ben waited while Keith sipped, relaxed, sighed. 'That's better. Now, what's happened?'

Jenny and Ben were like happy conspirators. 'The bag

on the table behind you. It's for you but it needs handling with care. Hold it by the handles,' Ben told him.

Cyclamen swirls covered the paper of the container which must have been used for a small present. Cord handles were white and Keith used them to lift the bag, finding it heavier than expected. He pulled the top apart and found inside a plastic bag surrounding a plain but sturdy glass. Not understanding, he looked at Ben.

'I got to thinking as you drove off yesterday. Miss Greenwood – if she's who she says she is – how would you be able to tell? I knew when she was due to leave so I went up to her room to ask if she wanted her cases carried down. I made out I fancied her and she got a bit huffy – said she'd go down and settle her bill. That's when I managed the swap, but I couldn't get away till this evening.'

Keith held up a standard hotel bathroom tumbler by its plastic cover.

'I know you can't use it in evidence, no warrant and so on,' Ben said, 'but it might help you nail down who she is.'

Chapter Four

Keith Tyrell sought peace in his own office. He was steadily updating files on the main computer and a ringing phone was an annoyance.

'Inspector Tyrell?' a strange voice demanded to know.

'Yes?'

'I am speaking from Chief Superintendent Bayliss's office and have here up-to-date reports on your activities.'

The DI waited. Bayliss was officially the 'desist' man who had tried to cut short the investigation into the disposal of Harding's body but Bayliss was a Geordie and this man's origins were in the south.

'Recently,' the pedantic voice continued, 'instead of obeying the orders you were given, you tricked senior officers into letting you continue to waste money. Then there was the cost of using covert surveillance equipment in a case where the man had already been arrested and charged with a minor crime –'

'I presume you are referring to Joseph Cutler?'

'Of course. ABH on a police officer? Hardly the crime of the century as you insisted on treating it, especially as the man claims he was assaulted first. That was bad enough but what do I find on my desk? Plans for keeping a twenty-four-hour watch on a completely insignificant female as well as getting permission for a detective constable to work a full day in a hotel office? This is in addition to tying up yet more staff collating information from national sources as well as you and Detective Sergeant Clarke wasting time in a hotel car park! I don't care if your father is a judge – it doesn't give you the right to play fast and loose with scarce resources!'

The tone had been thin, peevish, and as Tyrell listened he became certain the original interference had nothing to do with DCS Bayliss. 'To whom am I speaking?' he asked.

'That is quite immaterial. This matter is being handled by Chief Superintendent Bayliss's office.'

'But you are a person and you are using my name. I would like to be able to be as courteous and use yours.' The DI did not realize how firmly he was speaking.

There was an uneasy silence then, 'Campbell. Marcus Campbell.'

'Well, Mr Campbell, my father's occupation is not relevant but being related to him does make me aware of the necessity of at least attempting to follow all possible leads – it ensures fewer convictions overturned because of sloppy evidence gathering. You will agree even one such reversed conviction can be a very expensive business indeed?'

'I have to deal with cases at present under investigation.'

'I quite understand, Mr Campbell. I must notify you I have switched this call to record – after all, you should be entitled to the credit for saving your department, indeed the whole force, a significant share of the money available to every division.'

'That's not necessary!' was said hastily.

'I think it is, Mr Campbell. All communications within the service should be open and above board. I am happy to go on tape, surely you are too? After all, you are speaking on behalf of Chief Superintendent Bayliss and I know he will be anxious to hear anything accredited to him.'

'There's no need,' carried a sense of urgency.

'There is every need. All the actions of which you have accused me, including the waste of money, have been discussed with and approved by senior officers.'

'You've obviously been able to fool them – taking something simple and turning it into a three ring circus!'

'Not my style, Mr Campbell.' Tyrell had to restrain
himself. His grandmother's family was Scottish and he
was related to generations of McDonalds. As was his
nature, Keith Tyrell had tried to be fair and he had encountered innumerable delightful Campbells but there were
always exceptions.

'Style! You swan around thinking you're God's gift and
I have to clean up the mess you make of the finances you
spend in such a cavalier fashion. It's my duty to ensure
available money is spent properly and sensibly.'

'If that's what you've been doing, then I'm grateful to
you, Mr Campbell, but everything I do in an investigation
is in the line of duty. All I ever attempt, when I'm prepar-
ing evidence, is to see that my efforts and those of my
colleagues lead to a fair and just conclusion – with no need
for an appeal and no chance of a conviction being overturned. Now, if that is all? I am rather busy today.'

As the DI was putting down the phone with greater
firmness than usual, Brian Clarke came into the office. He
was in time to hear Tyrell deliver a few choice phrases, the
vibrant voice controlled and yet with determined civility.

'Who's upset you?'

'Someone working for or with DCS Bayliss. I called him
"mister" often enough. If he had rank I'd soon have been
told.'

'Campbell?'

Tyrell was surprised. 'You knew?'

'Thanks to one of Bayliss's sergeants the grapevine's
been full of the twit's antics for the last few days. He's
some half-baked number cruncher moved in by the police
authority to "help targets be achieved more efficiently".'

'Well, I've recorded some of my conversation with
Campbell. It's not damaging but it is revealing. Apparently, I'm interfering with the smooth running of CID by
following what he considers unnecessary leads. The
sooner I go home crying, the happier he'll be.'

Clarke chuckled. He had a fair idea how the DI had

dealt with Campbell. There would have been no heavy-handedness but Keith Tyrell's polite, incisive diction was enough to chill the blood of the most awkward of individuals. 'Give the tape to Bayliss. He's been trying to get rid of the little twerp from day one.'

'I'll keep it for now. One day it might come in handy.' The DI stood, was restless. 'Enough of him, any news from Mickey?'

'I think he's enjoying himself. Says he's got loads of paperwork for you and a way into the hotel software – should you need it in the future.'

Tyrell shook his head in despair. 'Mickey's enthusiasm with passwords will get me the sack one of these days. I hope you told him to do it by the book?'

'Of course, but when he's got a mouse under his fingers I'm not sure whose book he's using. By the way, he said he's got the print you wanted.'

'That's great! Is there any result yet from the glass you were going to check for me?'

'The one delivered by your mysterious friend?'

'There's no mystery. We used to fall out of trees together.'

'That's all right then. Actually, it's why I'm here. He got you a lulu,' Clarke said as he opened a folder. 'The lady is called Brosca, then something unspellable and totally unpronounceable. Born in Budapest – she came in as an illegal six years ago but disappeared. She surfaced almost immediately when she married an upright British citizen – well, he must have been standing the day they faced the registrar. A couple of months after that she first established herself in police records on a charge of soliciting.'

'Couldn't Immigration do anything?'

Clarke shook his head. 'Apparently not. There's been no sign of hubby – and no, he's not in our computer so it does mean Immigration are prepared to believe Brosca Thatcher is legally British.'

The DI was startled. 'Mrs Thatcher?'

'Don't laugh. She's been done under the name of

Thatcher for soliciting, prostitution, brothel keeping – you name it.'

'That'd be right. The lady in Broadway looked like someone intent on moving up in the world. She was obviously used to dealing with men – and women – in the money and I guess she likes to hang out where they can be found. It would be useful if she is the same one we saw at the Pinemount but we'll just have to be patient until Mickey's haul is processed.'

'Like the ones from your tree-climbing friend, the prints can't be used in evidence.'

Tyrell grinned and allowed himself a tension-cracking stretch. 'If we're about to be chucked off the case it'll be down to the team taking over to deal with that little problem.'

Brian Clarke was glad to see his friend more relaxed than for some time. 'I haven't had a chance to ask you before. Did you have a good day with your folks?'

'Yes, thank you, it was great. My parents wanted to know all about you and Brenda and they sent their regards. And I met up again with Emma and Clay Gifford – they were in the same place for lunch.'

'No kidding! What were they doing there?'

'Clay's on a sabbatical so he can write the great American novel and Emma's being a housewife.'

'Never! Clay and a book?' Clarke's expression mirrored the extent of his surprise. 'You're telling me Emma's content to play house?'

'That's what they said. Newly-wed, they could have wanted to be on their own, away from the embassy and all the political games being played out there.'

The sergeant studied the DI, who was making it clear he was at ease with what he had encountered. 'You don't sound convinced.'

'Well, you know Clay.'

The careful evenness of Tyrell's voice gave Clarke a distinct feeling of unease which he made an effort to suppress. 'Jenny would be glad to see Emma.'

'Yes, she was.'

Brian Clarke tilted his head, assessing his friend. 'Jenny enjoy her day?'

'Yes, she did. She's more or less back on an even keel, thanks to Brenda and her woman's instinct.'

'Tell me about it!'

'You're lucky your wife's so shrewd,' Tyrell said quietly. 'I'll always be grateful to her. Not only did she make Jenny tell me what had happened, remember it was Brenda who talked to her friends working in that damned clinic and got them to speak out about Ackroyd.'

'Is the creep still a prison psychiatrist in Belmarsh?'

Tyrell's face was dark, implacable. 'Yes, and apparently annoyed it's south of the Thames. The prison work keeps him busy and he spends his spare time in his club in St James's. Very keen on London's social whirl, is our Dr Ackroyd.'

'You've got an informant?'

The DI nodded. 'A retired sergeant I know from Savile Row. He's on the club staff and keeps an eye on Ackroyd for me.'

Clarke eased himself into comfort on the edge of Tyrell's desk. 'It just doesn't seem possible – all that going on in the clinic and none of us guessed.'

'How could we? I knew Jenny had occasional problems at work, some of them keeping her awake at night. She'd get phone calls at home and when she said it was to do with her work at the clinic, I'd do what she did for me – leave well alone. Even Jenny didn't fully realize what was happening until it was too late, and don't forget, she blamed herself. It was only a week or so after she started working there Ackroyd tried to kiss her. She pulled away and made it clear to him she wasn't interested.'

'Pity she didn't get him on sexual harassment then.'

'I did ask her if she considered it but she said it wasn't really an option. New member of staff, no witnesses, and Ackroyd very much her senior in status as well as experience, who'd believe her? It seemed easier for her to keep going and hope he'd soon look elsewhere.'

'That would make sense to most people but not Ackroyd.'

'Not his way, as we discovered from Brenda's friends. It was all done very subtly so there was no sign of cause and effect but any rejection and Ackroyd would start his mind games.'

'God, I hate his sort! I had an aunt that way inclined.'

'The constant playing on a victim's nerves, convincing them what was happening was all their fault?'

'Yep, and he sounds like all the battering husbands we've had to deal with.'

'Same difference, it's all to do with control. When Jenny thought she was at last getting free of him, Ackroyd started working on Jessie Whitton.' Tyrell shook his head. 'Poor, deluded Jessie, she didn't deserve what happened to her.'

'No? She bloody nearly killed your wife!'

'And she's been locked away for good because of it but that sad woman was only ever Ackroyd's tool.'

Brian Clarke was angry, frustrated, pushing strong fingers through the cap of black curls. 'Harassment, stalking, it all sounds so . . .'

'Banal? And the victim's written off as neurotic, yet in every case there's an overkill of hidden terror. The predator gets a kick out of knowing the victim thinks always and only of them – it's how they judge their success. Destroyed minds, marriages, lives, so what?' Tyrell's bitterness was quiet, deep and Clarke understood.

'If Jenny's OK again then Ackroyd's been defeated.'

Tyrell nodded slowly. 'He's out of our lives – and I hope to God he stays there.'

Running footsteps pounded along the corridor towards them and Mickey Walsh burst into the DI's office. He was laden with computer paper above which was a beaming smile. 'Got what you wanted, sir!'

'Good God, Mickey, have you brought everything they had in the entire Pinemount system?' Clarke wanted to know.

'No, Sarge, just rosters, customer details, staff personnel files –'

Tyrell was horrified. 'I never asked for those, Mickey. It's an invasion of privacy.'

'I know, sir, but they were there and I – got carried away.'

'The personnel data will have to be destroyed.'

'Of course, sir. I'll just park it all in a cupboard or something until I've a spare moment.'

'Prints?' Clarke asked.

The DC's happy face became radiant. 'You'd have been proud of me, Sarge. I polished up one of those hard plastic envelopes, took it down with me to reception and got the target to pass it to me. It's being dusted now.'

'Once again I thank Divine Providence you're on our side, Mickey,' Tyrell said with feeling. 'As a criminal you'd run rings round the opposition.'

'I'll take that as a compliment. Thank you, sir.'

There was a brief rap on the door and DCI Leggatt walked in, closely followed by two men. The first was short, broad, pugnacious, in a bulky leather jacket, his heavy features accentuated by an almost shaved head. Behind him was a tall man, equal in height to Keith Tyrell, with the same athletic build and minimal movements.

Joan Leggatt began the introduction. 'Keith, this is DCI Morrison and DI Gonwe from the National Fraud Squad.'

Tyrell shook hands with Morrison, being regarded with the greatest suspicion as he did so. He turned to DI Gonwe and grinned. 'Good to see you again, Jacob.'

'You two know each other?' It was clear from Morrison's glowering that the idea brought him no pleasure.

'Yes, sir. We were in Hendon together and served in various teams on occasion.' Like Tyrell, Jacob had no accent and spoke as precisely as his former colleague. Their voices had the same timbre and both had an air of natural self-control.

Morrison said nothing but even Clarke and Walsh could read his mind. He had expected to deal with a handful of hayseed coppers and had encountered a Met-trained professional, well thought of by his own DI. 'Very cosy,' he said at last to Tyrell. 'This identity business you think you've uncovered, someone in your management has the idea it's worth us having a look as soon as possible. We're here to take over what you've managed to dig up so far. I'll need all the paperwork and disks immediately.'

'Yes, sir. We expected someone like yourself once we realized the extent of the network. There's no way an individual force has the means to carry on, although we would have preferred to tie up all the leads before we handed over to you –'

Morrison sliced the air with his hand, waving aside any further explanation. 'We've not got all day! Are the records up to date?'

'Yes, sir,' Tyrell assured him. 'Mickey, the disks?'

'I'll get them, sir,' Mickey said and fled.

'You'll need a break before you go back to the Yard,' Joan Leggatt said. 'The canteen –'

'No time for that – and certainly none to waste on anyone having an old comrades' reunion.'

The two DIs could have been twins as they stared at the irascible mass of Morrison. Both had the same level, unblinking gaze and easy assumption of authority. Even their fine wool suits were similar and fitted with an equal casual elegance. The difference was in their skin colour which appeared to matter only to DCI Morrison.

Joan Leggatt decided she should break the tension quivering like a taut violin string. 'Keith, will you and Brian explain the beginnings of this case to DCI Morrison. I would not like him censured on his return for not gleaning all he could from our division. I'll have sandwiches sent in to you.'

Jacob and Keith smiled briefly at each other, setting out chairs while Clarke assembled a stack of files, hoping Mickey would stay away long enough to make copies of the disks being taken to London. DCI Morrison reluctantly decided he must delay his return to civilization and removed his jacket, turning the chair he selected so he could sit astride it and lean his arms on its back.

'Ready?' he snapped at his DI who simply opened his notebook at a fresh page and began to write. Tyrell knew it would be date, time, place, and marvelled at his friend's calmness. In the old days Jacob had never been one to suffer fools.

The questioning started. It was abrupt and, on DCI Morrison's part, confrontational. Jacob's queries were inserted quietly and Tyrell realized they were an ideal pairing. Morrison got what he wanted by bulldozing a witness, Jacob by watching and waiting, then asking in a few words the vital question. By the time Mickey came in with a laden tray, all Tyrell and Clarke knew had been passed on.

Morrison stood and helped himself to a sandwich. 'Disks? Where are they?' he demanded of the young DC.

'Nearly ready, sir.' Mickey, doing the wide-eyed innocent act, was young enough to be convincing. 'I'm trying to make sure you have everything you should, sir.'

Brian Clarke hastily put down his sandwich as he almost choked and it was left to Tyrell to pour coffee and tea.

'For Christ's sake, get a move on – we don't want to be here all day!' Morrison bellowed at Mickey who assumed appropriate meekness and scurried from the room.

When the door closed, Tyrell and his friend Jacob exchanged news over their cups while Clarke turned away, dragging a handkerchief from his pocket. Blowing his nose hard helped and he was red-faced but in control when he turned to the others and handed round plates of sandwiches.

The young DC was not away long, returning with carefully labelled disks in one hand, a sheet of paper in another. Morrison grabbed the disks and held out his hand for the paper.

'Sorry, sir, that's for DI Tyrell. Another case.'

'That's the trouble with trying to do the job in the back of beyond,' Morrison growled. 'Too many different directions to go in all at once.'

'For me, that's the attraction,' Tyrell told him. 'I found when I was working in the Met you could only go so far with a case which might be proving interesting and a special unit would take over, excluding you completely. Of course it was possible to apply to join such a unit but then you spent all your working time on one type of crime.'

'And becoming an expert, Tyrell, don't forget that.'

'I agree, sir, but in this county we have such a variety of situations you never know what the next day will bring.'

'Comes to something when you thought a dead man in a car was a challenge!' Morrison scoffed.

'In a way, sir, it was. It's officially death from natural causes but if a sick man is given a potent drug in the commission of a crime and he dies, shouldn't it be considered murder? Manslaughter, at least? Add to that the concealment of a crime, failure to report a death. Criminal offences, sir?'

Morrison snorted his disgust. 'And from all that you decided on this money-laundering theory? Don't you realize we crack that kind of crime on a regular basis? Only the other week we closed down an operation where money was being fed into legitimate bank accounts and passed on electronically to the Far East. Millions had gone before we closed that hole.'

'That's my point, sir. You're in a position to notice large amounts of cash on the move. Let's face it, whatever the crime, following the money nets you the criminals. This set-up is different.'

'Yeah,' Morrison said, his upper lip curling, 'tell me about it.'

'My guess is a very loyal network has been building up a mass of data. They can open accounts for genuine people and about which the named holder knows absolutely nothing. Constantly using fresh names and identities, they can close accounts they've used and escape detection. Money in relatively small amounts can then be moved around legitimately, possibly buying shares in one company or another, purchasing houses, blocks of flats, hotels, factories. There could even be donations to charities or political parties. It could earn the organizers tea in Downing Street and perhaps a mention in the Honours list.'

'And all this from a dead man in a car? Give me a break, Tyrell!'

Morrison was offered a cool smile and then, 'I was hoping you'd give us one, sir. You have the facilities to go over the banking arrangements of the men and women on the list DC Walsh has given you and which he says is the tip of the iceberg. I have a hunch you'll find some of those mentioned have accounts which are regularly very healthy and of which they have no knowledge. With luck, you'll have the solution before the Inland Revenue gets on to it.'

Morrison raised a hand. 'Leave those bastards out of it!'

'I'd like to, sir, but I can't help thinking of a worst case scenario when a number of blameless and worthy citizens suddenly find themselves owing millions in tax for money they never knew they had.'

Jacob, like Keith, had a law degree. 'I suppose if we don't clear it up fast we'd be liable, sir?' he asked his DCI. 'We've assumed responsibility for the case. A good lawyer could argue –'

Morrison hung on to his temper with great difficulty. 'Don't give me lawyers! Let's get back to the Yard – and don't think you're going home early tonight,' he shouted at Jacob before grabbing the disks and paperwork Mickey had prepared. Muttering to himself the DCI stormed out of the room, leaving Jacob to say his goodbyes for him.

'Good luck,' was Tyrell's wish for his friend.

'He's OK really and he is good at his job. Very good. Yes, Morrison's unpleasant but it's because he cares. He has a burning hatred for the swindlers and embezzlers who cheat ordinary people and think it clever.'

Keith Tyrell kept a straight face but his eyes sparkled. 'And you'll learn all you can from him before you play leapfrog and he has to call you "sir".'

Jacob's laughter was a warm, rich sound, lingering after he had gone. Mickey set about tidying up, watched by a surprised Sergeant Clarke.

'By the way, sir,' Mickey said as he picked up the report denied to DCI Morrison, 'this was for you. The result of the print I brought from the Pinemount.'

Tyrell read as quickly as he could, Clarke peering over his shoulder. 'Brosca! It is her. You and your backs,' he told Tyrell.

The young DC stopped filling a waste bin to stare at Clarke. 'Backs, Sarge?'

'Yes, Mickey. If you've time to learn, always remember people take great care how they look from the front. Their backs, especially when they're walking or running, give them away every time. That's Mr Tyrell's theory and he's been proved right on a couple of occasions – this being one.'

The DI had not heard the exchanges going on behind him as he concentrated on the information Mickey had brought him. Frowning, he turned to Clarke. 'OK, so we've proof she's leading a double life, the stolid receptionist and the wealthy lady of leisure. It still doesn't help us tie her in to Frank Harding's death.'

'If you need to solve that little problem, then you can pass it on to Morrison and make his day.'

'I wonder,' Tyrell said slowly, 'did she follow Harding to Northampton? She's daring enough to want to play the dowdy girl as well as the glamorous businesswoman, with her helper somewhere handy.'

'Let it go, Keith. It's not your case any more.'

'Maybe not but when they cleaned so efficiently they robbed us of evidence. Don't forget Anita McBride's PM notes said Harding's ears and nostrils had been swabbed, presumably to clear out any insect eggs.'

'Are you surprised? Everybody's a forensic expert these days with all the TV shows – especially when they see an actor pop a DNA sample in a machine, press a button and get a complete profile in thirty seconds flat. If they ever really needed one they'd have a fit finding out how long they had to wait.'

Tyrell smiled, was silent, as he followed a train of thought. 'The only reason Brosca would have left the body on our patch was to allow her or her accomplice to get back to work on time for a shift. We were agreed on that.'

Clarke nodded and then pointed to Mickey's harvest of paper from the Pinemount. 'Somewhere in there are the answers to the roster problems and it's Morrison's headache now.'

'You're right, Brian.'

The DI shuffled paper into tidiness. During the handover to the Yard men he had often thought of Mrs Harding. At the end of the investigation would the brusque DCI explain to the widow how her husband had died? Would he even bother to tell her? Common courtesy was an essential part of the job but Tyrell asked himself a harsh question. Could he be as open with the Hardings if there was no real need, no way for such an effort to further the investigation? He hoped he would take the time. Mrs Harding and her children had been victims too. Justice might be out of the question but they were at the least entitled to an explanation.

'Have you a moment, Keith?'

No one had noticed DCI Leggatt come in.

'Of course, ma'am.' The DI followed Joan Leggatt to her office.

'Close the door, will you?' she asked Keith as she picked up her phone and dialled. 'And sit down.' Her call was answered quickly but even so the DCI showed a trace of impatience. 'Assistant Chief Constable Hinton,' she snapped at an unseen listener. 'Please connect me now.'

The request was undoubtedly an order and in seconds Tyrell could hear the booming voice of ACC Hinton reverberating at a distance. Without saying a word, Joan Leggatt handed the instrument to her DI.

'Keith? Listen, lad, we've a damned sticky situation building fast. A local paper's got wind something's up and it can be only a few days before the worst of the red tops come crawling under the door. It's this blasted girl lobbying on behalf of the mother – says she's dying any minute now. We're checking it with her GP in case it's all hogwash but we need the facts of the case gone over as thoroughly as humanly possible in case there's a hole in the evidence which got the son convicted. The Chief's tamping and I don't blame him, but I've convinced him you're the man for the job.'

Hinton stopped for breath and Tyrell had an opportunity to try and make sense of all he had heard. 'It's very kind of you to say so, sir –'

'No "buts", I'm not flannelling you. You'll do a good job, as you always do, and you have an advantage nobody of your rank or above has. You were away in the Met and not on our payroll when it happened. Now, your super, Copeland, is in a Home Office conference he can't wriggle out of so DCI Leggatt'll explain what has to be done. She says you're doing a handover to the Fraud Squad wallahs so get those buggers satisfied and out of the way. I've seen to it you'll have all the help you need. No point in saying we must have the truth – it's what we'd get from you anyway.'

The phone crashed into silence and Tyrell handed it to the DCI. 'I gather you're the one who'll explain, ma'am?'

Joan Leggatt paused for a moment, assessing the man in front of her. He was young for his rank and had just been faced with handling an unknown crisis. She looked for excitement, apprehension, seeing only the calm, capable individual she had already come to trust.

'I wasn't here when it happened – in a different division – but I followed the case as best I could,' she began. 'Almost five years ago a young girl went missing. Abby Jenkins, aged nine. Her parents were frantic, there were immediate searches and next morning she was found tossed into some bushes like a rag doll. Extensive bruising and defence wounds showed she had put up a terrific fight. Slashes on her arms and body suggested she'd been attacked with a knife of some sort, one with a short, very sharp blade. She bled out and died while she was being raped.'

'I read about the case. The girl lived near Soudley?'

Joan Leggatt nodded, her face shadowed with harsh memories. 'Disappeared on the way home.'

Tyrell frowned as he concentrated. 'The investigation was rapid, if I remember rightly. A local man?'

'Carl Joseph Miller. He had a small garage, a one-man affair, and his van was seen in the area where Abby was found, around the time her body must have been dumped.'

More facts rose in Tyrell's memory as he recalled newspaper reports of the trial. 'Bloodstained clothing in his home and no alibi?'

'Yes. Forensics clinched it. Miller pleaded not guilty but the jury disagreed with him and he got life.'

'As a child killer he'd be sectioned in prison.'

'And he was. We thought that was the end of it.'

The DI shook his head, puzzled. 'I can't remember an appeal.'

Joan Leggatt looked tired. 'No grounds for one. No, it's his mother. She always insisted he was innocent and fought like a tiger for her son. Over the years she's become exhausted and ill so his girlfriend's taken over the protest. She's a nurse, young and fit, and using everything she can lay her hands on to get him released.'

'The local paper?'

'It's taken a while but at last the editor's interested.'

Tyrell began to understand the panic at HQ. 'I see the Chief Constable's dilemma. If one paper takes an interest, the rest may follow.'

The DCI was silent, then she straightened in her chair. 'That's not all. This nurse is insisting police procedure was flawed and biased against Miller. She says witnesses were ignored – some never interviewed. Once Miller's van was identified at the scene the investigating team never attempted to look for anyone else – so she claims.'

'Is there any truth in what she says?' Tyrell asked softly.

'That's what you've got to find out. I've been through the files, so has Mr Copeland. Everything seems in order – it was almost a textbook investigation.'

The DI sensed Joan Leggatt was uneasy. 'But?'

'I've talked to people who've met this Shona McGuire. Without exception they were impressed by her. She's no fool and would understand the forensics and all they implied but she's still adamant, like the mother, that Miller's completely innocent. It's strange because I gather she's a very logical person yet she appears to ignore all the facts. As far as the media are concerned, Shona McGuire's just getting into her stride. If she's listened to nationally . . .'

'The Chief Constable could end up with a red face smothered in egg.'

'Got it in one. It was Mr Copeland suggested you to the Chief and the ACC. He thought you could handle an internal enquiry discreetly and speedily. Who would you have with you?'

Tyrell did not hesitate. 'Brian Clarke – with DC Walsh and a computer.'

The strong planes of Joan Leggatt's cheeks were illumined by her smile. 'He said you would.'

'The files, ma'am?'

'Sergeant Willis is organizing those. You should find most of them in your office when you get back there. Anything else you need, Sergeant Willis will get for you. Now, is there anything outstanding which is likely to get in the way?'

'No, ma'am. The sudden death in Tutnalls was thought to be suspicious but it appears to have been a minor skirmish between neighbours. The victim started the ruckus, then collapsed with a massive stroke.'

'I'll keep an eye on it. Anything else?'

'A worried shopkeeper. He's had a demand from some organization to do with data protection. It all looks very official –'

'But there's a smell?'

Tyrell grinned and looked younger than his years. 'It was the thought of being expected to pay out a hundred or so to an apparent government agency which got him running to us. It didn't take much checking.'

'No such agency?'

Tyrell shook his head. 'Of course it's a scam and will soon be wrapped up but in the meantime small businesses could be ripped off. The trouble is, we can shut down the fraudsters but in a week or so they'll pop up with a new idea, a new address and a new mailing list. I was going to have a word with the local Chamber of Commerce – alert them to the fact they're a target area.'

'Now she's free of the Cutler business, Bryony Goddard can handle it. The Chamber's chairman is very susceptible to female officers,' Joan Leggatt said with feeling.

'Thank you, ma'am. I'd better get started.' Tyrell prepared to stand but saw the DCI seemed to want to say more. He waited.

'It won't be easy, Keith. You'll be seen as checking up on working colleagues. They won't like it and you could get a rough ride.'

The DI had had bouts of difficulties since he first arrived in Lydney, finding out the hard way he had to keep going and work to the best of his ability. There were enough men and women in the station determined to make up their own minds. It was all he asked.

'Part of the job, ma'am, but it will be nothing as bad as Carl Miller's already endured if he has been wrongly convicted. Protected by a 47 he may be but it will still have been hell on earth for a supposed child killer.'

'Remember, you'll be seen as someone trying to get him released and possibly pardoned,' the DCI said quietly. 'If you do that you'll have to prove men and women who worked here, on that case, presented flawed evidence to secure a conviction. It won't go down well, Keith.'

He saw genuine concern for him in her expression.

'Watch your back,' she said quietly.

'You wanted me?' Clarke asked as he pushed open the door and saw Tyrell working his way through a pile of folders, Mickey intent on a screen nearby.

'Yes, Brian. Have a seat – and Mickey . . .'

The young man looked up, his eyes still dreamy, focusing as he looked away from the screen. 'Sir?'

'Take a break. I don't want you losing your sight on my account.'

Mickey was pleased and grabbed his jacket.

In the quiet aftermath of the DC's departure, Clarke was puzzled. He saw boxes of files on every available surface, including the floor. 'This looks ominous. What's going on?'

'Does the name Abby Jenkins ring a bell?'

'Oh God, no!'

Tyrell could see remembered agony in his friend. 'I'm sorry. It must have been hard on you all, Abby so young.'

The sergeant bowed his head, still grieving for the child ripped from innocence. His own daughters had been little more than babies then and he had suffered with Abby's parents. He lifted his head and stared at the DI. 'What's happened?' he asked quietly.

It took few words for Tyrell to explain and, as he watched, he saw Clarke's fury flare. 'There's a chance the bastard will get out?'

'Only if he's not guilty, Brian.'

The sergeant began to pace the small room. 'Not guilty? By whose standards? Ours? Or some smart-assed brief's?'

The DI let Clarke keep moving, knowing the short, strong steps would help ease a flare of emotion. 'All we're going to do is go over the evidence presented in court and make sure there's no possible crack in it – ahead of the media. We don't have a lot of time.'

Clarke stopped as though he had been hit. 'But I was there! We all did our damnedest and it was a good case. Watertight! OK, so it was mostly circumstantials but Eric Livermore came up trumps and the jury went along with what he found.'

'Bear with me, Brian. I've been handed a mammoth job to do in a matter of days and there's all this to wade through,' Tyrell said, gesturing to the heaped files and waiting boxes. 'I'm going to ask you to do something a bit odd. I want you to have an ordinary notepad handy – not your official one. Then I'm asking you to cast your mind back to the moment you first heard Abby was missing. I don't want anything from you I can find in these reports and statements. What I'm after are the thoughts and memories you have, the smell of a witness, for instance, or anything which seemed odd at the time – impression of parents, medical staff, Miller himself.'

'Write notes on it all?'

'Just jot down enough to hold the memory and let your mind hop around.'

Brian Clarke stared at his friend. 'You want me to relive the case?'

'No, Brian, not want. I need you to relive it. You were there and I trust your instincts but we don't have time on our side. Once there's a media circus outside the gates we'll have an outside force – or two – going through every dot and comma on every scrap of paper in the building. Anyone who was working on Abby's murder will be put through the wringer.' The DI was grim, seemed to have aged. 'I won't get much sleep tonight with all this to sort through but it'll be worth it if it stops a guilty man from going free – or frees an innocent one.'

Clarke had no illusions. 'You could have the major problems right here, especially with the older ones. They'll see you as the enemy,' he warned.

Chapter Five

Tyrell was weary next morning, hiding it behind freshly shaved skin and the invigoration of cold water at the end of his shower. Clarke was no better, rubbing his eyes as he walked into Tyrell's office and murmuring 'Good morning' to the DI and Sergeant Willis.

'How's it going?' Clarke asked, nodding towards paper and folders massed on the desk.

Tyrell stifled a yawn. 'A long way to go yet but I can see why the CPS thought they could make a good case – and why the jury convicted. How about you? Any useful memories?'

Clarke was silent, his features dour. It had been a long night. 'Nightmares, more like – I was at little Abby's post-mortem. Still, I did what you asked.' The sergeant pulled a notebook from an inside pocket of his jacket. 'It's all disjointed,' he said, offering the book to the DI who raised a hand in negation.

'It's not for me to read. I only want you to recall any oddment and add some colour to all this paperwork. What about you, Roly? You'd have seen how the investigation went. Can you help out with any memories which might be useful?'

'Odd scraps not in the files? I could try, I suppose. Don't you want to ask any of the others?'

'Not at this stage. Later, perhaps.' Tyrell smiled at them, a bleak effort that time in the morning. 'When I've harvested all I can from you two.' He started checking his pockets, making sure he had all he needed. 'We've an appointment, Brian. Mrs Miller and Ms McGuire are expecting us.'

'That was quick!'

'Logical next step. DCI Leggatt rang last night and organized it. The Ms McGuire's a district nurse and we have to see her before it interferes too much with her rounds.'

'She's a tough one,' Roly Willis warned. 'As for Mrs Miller, she's a nice woman but I've heard she's not so good. Nothing physical, just that she's been fighting for her boy so long she's worn out and on the point of giving up.'

The morning air was cold, bracing, and it heartened the two detectives until they were in the car and heading east on the A48. The heater warmed them and tiredness deep in bones dragged at them.

'What are we after?' Clarke asked.

'Nothing specific. The women believe they have evidence not presented at the trial, so we let them talk.'

Clarke's surprise almost woke him completely. 'Is that all?'

'After so many years struggling with lawyers, neighbours, police – and largely being ignored – it's about time someone heard what it is they have to say.'

'Better us than a national daily?'

'I think so.'

The countryside had been washed by heavy rain in the night and a fitful sun sparkled water on branches and grass. The turn to Soudley was soon reached and Tyrell ran the car smoothly between cottages scattered on the banks either side of the road. Slowing down as the end of the village came in sight, he stopped the car and switched off the engine.

'Which one is it?' Tyrell asked.

'Last on the right. You can tell it by the graffiti showing through all the new paint.'

Someone had made a great effort to remove the word

'murderer' from the garden wall but it had originally been applied in a strong red enamel. In what was an idyllic setting the cottage would have been charming had its windows sparkled and not been dulled by time and neglect, wooden frames dry of preservative of any kind. The roof looked sound enough, the DI decided, although a few slates were cracked and moss greened where it could.

'Is that where he worked?' Tyrell asked, pointing to a rickety structure of corrugated iron in a space beside the cottage.

'Yep. Miller was a good mechanic by all accounts. He was saving to build a bigger and better workshop but all that cash went to pay for his defence.'

A large red gash across the garage door blotted out the name 'C. Miller'. Underneath had been two telephone numbers, Tyrell presuming one was for Miller's home, the other his mobile. The rusting iron sheets looked as though they had been battered by many stones and windows had been replaced by slabs of wood.

'It would have looked welcoming, prosperous even, before the murder,' the DI remarked.

'Blast the man!'

'What's the matter, Brian?'

'The car that's stopping.' It was long, sleek, silver. 'Unless I miss my guess we'll have Jonathan Hedges with us when we go in.'

'Hedges?'

'Father, Philip, was Miller's solicitor. Very good at the conveyancing, our Mr Hedges senior – at least his clerk is. This time in the morning Daddy's probably too busy getting ready for a round of golf to be bothered with the family of a past client. I'll bet Baby Hedges must've got a sniff of the media and fancied himself on TV.'

Tyrell was annoyed. 'I didn't bargain for this. We need everything calm and quiet to get the women to talk freely.'

'No chance of that with our Jonathan, I've heard him in court. Thinks he knows it all but his law degree's so new and shiny you could use it as a mirror.'

With a glance at the dashboard clock, the DI prepared to move. 'Let's get at it then – and remember,' he said, fixing Brian Clarke with a sharp stare, 'calm and quiet.'

'As a mouse,' the big man assured him.

The garden gate creaked and wobbled as it was opened. Concrete steps and paths were slippery with algae, flower beds empty of all but dead plants and thriving weeds. The front door may have received its quota of graffiti but a certain defiance had driven an unknown hand to cover it with a shiny new coat of bright red.

Clarke's knock was answered by the nurse, her navy blue dress brightened with the kind of badges Tyrell knew to be hard-earned in training. A pendant watch was pinned to her right breast and he saw she checked the time using her left hand. The DI introduced himself and DS Clarke but there was no reaction. The woman stared at them and they returned her gaze. Shona McGuire was very attractive, with broad cheekbones and large eyes. Her clear skin was dusted with the brown of the Caribbean, although her features had strong links to native British stock.

'You'd better come in,' she said at last, pointing to a door in a side wall of the narrow hall.

As he led the way into the room indicated, Tyrell decided the nurse had grown up in Scotland, possibly Glasgow. Was it there she had learned to stand up for herself?

'Mrs Miller.' The DI held out his hand and she slowly raised hers to greet him, not knowing how disturbed he was by the feel of fragile bones hardly capable of movement. 'Thank you for letting us see you. This is Detective Sergeant Clarke and I am Detective Inspector Tyrell.'

The woman looked old, exhausted, and at the end of her strength. Keith Tyrell had seen many women of eighty with the same appearance but he knew from the files Winifred Miller was only sixty-two. She had been tall and strong, her big bones angular. They were awkward now, her clothes dull-coloured and hanging on a once robust frame. Only her eyes were alive in the wrinkled skin, eyes from which blue had been washed by despair to a pale grey under whitened hair thin and limp, her brushed scalp barely pink. Mrs Miller did not blink as she stared first at the DI and then his sergeant. She nodded, her decision made.

'Inspector Tyrell, I am Jonathan Hedges and Mrs Miller's legal representative. I warn you I will have no –'

He was silenced by Tyrell's steady regard, the smaller man swollen with puppy fat and indulgence. Brown curls had been gelled to add age but he was still the kind of obnoxious small boy loathed by teachers and pupils alike.

'Mr Hedges, we are here to listen to whatever it is Mrs Miller and Miss McGuire wish to tell us. Nothing more and nothing less. I would be grateful if you did not interfere,' the DI informed him, his manner, as always, civil.

'I will not allow you to harass them!'

Tyrell turned to the two women. Shona McGuire was standing beside Mrs Miller, a hand on her shoulder to give them both comfort. 'Did you ask Mr Hedges to come here this morning?'

'I just rang to say a DCI Leggatt had set up an appointment,' the nurse said.

The DI swung to face the lawyer. 'So, you've come on your own initiative? How very enterprising of you, Mr Hedges, since you cannot then charge anyone for your time. Please, do take a seat. You may make notes but I ask, since you were uninvited, you keep quiet and let these ladies do the talking. For our part, DS Clarke will also take notes –'

'While I suppose you question these poor women!'

'I will ask you just once more, Mr Hedges. Please sit down and be quiet – or leave.'

As he prepared for his note-taking, Brian Clarke concealed a smile. Tougher men than young Hedges had done as they were told when the DI was not prepared to tolerate interference.

Tyrell lifted an upright chair and placed it in front of Miller's mother, seating himself so she could look directly at him without strain. 'Mrs Miller, I was not in the area when your son was under investigation. At that time I was a member of a different police force altogether. I've read most of the files of evidence but I need to hear what you have to say. It doesn't matter in which order it comes but it may help to start with the night you went to the whist drive.'

Moments passed, Mrs Miller looking up at the nurse for reassurance.

'Go on, tell him,' the younger woman urged.

Winifred Miller began to talk, slowly, quietly. Then came anger, frustration, and Tyrell rode the storm. He was attentive always for a fact, a tiny detail which might help clarify the puzzle. There was no doubt in his mother's mind Carl Miller was innocent. Blood had been put on Carl's clothes by another person, she insisted. There had been a phone call, a motorist asking for help. Carl had said it was to his mobile but the only call traced was to the phone in the house, a brief connection with the caller not speaking when the answering machine cut in.

Then memories became rambling, details increasingly hazy as her weariness drained Mrs Miller. She was fighting yet again for her son but hope was weak. As she gazed at Tyrell, there was a silent pleading in her eyes and in every line of her.

'I think you could do with a cup of tea, Mrs Miller. Brian?'

Willingly, DS Clarke rose and headed for the kitchen, needing no one to tell him where everything was kept. He had been one of the searchers all those years ago.

'Don't you want to ask me any questions?' the frail woman asked the DI.

'I promised I was here to listen,' he reminded her.

'I've got some questions,' Hedges persisted but was ignored as Tyrell looked up at the nurse.

'Miss McGuire?'

'You want me to talk?' she asked bitterly, her fury barely controlled. 'I talked when your people came here and ripped this place apart. I screamed at them when they handcuffed Carl and bundled him into the car, not caring if he hurt his head when he was pushed into the back seat. Who listened then? No one!' She drew breath, air rasping in her haste. 'Why should I talk to you now? Better I wait until reporters come, then let's see how you like it when it's your names in black and white – guilty as charged – all of you! You're only here today to stop that happening. You, Inspector Tyrell, with your nice manners and your smooth ways, you're the defence for those bastards who got it wrong. Well, I hope you make a better fist at it than that fool's father did for Carl. "My dear, I'm not used to criminal work, you know," he told us.' Her imitation of Hedges senior was good enough to bring his son out of his chair. 'Useless, he was – and that barrister, Haliburton. Both were being buddy-buddy with the prosecutor. He was a QC and they made his job easy for him.' Tears in her eyes were ready to fall. 'Carl didn't stand a chance.'

A stern expression and a slight gesture from the DI had Hedges seated again.

'Miss McGuire, I've only the records of the investigation and the trial transcript to go on. You know as well as I do, for an appeal to succeed there must either be new evidence presented or a fair and reasonable criticism of the way the trial was handled. You may rightly have grave doubts as to the efficiency of Carl's solicitor and barrister, in which case the Law Society would be interested in what you have to say. Unless you talk to me, remember any detail I don't have in all the paperwork I'm wading through, how can I get at the truth?'

'Truth? You want truth?' The girl's laughter held a strong element of hysteria.

'Yes, Miss McGuire, it's what I've been asked to determine and with Sergeant Clarke's help I will find it,' Tyrell said quietly, firmly. 'If there has been a miscarriage of justice and any member of this county's force is responsible, they will be dealt with. You have my word.'

Mrs Miller turned her head, a slow, stiff movement. 'Trust him, love,' she said to the girl who was as a daughter to her.

Shona McGuire fought her emotions before breath escaped her in resignation. She had little to add to the few facts supplied by Mrs Miller, only emphasizing Carl's shock stunning him into bewildered silence as hordes of detectives and uniformed men and women invaded his home, upset his mother and girlfriend, then removed him from them for ever.

'I'm telling you, Inspector, Carl had no idea what had happened. He kept being questioned about how he'd picked up Abby the day before, how he threatened her with a knife, then raped and killed her. He had no idea what any of them were talking about. I tell you, he had nothing to do with it! As far as I could tell, the two policemen we saw most often never considered any other suspect but Carl. We told them about Duggie Beech going past the garage and hearing Carl working there when he was supposed to be harming the child. We even tried to tell your dad,' she stormed at Hedges, 'but he wouldn't listen either. Duggie's been dead a year so it's all too late now.'

The DI said nothing, watching the nurse's face, her eyes, the way she twisted her fingers.

'Why won't you believe me?' she pleaded.

'Because I have to work on evidence, Miss McGuire. I will check out what you and Mrs Miller have told me and I ask you to give me time to be thorough.'

Jonathan Hedges had been quiet too long for his own self-esteem. 'So you can brush it all away as was done last time?' he sneered.

'I would be very careful, if I were you, Mr Hedges. Your father and his friend, Mr Haliburton, were responsible for Carl Miller's defence. Should we find a miscarriage of justice, the practice you represent must take part of the blame.'

'Don't be ridiculous! There's nothing with which you can charge us.'

'I won't be trying, Mr Hedges, nor will I be reporting you. The Law Society has its own ways of dealing with the slipshod.'

Hedges drew himself up to his full height, annoyed he had to crane his neck to face DI Tyrell. 'What do you police know of the law and its officers?'

DS Clarke had kept an ear on proceedings and decided it was time to carry in a tray of tea. He heard the lawyer's question. 'Come now, Mr Hedges,' he intervened in a heavy whisper. 'The inspector's father's a judge, his brother's a barrister and he himself has a law degree from Oxford – first class, too, so if you want to pull rank, you'd better pick on someone else.' The sergeant bulked large as he stood over the solicitor who seemed to get smaller by the second.

When Hedges had shrunk to complete silence, Clarke handed round the reviving tea, helped by Shona McGuire. Unobtrusively, Tyrell watched Mrs Miller, seeing the hot beverage bring colour to her cheeks and an easing of taut muscles. He reached into a pocket. 'Here's my card, Mrs Miller. It has my mobile number so you can reach me any time. It's been very hard for you today, I appreciate that, but maybe a few items will begin to surface now and they could prove useful. Don't forget, we're here at the express order of the Chief Constable to get at the truth. Like DS Clarke, I'm Gloucestershire born and bred, and if any procedure's been carried out wrongly, we want it cleared up.'

Winifred Miller nodded as she took the slip of cardboard. 'I believe you will at that. Thank you.'

'And my numbers, in case you can't get hold of Inspector Tyrell for some reason,' Brian Clarke added as he gave her his card.

She looked at the sergeant. 'I remember you from before. You didn't judge me as all the others did. "Ye shall do no unrighteousness in judgement,"' she quoted softly.

'"And thou shalt not respect the person of the poor nor honour the person of the mighty, but in righteousness shalt thou judge thy neighbour,"' Clarke answered, surprising his listeners.

'You know your Bible,' Mrs Miller told him.

'Not really. It was my old Nan used to use it all the time

when my Dad was around – said if she had to have a policeman for a son-in-law, she'd make sure he did it properly.'

'Did you learn what you wanted?' Clarke asked as the DI pulled into a lay-by on the Forest route back to Lydney and the bustle of a busy station.

'It set the scene. We've lanced the mental boils of those two women so they may be ready to allow useful images to float up from the depths.'

'I've just realized you and DCI Leggatt set up the meeting in Emanuel Cottage for a purpose. You wanted to trigger off thoughts in me, too, didn't you?'

Tyrell said nothing, watching a man walk with his dog as it sniffed at interesting clumps of grass along the green verge of the roadway.

'You're a devious bastard!'

The DI grinned, was suddenly younger and less tired. 'Did it work?'

'Yes, damn you, it did. For a while I was back that day as the house was torn apart. Mrs Miller was turned to stone and Carl . . .'

'What about Carl?' Tyrell asked softly.

'He was so bemused by it all – kept asking what we were doing. I tried to explain but he couldn't take it in a child had been horrifically killed and he was being blamed.'

'Did he strike you as intelligent?'

'Not at first, he was like a zombie. Then I had to collect his paperwork, go through magazines and books in his room. No smut at all, just trade journals and books.'

'What sort of books?'

'John Grisham, Dick Francis. He obviously liked a good story with plenty of detail.'

'If that was his choice of reading matter, would he be the kind of man likely to leave such an obvious clue as the victim's blood smeared on overalls waiting to be washed?'

Clarke was restless, his mind roving one way, then another. Startled, he sat erect. 'That's it! That's what I thought of at the time. Funny. You think your mind has everything organized.'

The DI waited.

'I had to bag the evidence,' Clarke explained. 'I was in the scullery and as I lifted the overalls it struck me as odd. You used the word "smeared". The stains hadn't come from blood gushing from a child's artery.' Clarke closed his eyes, the better to concentrate on the image he was seeing. 'I remember thinking it looked as though someone needed to wipe off blood and had used the overalls.'

'What else was ready for washing?'

The sergeant raised his eyebrows. 'I don't know – or maybe I do,' he added slowly. 'Some of Mrs Miller's things. A blouse, an apron, stockings. Towels, there were towels.'

'The overalls, where were they in the basket?'

Clarke closed his eyes, frowning as he tried to relive the moment. 'At the bottom,' he said at last. 'They were on the top of the pile I had to search but that was because I'd tipped the contents on to the washing machine.'

'And a normally careful man left them for his mother to wash when it was a good drying day?'

It was quiet in the car, each man intent on his own thoughts. It was Tyrell who broke the silence. 'Brian, there are two possibilities. Carl Miller abducted, raped and killed Abby Jenkins –'

'Or someone else was the murderer? Trouble is, who?'

'That we come to eventually, if necessary. Our first priority is to find out if the evidence left at the scene and in the Miller home was doctored to fit Carl Miller exactly.'

'One of us?'

'It's possible but not because they're the killer. Pressure of getting a result – was it severe?'

'Are you kidding? After Fred West and Cromwell Street?'

'There is a third possibility.' The DI saw Clarke's doubts. 'The murderer outlined a frame to fit Miller and overzealous officers helped things along. Could that have been accomplished by just one of our people?'

'I suppose so. If they had enough rank.'

The DI mulled over what Clarke had said. Determined to be as fair as possible, Tyrell had so far allowed no mention of any individual officer's activities in the previous investigation. It had become increasingly clear he could no longer afford the luxury.

'You've been pretty good at stirring up old ideas but what about you?' Clarke asked. 'OK, you're new to the case but you must have a first impression.'

'I've tried not to – until now. Seeing Mrs Miller, the girlfriend, listening to them in his home, the man doesn't match up with the crime.'

The sergeant riffled through his notebook and found an entry. 'Snap,' he said, showing a page to the DI. 'I thought at the time the way Abby had been picked up, it was so quick, so – slick.'

'And you thought, as I did, it wasn't a one-off crime. It had been done before?'

'Yes. After the searches it was even more puzzling.'

'Plenty of reading matter but not a single scrap of paedophile material. Was there any history of Miller watching small girls, taking photos of them?'

'Nothing.'

'If you'd been in charge of the operation what would have been your first move?'

Clarke had no hesitation. 'Look for similar murders elsewhere. I'd have put out a call nationwide.'

'Do you remember it being done?'

Slowly, Clarke nodded. 'In the first big briefing, the DCI in charge asked for a check with all forces.'

'The only mention in the records of the case is a note to say Abby Jenkins's death could not be linked with any others as Miller had never left the area.' Tyrell paused, needing to choose his words carefully. 'Who was asked to cover that part of the investigation?'

'One of the DIs. Pete Simons.'

It was quiet in the warm car as a white face with a cruel

mouth and supercilious sneer beneath a dark widow's peak flooded Keith Tyrell's mind. How Pete Simons had hated him and a harmless boy died because of it. The DI opened a window, feeling the air in the car suddenly oppressive. 'And of course the DCI was –'

'Whittaker.'

Richard Whittaker. No matter what had happened he had always been an excellent detective. Had Simons not been his right-hand man Whittaker could still be active, working well and climbing the career ladder as he had planned instead of being invalided out of the service he had loved.

The DI lay back in his seat and closed his eyes. 'Was this one of the cases where Pete Simons cut corners?' he asked softly.

There was a rustle of paper. 'See for yourself.'

Tyrell took the notebook. In his clear writing Brian Clarke had recorded, 'Whittaker was on the ball. Simons seemed to get his answers too quick for comfort.'

Keith Tyrell knew what it was like to be hounded by Whittaker and Simons. He had suffered from DCI Whittaker's jealousy of a younger man and, having given evidence against Simons in a case of an assaulted prisoner, had seen that DI reduced to a sergeant's rank. It had earned him enmity which ended only with Simons's death.

'When I opened the first file I could see I'd be walking a tightrope,' Tyrell admitted.

'Rope? More like a thin wire with those two involved.'

'You're right, Brian. Even from the grave Pete Simons is on my back.'

'Forget him!' was good advice for Tyrell. 'Mickey's done with the identity business now Morrison and your friend Jacob have taken over. Shall I get him on to chasing past child murders with any similarities?'

'A good idea, Brian. Let's open it right up the middle. It'll mean some flak from the original team but I can stick it out if you can?' He turned and there was a wry smile for his friend.

'Brenda tells me I've the hide of a rhinoceros, so go for it. What's first?'

'I'll have to run the three possibilities past DCI Leggatt but she's a stickler for the truth so we should have no difficulty following our lines of enquiry. As for me, I'll get stuck into the forensics and see if there are any discrepancies.'

'There were no problems at the trial,' Clarke reminded him.

'No, but I want to make sure every scrap the forensic people collected was fully examined and considered.'

'You've got one of your hunches, haven't you?'

'Not really. I've been making my own list of odd ideas, as you have, and one line reads, "too neat".'

'Yes,' Brian Clarke agreed. 'That's what made me uneasy at the time.'

DCI Leggatt had listened intently. 'You're telling me that not only was the victim selected, the individual to take the blame was also picked out in advance?'

'It's only one possibility, ma'am. If we're to keep an open mind, that particular scenario has to be considered.'

'Phew! I must admit it's an idea which would please Mr Hinton and the Chief Constable. Then it would also take the heat off all the men and women on the first investigation.'

'But not completely off the hook, ma'am. I think it was accepted at too early a stage in the enquiries that Carl Miller was guilty –'

'And anything not pointing that way was discreetly lost?'

'That, I can't say at the moment. I'd need to do more interviews with personnel active at the time and I'd prefer to keep those to a minimum – it would be less disruptive.'

'I'm sure it would! Get on with it, Keith. Dig up the dirt

as quickly as you can. If it's thoroughly exposed it'll smell less offensive in the end.'

The noise level in the canteen dropped as soon as the DI walked in. He appeared to take no notice but his quick glance had seen it was small groups of the older men and women, uniformed and CID, who had stopped talking and watched him with a mixture of wariness, anxiety, suppressed anger. Tyrell felt a chill between his shoulder blades and recognized primeval fear rising to warn him.

He still missed some of his colleagues who would have defended what he was doing. Bob Vidler was part of Gloucester CID and Penny Rogers's admin expertise had at last been recognized. She had earned her promotion but being a desk-bound DI would not really suit such a good detective. At least she was at HQ. Then there was Emma. She had always been a fiery stalwart until marriage had transferred her loyalties to Clay Gifford and whatever he was up to in Stanton.

'Chips with it, Mr Tyrell?'

'What? Oh – sorry. No thanks.' He smiled at the patient woman behind the counter. 'I might enjoy myself too much and nod off later. I've got to keep my wits about me.'

'Sorry, darling,' he apologized into his phone.

'I know, you'll be late home. Never mind,' Jenny said cheerfully. 'I'm meeting up with Brenda for a girls' night out and she's coming back here so Brian can collect her on his way home.'

'It could be very late,' he warned.

'No problem. We get tired, we go to bed. You and Brian can decide who has our couch – if you don't plan to spend the night in one of the cells.'

Tyrell was smiling as he replaced the handset.

'Jenny OK about you working late?' Clarke asked.

'Very chirpy, considering. You, on the other hand, may not be. If we don't finish early enough for you to transport

Brenda home, you get to sleep on our couch while I get the floor, apparently.'

'Cheeky little madams! And what about the girls?' Clarke asked of his daughters.

'I'm assuming they're having a sleepover at Grandma's.'

'It's probably just as well. I've had a shufti at what Mickey trawled up. Seven cases.'

Tyrell was stunned. 'My God! Identical?'

'More or less.'

'Carl Miller can't have done any of them,' the DI said slowly.

'His comings and goings we all knew parrot fashion in the end. At the time, had we known this data, any one of us could have flagged at least two or three of those deaths as being like Abby's.'

Tyrell frowned. 'They must have been written up in the papers. Didn't anyone ever query if the killers of the other children could have been responsible for Abby's murder?'

Brian Clarke was clearly uneasy. 'It was raised at a briefing but in each of the other cases there was already a suspect and plenty of evidence for a conviction, if the supposed killer hadn't already been banged up.'

'Go on.'

'A young PC questioned not collating data with other cases. She was shot down in flames.'

'Don't tell me. Pete Simons?'

'It was his normal reaction to any woman with an idea of her own but to be fair, each force seemed to think they'd already got their man. After that, no one mentioned it again.'

Mickey Walsh hurried in, brandishing a sheet of paper. 'Sir! The murder of a ten-year-old girl in Scotland – there's a note added about Interpol.'

'Follow it up, please, Mickey. Discreetly. We don't want another national squad breathing down our necks.'

'They'd have to get past the Chief and ACC Hinton first,' Brian Clarke said as Mickey raced away. 'Neither of them will want any of this to go "out of house" yet.'

101

'Maybe not but the ball's in Ms McGuire's court. If we've managed to influence her in any way, we should be safe for a day or two.'

Clarke was not so sure. 'But not much longer if she keeps to her original plan and gets us blasted in all the papers.'

Chapter Six

'All those years she's spent fighting for her son and it's only now you're interested?'

Shona McGuire stood at the door of Emanuel Cottage. She was ready for work, fresh, pretty, angry.

The DI waited until her breathing steadied. 'This is only my second full day on the case, Miss McGuire. Yesterday I spent quite some time here and asked very few questions. Today I would like to continue that process.'

She was restless, unsure. 'I've got to get on my rounds – patients are waiting and they need their injections on time.'

'Then please don't let me detain you any longer.'

'Mrs Miller –'

'Will be fine. I have no intention of causing her any kind of distress.'

'Just being here and bothering her's enough.'

Shona McGuire experienced Tyrell's steady gaze. 'Miss McGuire, it's time you faced facts. I am doing my best to see if Carl Miller was treated fairly when Abby Jenkins died. You, on the other hand, are intent on making it as public a fight as possible. If you can't bear the thought of me sitting with Mrs Miller this morning, how do you think she will cope with the very persistent men and women of the nation's media you are determined to see massed at that gate and peering in her windows?'

The nurse hesitated, grudging to herself that his words made sense.

'I can appreciate all Mrs Miller's efforts – and yours,' he said less forcefully, 'but you have what you say you wanted, a review of Carl's conviction. Granted, it's within the force which put together the evidence that helped a jury decide he was guilty. I'll say it again, you have my word that should I find anything at all which casts doubt on his conviction, the Chief Constable will be the first to be informed and an independent organization brought in to go over my data and my findings.'

She savoured his words for a moment. 'How come you're on your own?'

'I thought Mrs Miller might prefer it that way. As for Detective Sergeant Clarke, he's gone to talk to Mrs Beech.'

'Why? I thought you couldn't use Duggie's evidence.'

'In court we can't but we can find out from the one person he'd have talked to, what it was he wanted us to know.'

Shona hesitated, was anxious. 'Oh, damn you! Go on but take care with her, mind. She's very frail – and very precious,' she added, her tone suddenly plaintive.

Mrs Miller was dressed, ready for her lonely hours, and Tyrell was pleased to see a hint of pink in her cheeks. Today, she had chosen her clothes with care, a dark blue skirt, lilac blouse and a soft purple cardigan. Her hair had been washed since he last saw her, fluffing in a grey halo, but it was her eyes which surprised him. They seemed darker and in them he saw hope.

'Inspector Tyrell, come in and sit down. Take your coat off, do. It's warm in here – Shona sees to that, bless her.'

'Has she lived with you long?'

'Since Carl . . .' Sadness returned and she wilted.

'I believe she was nursing you at the time?' he asked, his voice gentle.

Winifred Miller made a supreme effort and faced Tyrell with a fortitude he admired. 'I'd had a new hip. Shona came to see me as she should and when the first week was over, she kept coming. That was when she and Carl became – friends. There wasn't time for any more.'

'I'm sorry.'

She looked at him, her hands tightening on the arms of her chair. He was patient, knowing she needed to make up her mind. There was a slight sigh and he could see the almost fleshless bones of her fingers relax. 'Yes,' she said. 'I think you are.'

Her Forest vowels and intonations were stronger than he remembered from the previous day and Keith Tyrell began to be optimistic she might shed more light on his puzzle.

Mrs Miller gazed at him for a long, silent moment, then sighed again. 'What do you want from me?'

'May I ask you some questions? It will mean going over some of the events we talked about yesterday.'

She stiffened, then lifted her chin and he saw the proud woman she had been. 'If that's what you want.'

'Thank you, Mrs Miller. Can I take you through the night Abby went missing?'

'Again?'

'I'm afraid so.'

She drooped in her chair as thoughts and memories were dragged from the past. The DI watched her, patient as she relived the last happy time she had known.

'Poor little Abby. We knew her, you know. Her mum was older than Carl but they'd catch the same school bus together. Then she married and moved away, almost to Cinderford.'

Tyrell let her ramble on, knowing a mind full of memories needed more time than a young one to sort out what must come to the fore and be put into words.

'Of course, when Carl took me out that night, we'd no idea Abby was missing. I'd been sat here and he'd been in his workshop until he washed in the scullery and changed his overalls, ready to take me out. Shona had said I must get out and use my new hip more so that night Carl put cushions in the passenger seat of his van and loaded me in. The whist drive it was. A while since I'd been but everyone was so kind, welcoming me back. Didn't stop Betty Thomas trumping my Queen of Spades, though.' Winifred

Miller was quiet, remembering a pleasant interlude before horror. Her mind returned to the present and she shivered, silently apologizing to Tyrell for her lapse. 'Carl came back to the garage to work so he was late picking me up from the hall. I didn't mind. It was nice there, warm and with friends.'

Her voice tailed away and the DI let her rest for a while.

'Did Carl say why he was late?'

'Right annoyed, he was. I told you someone had rung and needed help with his car. Carl stopped what he was doing and went to where the man told him he'd broken down. Right by a phone box it was but there was nobody there. Carl waited. My boy'd been rung on his mobile and he had that with him so he guessed if he was in the wrong place the man'd ring again. In the end, Carl gave up and came back here to work on a car. Tony Gilbert's it was. After that he came for me.'

'How was Carl then?'

'All right – apart from being angry. It meant he wouldn't even stop for a cup of tea when we got in. Said he had to go out to the garage and finish what he'd been doing.'

'His clothes. Clean overalls when he took you and clean overalls when he collected you?'

She was bemused by his question. 'Same ones – the clean pair. Dirty ones to work in, then use the clean ones for tidy until I do the washing and take the mucky ones off him. Waste of money having more pairs than that.'

'How long had he been wearing the ones needing washing?'

'Like usual, best part of a week.'

'And because you were going out there was a dirty pair on the top of the washing basket?'

'Course they were.'

Tyrell did not allow his expression to change. 'Who could have known you'd be at the whist drive?'

She frowned, puzzled by the question as well as struggling to answer the DI truthfully. 'Anyone – not many.'

Tyrell took her through the previous few days, helping

106

her to recall the weather, her visitors. She was tiring fast and Tyrell offered to make tea. 'Or would you prefer coffee?'

'Tea would be good. Can you manage?'

His grin cheered her. 'I've made tea in some strange places, Mrs Miller. I'll bet your kitchen'll be one of the cleanest and tidiest.'

It was as he expected, immaculate. Waiting for the kettle to boil, aching tiredness began to encroach and the DI longed for strong, fresh coffee. Mentally, he shook himself. Tea it would be and he must remain alert, watching for the half remark, or the hesitation, which could help him. The kettle took its time, allowing the DI to reflect there was always someone making tea in an investigation. It relaxed the questioning, subtly shifting control to the inquisitor, and often resulted in some very useful answers.

Whatever the reason, the hot tea helped them both but Keith Tyrell waited until Mrs Miller was ready to talk again.

'Did you go to bed before Carl?'

She nodded. 'He insisted – but not before he'd fiddled with that thing over there,' she said, pointing to the answering machine. 'One message there was supposed to be but it was one of those when nobody says a word.'

'Did he cancel it?'

'Muttered something he didn't want me to hear and switched it off. I went up to bed and Carl came an hour or so later.'

'Did he take his van out again?'

'No. I almost wished he would, that night. Whatever he had to do it meant banging and hammering and I couldn't sleep till he stopped. When he did he cleaned himself before he came upstairs, bless him. He's so like his father – always getting rid of the grease and dirt on him in the scullery.'

'Just a little more, Mrs Miller. Carl's old overalls. What happened to them when they were worn out?'

'When I'd made him buy a new pair, you mean? I'd wash the worst he had, then cut it up for him to use the best bits in the garage.'

'The last time you did that?'

'Oh, it was before I went into hospital.'

The DI knew from the files the general belief Carl had worn an old pair of his overalls to commit the murder and then burned or hidden them. He glanced round the room. This would have been a careful house, not cluttered. The furniture he could see was good, solid and well cared for. Chrysanthemums were splashes of bright yellow on the table, the ornate pot separated from polished wood by a lace cloth he guessed was handmade. Photographs of Carl, some with his parents, were placed carefully so the occupant of the main chair by the fireplace could see them all. Every item in the quiet room was free of dust and cherished. How devastated Mrs Miller must have been when the CID teams had finished searching, especially if Pete Simons was involved.

'Could anyone have got into the house without you knowing?'

'Certainly not! One thing Carl made me do was to lock up careful.' Her features moved, showed sadness. 'It's not like it was when I was growing up. My Dad lost the front door key once but he never got a new one. Didn't need it then.'

'Have you never left a key handy – in case you locked yourself out?'

'No, not now. Course, I did before I went into hospital. I mean, if Carl was called out, how could the nurses get in when I was back home?'

'Who would know?'

'Just the nurses. No one else needed to.'

Tyrell's smile was gentle. 'And when did you stop leaving it hidden?'

She closed her eyes as agony washed through her. 'When your lot had gone and taken Carl. Everywhere was such a mess, I had to make sure I had no more visitors I didn't want.'

The DI answered the summons from his mobile as he settled in the driving seat. 'Good morning, darling. You looked so comfortable when I left I hadn't the heart to wake you.'

Jenny's chuckle warmed his day. 'I hope that's not how you greet DCI Leggatt when she calls you.'

'All this modern technology, I knew it was you.'

There was another chuckle. 'Just think of husbands after a naughty night out who are too bleary-eyed to read numbers correctly or focus on the text on their mobiles.'

'You need reminding, madam, it was you and Brenda who whooped it up, not us. Brian and I were working!'

'I know. In late and then off so early you didn't wait for breakfast.'

'No time. We've got the hounds of the fourth estate about to be unleashed on us.'

'Poor darling – you've had enough of reporters this year already.'

'And how! By the way, Brian says if you and Brenda want a repeat performance of last night, can you make sure she carries a clean shirt for him? He claims the collar on the one I loaned him is choking him.'

DCI Leggatt was waiting for them. She gestured the two detectives to chairs and when they were seated, 'Update, please,' she asked Tyrell.

'I've gone through all the records to hand as carefully as I could in the time, ma'am, and I would say the original investigation was, by and large, as fair and accurate as possible.'

Joan Leggatt sensed Tyrell was holding something back. 'Go on.'

'The officer in charge, DCI Whittaker, directed enquiries as procedures demanded he should have done. This is obvious from all the files and is confirmed by officers I talked to who worked on the case.'

He did not tell her of the ones who had answered him grudgingly, convinced they were being set up as scapegoats. Over the years the DI had encountered difficult individuals in interviews, but few had needed such careful handling as those he had interrogated during the last two days.

'I'm glad,' the DCI said, hiding her relief.

Keith Tyrell knew he had passed some kind of test. 'However, not all orders given by DCI Whittaker were carried out as fully as they should have been. Assumptions as to the identity of the child's killer were made early on. Unfortunately, these assumptions appear to have been based on scanty evidence. Miller's alibi for the abduction of Abby was provided by his mother and ignored, it being decided she must have been lying. As for the body being found, Miller was seen waiting near the spot where Abby's remains were eventually located, the van with his name on it making identification easy. He must have been seen very shortly after the dead child was tossed into the bushes.'

'Could all this have been cleared up in the first investigation?'

The DI looked at Clarke and waited for him to speak.

'Yes, mam. As soon as Carl Miller was picked up Duggie Beech tried to give a statement. He'd been walking his dog past the garage at the time Abby was reckoned to have died somewhere other than where she was found. Through the open door he saw Miller's shadow moving about, heard his radio playing and Miller whistling to the music.'

'You're saying no statement was made?'

'No, mam. According to Duggie's widow he was furious about it but a police officer, not in uniform, persuaded Duggie there was no need to go to the station. He had only seen the shadow and not the man himself.'

'Do we know the identity of the officer?'

'Mrs Beech didn't know his name but she gave a very good description.'

110

'He was?'

'Pete Simons, mam. He was a DI then.'

In a hard fight for her career, Joan Leggatt had learned not to show her emotions. 'Was that the only way a witness was influenced?' she asked Tyrell.

'No, ma'am. When Miller was arrested his home was taken to pieces – as you'd expect. Mrs Miller told officers present her son never had three pairs of overalls. She was completely ignored and the man in charge of the search entered the information Miller was known to have three pairs of overalls, burning or hiding the pair he wore when committing the crime.'

'Do you believe her, Keith, because she's a nice old lady?'

'No, ma'am – and she's not that old but she is in the habit of telling the truth.'

Joan Leggatt sat back in her chair and swung it gently from side to side. 'Two small pieces of data, Keith. It's not enough, especially since the dead girl's blood was found in the house. Some of it on overalls, I believe?'

'That's just it, mam,' Clarke burst out. 'It wasn't blood which had spurted. Pathology said Abby must have lost blood very quickly. What was found on Carl Miller's stuff was smeared.'

She frowned, remembering. 'He was supposed to have wiped his hands.'

'And he was supposed to be that much of an idiot?' The sergeant was red-faced with anger, or it may have been the DI's borrowed collar.

'You asked me to look for inconsistencies, ma'am,' Tyrell reminded her. 'I think you see they exist. As for Mrs Beech's testimony, it's hearsay and not usable but if the press get to her they can exploit it to the limit. It would be a damning indictment of the first investigation and that would be unfair. Forensic details are straightforward and most reporters can grasp their significance, but if they even suspected a detective had been sitting on a potential statement – or two – they'd all be going for the Chief Constable's jugular.'

'Mm. Tricky. You say, Keith, the enquiries pursued five years ago stand up to scrutiny?'

'On the whole, yes, ma'am.'

'Your reservations appear to incline you to Carl Miller's innocence. Did a member of the division frame him?'

'Not really, ma'am.'

The DCI stared at Tyrell. 'Qualify that.'

'Any manipulation of evidence was done out of a misguided intent to get a speedy trial and a quick conviction of a man most thought had committed a particularly brutal murder.'

'Why should that be the general belief if there was even the slightest chance Miller was not guilty?'

'It's just a hunch but I think Miller was set up, but not by a member of this force. I'm as sure as I can be that evidence against him was planted ahead of Abby Jenkins even being picked up.'

The DCI was startled from her normal composure. 'Your third scenario. Are you sure?'

'No, not certain but if I'm right this was done by a very clever individual who spotted ways he could get some poor devil to take the blame for a crime yet to be committed.'

Joan Leggatt pursed well-shaped lips as she studied Tyrell, then assessed Clarke. Each man accepted her gaze calmly. 'Why did you decide on this MO? Reasons, please,' she demanded of Tyrell.

'That's just it, I can't give you any. Neither can I find an explanation for not one of Carl Miller's fingerprints being found in the bathroom where at least a few should have been. Somebody had done a very good job of wiping down. Then there's the key. Around that time Mrs Miller and Carl had been leaving one hidden outside for her nurses' use. They knew where to find it because the information was in her medical notes. Brian checked.'

'Is that all?'

'Not quite. With DS Clarke's help I went through all the forensic notes, diagrams, results. Everything possible appeared to have been done but there was a small group of blood spots – not smears – which were found in a dark corner of the bathroom. Not Abby's blood. What was found of hers in that bathroom was always in the form of smears. Drops mean fresh blood falling. If Abby had fought back and knocked the knife into the murderer, he would have lost blood.'

The DCI understood his arguments. 'The knife which was never found.'

'But must have been very sharp indeed and with a very short blade. It was supposed a Stanley knife had been the weapon of choice. Often dangerous for the user unless held carefully.'

'I see. You want further testing on these blood spots?'

'It would be advisable, ma'am. Of course, there may be not much of that particular blood sample left in store and if there is, deterioration is possible.'

'What do you suggest?'

'A try for DNA in case there's a match on the database. Failing that we could ask for a mitochondrial DNA test.'

Joan Leggatt was shocked. 'That'll take for ever and it won't come cheap! If we can get it done, what could it show?'

'It can only be compared with a maternal sample. If there's a match with Mrs Miller then the blood is most likely Carl's – of no use in our argument.'

'And no match with his mother means another person was bleeding there – someone not related to the Millers.'

'Yes, ma'am.'

'You mentioned nurses?'

'They would need testing, too.'

The DCI stretched, pushing back her head. When she settled again she was smiling. 'Our resident helper in Chief Super Bayliss's office is likely to faint when he sees all your proposals, Keith, but you have my backing and the Chief Constable said to pull out all the stops. Is there any other line of enquiry which might prove useful?'

Tyrell gestured to Brian Clarke who cleared his throat and tugged at his collar before speaking. 'DC Walsh, mam. He's ferreting around in past cases and talked to a DS in

Dunfermline. The guy had offered help when Abby died – they'd had a similar death. This DS McBain was told, no thanks, Carl Miller had never left his home patch so there could be no link.'

'You weren't happy with that?'

'No, mam! The question should have been, "Could the Scots killer have been in Soudley and murdered Abby?" It was never asked.'

'Did this DS McBain tell DC Walsh to whom he spoke?'

Clarke nodded, his features dark, grim. 'Simons.'

The DCI stared down at the neatness of her desk as she frowned. Lapses in the original enquiry must be faced. The Chief Constable would not be pleased but it had happened. She looked up at Clarke. 'You said other cases?'

'Yes, mam. Very strong similarities with at least two other child killings in the UK – possibly more. And Walsh's dealing with Interpol.'

Tyrell leaned forward. 'We would prefer to get a lead to this unknown suspect before we get taken over by yet another national squad. What evidence is left, here in the Forest, is deep in memories and there's no way strangers will help them out into the open.'

Clarke undid the top button of the cream shirt he was wearing; the congestion around his neck had enhanced his anger and he needed calm reason. 'Abby had the right to grow up here, mam. We owe her – and her parents.'

'Then go and get on with it!' the DCI told them and watched as the two men strode from the room.

She understood their frustration. Local knowledge was essential in a country area, the hunters knowing where to look for clues. A national unit might have more cash and more officers but it was always easier for locally based men and women to track an alien predator, especially if the trail was cold.

It was the first day in the week they had both been home early enough for a quiet dinner and a peaceful evening.

Keith was restless, prodding logs in the fireplace. Wrapped in a favourite nut brown housecoat and curled in a corner of the sofa, Jenny watched him but said nothing. The room was warm, its muted pastel shades soothing, cushioned chairs inviting, yet all evening Keith had been silent, lost in thoughts which disturbed him. As soon as he had come home late after his shift ended, he had had a shower, standing for ages under the hot water. Dressed in ancient chinos and a thick red sweater he had seemed relaxed, enjoying his dinner and chatting as they finished their wine by the fire. The logs crackled and Keith stared at them, melancholy returning.

'What is it?' Jenny asked. They both had careers which needed confidences kept. In the last few days Keith had been preoccupied, intent only on what was absorbing him at work. 'Can you talk about it?'

He sighed, a defeated sound. 'It's me, I suppose, not just the case. The way things are done now – my reactions. For instance, Harding, the man found dead in his car. The investigation and what we began to find out has been handed over.'

'You've been sidelined?'

'Very much so. It was our case and in our territory. I'm sure the link which would have unravelled a network of fraud is here – right on our doorsteps. No, a DCI Morrison hares down here from the Met and we are, as you say, sidelined.'

'You and Brian could have done it better?'

'On our patch, yes. Morrison will go at it from the top, as if he was opening a clam with a hammer. Very effective but the meat inside is useless!'

'Except for soup.'

Keith smiled when Jenny had hoped for laughter but it was a start, she decided. 'Was it only the Harding case?'

'No. There was the Cutler business. Over the years the CID and uniform did what the law said they must and Cutler got a clean record which allowed him to be free to wreck yet another girl's life.'

'I thought you put that right?'

'Using information we weren't supposed to have – and be politically correct? In a sense we had to be devious to get a result.'

'Was it worth it?'

Keith grinned at her. 'And how!'

'Well then, swings and roundabouts. So why are you still itchy?'

'An itch that needs scratching and you don't know where?' he asked softly, remembering a conversation with Brian. 'Almost immediately we're involved in a situation which has panicked HQ. Five years ago a child was abducted, raped and killed.'

The creamy skin of Jenny's brow became a frown as she tried to recall vague details. 'I remember your mother talking about it. She was horrified by what she read and very relieved the murderer was picked up so quickly. It can't be that case, surely?'

There was no answer and Jenny realized Keith's thoughts held him. She uncurled her legs and moved close to him, hoping the warmth of her nearness might console and relieve.

'An article in the paper this week,' she began conversationally, 'the murderer's mother's very ill and his girl-friend wants a review. She was insisting – Miller – was that the name?'

Keith managed a nod.

'Miller is innocent and she's threatening to sue the police?'

'That's the least of it.'

Jenny waited and watched Keith's expression harden, become grim. 'I've got the task of seeing if there were any police cock-ups in the original investigation. The Chief Constable wants to be forewarned if there are.'

'Who was in charge last time?'

'Whittaker.'

On hearing the name and all it had implied for Keith, anger flared through Jenny and she was shaking. Keith reached out and held her.

'No, you don't understand. Whittaker did nothing wrong. The way he handled things was first class.'

She was not mollified. 'So why are you the one who's got to review what he did?'

'Because I was still in London, in the Met, when it went down. I'm as near as damn it independent but Whittaker's DI and right-hand man was Pete Simons.'

Jenny was aghast. 'That devil? He got an innocent man convicted?'

Keith pulled her to him, leaning his cheek against the scented silk of her hair. 'It's not that simple. Oh, yes, Simons bent facts here and there and made the prosecutor's task easy for him. He may also have helped sway the jury but no, Simons didn't frame Carl Miller. I think Simons and Whittaker were fooled by the real killer.'

'You're joking! Why on earth would anyone want to get the blame landed on this Miller person?'

'I don't know. The only explanation which begins to make sense is because he could.'

Jenny savoured the concept and decided it was a weird logic. 'And you're afraid you won't be believed?'

'I'm certain I won't. Let's face it, there's a dead man in a car. Brian and I come along and in next to no time we've got a nationwide investigation. Then Hinton sends me to find where the dirty linen's hidden and I suggest there's a serial killer wandering around the UK killing small girls and getting innocent men banged up.'

'It may sound odd but you could be right. What happens if you are?'

'Then it'll no longer be any of my business. Yet another high profile group of the young and the ambitious will take over.'

Jenny sat back and gazed at her husband. There was no sign of petulance but he was holding in a great deal of anger. 'Why does that aspect of your work matter so much?'

'Which aspect?'

'Being there at the end.'

He did not answer, arranging his thoughts and seasoning them with his feelings. 'Yes, it matters,' he said at last. 'I came into the police to make a difference, to be part of an investigation to the point where I have proved someone guilty to my own and everyone else's satisfaction. He or she is handed over to the appropriate authority which arraigns them in public in front of a jury. That's my part in it completed. Talk to any copper – whatever the rank – and you'll hear much the same thing.'

'And now?'

Pushing himself from comfort, Keith marched to the fireplace and used a poker to express his emotions on the logs burning there. 'Now? We do what we know works and as soon as we look like getting somewhere a clique frozen into their ambitions takes over.'

'Aren't they specially trained?'

'They can't be! Every case is different, so is every victim, every witness. You have no idea how much depends on the background – if you like, the habitat in which it happens. What solves crimes in Manchester may have no bearing at all on an incident in Carmarthen Bay or the Outer Hebrides, but these experts from on high think they have all the answers and they're coming from the wrong direction.' Kicking a log into place seemed to help. 'Oh, I grant you it all may have started out with the best intentions but nowadays it's down to targets and resources and people management, not to mention a career scrum of monumental proportions.'

'Then people like you and Brian suffer?'

'We all do – every one of us is supposed to feel inferior to the great ones who come to teach us to suck eggs.'

Jenny hugged her knees and rocked on the wide cushions of the sofa as she laughed. 'You sound just like a Luddite of old, fed up with the bosses controlling their lives as well as their work.'

Keith's smile was slow in coming, then he joined his wife on the sofa, pulling her to him and holding her until her giggles ceased.

'Is your suffering that bad?' she asked.

'No, I'm just annoyed with the system. The real victims

are people like Harding's widow and his children, Mrs Miller and Carl's girlfriend. They're pushed aside as if they're of no consequence and the autocrats out to score points never realize justice is for everyone involved in an incident – large or small – and not just for the criminal who commits the crime.'

'Whereas left to you?'

'Me? Not me. The likes of Brian and Roly Willis, Mickey and Rose – and so many others, they'd see it through and help the ones left behind reach closure – of a kind.'

Chapter Seven

The DI sniffed. Lemons?

He stood in the doorway of the main CID office, empty that early in the day, its windows closed against endless rain. Something was different. The stacks of paper and folders which normally strewed desks were neat, orderly. Keyboards were aligned exactly in front of monitors and all bare surfaces gleamed. Silently, he laughed at himself. The cleaners had been in and with a new polish.

In his own office and with his raincoat drying in front of a radiator, Tyrell stripped off his jacket and draped it over a chair before rolling his sleeves clear of his wrists. A sound night's sleep had released pent-up energy and the DI settled to his mental list of self-imposed tasks, working through files and using his computer at a steady and satisfying pace. The leaps forward made the previous evening had opened up several lines of enquiry and it was necessary to get all the background notes up to date.

There were interruptions as colleagues came on duty, checked with him for the day's objectives and went away again. One or two still carried resentment with them like a cloud, sure he was blackening their reputations with the DCI. They had been in Simons's original team and would be uneasy until they were cleared. Tyrell had refused to be affected by the antipathy, treating the individuals as he had always done. Only those with a five-year-old guilt on their conscience need lose any sleep and he was sure the only person fitting that description was already dead.

Brian Clarke came and stayed; his grin was cheering on a drear day. 'So, anything new in the pipeline?'

'Not really. The DCI's seen to it there's pressure at all points to get samples analysed – the blood spots, as well as samples from the nurses and Mrs Miller.'

'Mark my words, they'll take for ever.'

'ACC Hinton and the Chief wanted results in a hurry. Let's see what they can do to help.' Tyrell rolled down his sleeves and buttoned them. 'I need to take a run out to see Mrs Miller sometime today. Coming?'

'You bet. Can you make it after I've collected the tests from those last two nurses who attended her?'

'No problem, I've enough to do here for a while.'

'Damn,' the DI said under his breath. He could not remember if he had picked up the file for the DCI so he stopped short, not far from the open door of the canteen, quiet at this time of the day, searching through the paperwork he had brought with him.

'I tell you, watch yourselves with him. Oh yes, he's as nice as pie to your face but just remember, he was only here five minutes when he got Pete Simons busted to sergeant.'

Tyrell recognized the voice. Dave Beckford was a uniformed PC and nearing retirement. Overweight and unfit, he was always the voice of doom in the canteen and the last to get back to work.

'I heard Simons was lucky to get that,' a woman said. 'It was DCI Whittaker stopped him being busted back to uniform and no stripes.'

'Whittaker knew we always look after our own, no matter what it takes,' Beckford rumbled on.

'Simons was a right bastard, Dave, and you know it,' a younger woman added. 'He did as he pleased and we were all supposed to lie for him.'

'So what, if your pension's at stake? Little Lord Fauntleroy's got no worries there, has he? Lose his pension and Daddy'll see him right.' Beckford's spite was well seasoned with envy. 'You wait, when he reports back to Madam, we'll all get shafted – just like Simons.'

There was a general murmuring and Tyrell turned to walk away.

'Pete Simons's mistake was expecting the DI to lie for him – and Pete's not the only one who went offside and expected everyone else to make excuses.' It was a voice with a slight stammer and a faint Welsh accent, Tyrell recognizing it as belonging to Clem James, a quiet, balding stalwart. 'Who's at fault then, Dave? The DI or the bent bastards who put us all at risk?'

Definitely time to go, Tyrell decided and walked back to his office. DCI Leggatt would have to wait for her crime figures. Settling at his desk he reflected briefly on what he had heard. There had always been someone ready to stick in the knife but his father had warned him well and prepared him even better to cope with the unpleasantness. Today? There were fewer voices raised against him than a year ago as well as more colleagues willing to defend him. Perhaps he was doing something right.

The quiet knock did not augur a problem and the DI called, 'Come in,' from the corner of his office where he stood by an open filing cabinet. 'Rose. Anything I can do?'

'There's someone insisting on seeing you,' Rose told him. 'She's a sort of relative.'

Tyrell could see the PC's usually serene expression had been replaced by what looked like an apology. 'How sort of?'

'She's a great aunt of a cousin, sir.'

The DI kept a smile at bay. 'Anything else I should know?'

Rose hesitated. 'She's nosy but she means well – and she's a stickler for the truth.'

'Where is she now?'

'The small interview room, sir.'

'Any idea why she's here?'

'Zinna didn't say but she is a friend of Winnie Miller's.'

Tyrell picked up his jacket. 'Coming to sit in?' he asked Rose, and waited for her nod before leading the way out of the office.

Sergeant Willis was just leaving the interview room as the DI approached.

'And don't think I've forgotten what you did, Roly Willis!' was shouted at him in a woman's voice, her Forest vowels strong.

He turned to face the unseen virago. 'Me, Zinna? What did I do?'

'Smarmed me off when I reported being knocked off my bike by that bastard. Nothin'! That's what you did. Nothin'!'

'I did.' Sergeant Willis was determined to defend himself and yet be calm. 'What you could remember of the number plate was circulated and we followed up any possibles. I told you all this but you won't listen, will you?' The sergeant had had enough and walked away.

Tyrell glanced at Rose. Her expression did not change, she merely shrugged her shoulders and waited for the DI to precede her.

'Well, young Rose, you're not goin' to stop me speakin' my mind!' greeted the officers.

Rose Walker was unperturbed. 'Mrs Richards, sir,' she explained to Tyrell by way of introduction. 'Now then, Aunt Zinna, Detective Inspector Tyrell has come to hear what you have to say.'

The virago glaring at the DI was probably younger than she looked but an aged and grubby man's raincoat, grey trousers bedaubed with grease from a bicycle chain and grey hair escaping in witch-like tendrils from a careless bun on top of her head did not help Zinna Richards's appearance. Tyrell inclined his head in acceptance of her presence and waited, noting that she had finely boned features and the skin of a girl.

'I suppose you're goin' to stick your nose in the air like the other lot did when young Abby died – and then ask stupid questions.'

'Aunt Zinna!' Rose Walker's words were quietly spoken

123

but the strength in them thwarted anger and the old lady subsided as Tyrell and Rose faced her across a narrow table.

'I'm too tall to stick my nose in the air, Mrs Richards,' Tyrell assured her, 'and as for questions, I'm here at your bidding.'

'Huh!'

'Inspector Tyrell was working in London when Abby was killed,' Rose explained. 'He's been listening to everyone who could help. Is that why you came? To help?'

Zinna Richards drew a surprisingly white handkerchief from her sleeve and blew her nose loudly to clear tears. 'It was all wrong,' she said at last. 'Yes, with my bare hands I'd throttle the devil as did for Abby but Carl Miller? While your lot were pattin' themselves on the back for puttin' that poor boy away, the real murderer was getting' away with it.'

'You're sure Carl is innocent?' Tyrell asked.

'Course I am! No way the boy did it – and I've told Winnie that from the start. Why, he didn't even like little girls – not that way. I should know.'

'That's interesting, Mrs Richards. How?'

The deep, melodious voice caught her attention and diverted her from venting her spleen. 'I cycle a lot, always have done. I see things.'

The DI waited.

'Goin' about odd times, odd places, I see men with queer habits – women too.'

'Watching young girls and boys?'

She nodded. 'Over the years I've known who was up to what but it was never young Carl. Never, I swear it.'

'The ones you did see, Mrs Richards, did you know their names?'

'Course I did! And I let the mums and dads know so's they could take care o' their young uns.'

'Can you still remember who those people were?' Tyrell asked while at the edge of his vision he could see Rose Walker ready to make notes. He made no gesture in her direction, giving Zinna Richards his full attention as she

124

listed names, addresses, dates, sometimes even the children who had been targeted. Silent at last she sagged in her chair and Tyrell offered her tea, insisting he would fetch it for her himself.

'Why can't Rose do it?'

'Because PC Walker has something else she must do.'

He opened the door of the interview room for Rose to leave first and take the data she had just acquired to Mickey Walsh for checking.

'Are your ears still ringing from Zinna?' Clarke asked when the DI returned from escorting his guest from the station.

'Not at all. Do you know, Brian, most of the concierges in Paris helped the French underground and the Gestapo never stood a chance. Zinna's cut from the same cloth as those beady-eyed women. Without notes she's listed details of half a dozen on our list of possibles who could develop into child predators and she's added three characters so far unknown to us. Single-handedly she's been tackling them about their habits. I wouldn't mind betting Zinna's made each and every one realize an unhealthy interest in children is not socially acceptable.'

'Carl Miller not one of them?'

Tyrell shook his head. 'Zinna was adamant. Never under the slightest suspicion.'

'Who did she try to tell? Pete Simons?'

'Who else. You know, it explains Whittaker's present predicament. If the stalker who's made his life hell and wrecked his family and his career had been sent down by Simons using the same tactics –'

'He'd go after Tricky Dicky when he got out on parole because Simons is dead? Makes sense.'

'It's hard on Whittaker.'

'Oh yes, and you'll tell me he was good at his job,' Clarke said, 'but be honest, Keith. If Tricky Dicky was that good, shouldn't he have guessed what Pete Simons was up to and stopped him? Or did he find Simons's methods helped with the apparent clear-up rate and made our Mr Whittaker look good – promotion-wise?'

The DI was saved from answering as a uniformed figure approached. 'Sergeant Willis, how can I help you?'

'Actually, I may have some assistance for you, Mr Tyrell. There's a visitor in reception waiting to see you. One who's come a long way.'

Joan Leggatt met them in the corridor. Tyrell waited until they were inside her office and the door closed before he introduced his companion.

'This is Detective Sergeant McBain, ma'am. He's driven down overnight from Dunfermline.'

The DCI shook hands as she welcomed and appraised the newcomer to her station. Shorter than DI Tyrell and more slightly built, he was red-haired and alert, with the demeanour of a man inclined to be pugnacious. Under strong brows which would become bushy as he aged, DS McBain studied the DCI and approved of what he saw. He had already taken the measure of DI Tyrell and decided his rush south was worth it.

When all three were seated Joan Leggatt could see little sign of tiredness in a man who had spent the night behind a wheel. 'You have an interest in one of our cases, Sergeant McBain?'

'Rob, if you don't mind, mam. I'm more used to it at home. Yes, I was interested in it five years back when I was a DC and based in Cupar.'

'That's in Fife?'

'Yes, mam. Nearly a year before that we'd had a very nasty murder. Lorna Sinclair was only seven years old when her body was pulled from the Eden River where it widens to the west of Guardbridge. That's a few miles east of Cupar but nearer Lorna's home in Dairsie and to the south of Tentsmill Forest. The child had been missing three days when she was seen in the water just above Guard-bridge.'

The DCI remembered the briefcase DS McBain had carried. 'Do you have data with you, Rob? Photos?'

'Yes, mam.' With swift movements McBain unlocked his case and took out a stack of paper. From a folder he withdrew a sheaf of pictures, a record of the body in all stages of its discovery.

Joan Leggatt was made of stern stuff but she paled as she saw what had been done to a child until it looked like the remains of a discarded rag doll. Tyrell tried to remain professional but he, too, was shaken by what he saw.

'It's no' something you can forget,' Rob McBain said softly.

'No,' Tyrell agreed. 'Was the river in spate at the time?'

The sergeant was surprised. 'Aye, it was. We'd had some right heavy rain a day or so before the lassie surfaced.'

'We have some experience of the damage an angry river can cause,' the DI said quietly.

'Why have you come, Rob?' Joan Leggatt wanted to know.

'When your wee girl was killed we offered our help.'

The DCI's spine stiffened. 'Did you, or a colleague, talk to any of our officers?'

'Aye, DI McLennan did. He was near retiring but stayed on to get the case sorted. He spoke to a DI from here and was told there could be no connection. Your crew had a man bang to rights, McLennan was told, and there was no way the killer in custody down here could have been in Fife. He'd never left your area and certainly had never crossed the border. DI McLennan was put out, I'll tell ye. He found your man gae offensive.'

Joan Leggatt turned to her own DI. 'Do we know who it was, Keith?'

'It's in the records, ma'am. DI Simons talked to a DI McLennan.'

She turned to the Scotsman. 'I'm sorry. Simons should have brought you in at that point, Rob. I know it's a bit late for apologies but we're going to have to get used to that.'

'Forget yon man, mam. It's the rest of your case as matters. The one convicted – he insisted he was innocent? There was the child's blood wiped on stuff he owned, clothes perhaps? He had no alibi?'

Joan Leggatt was intrigued. 'That's all true.'

'I'll bet you, mam, if I sit down with DI Tyrell and we compare what we've got in our files, we'll come as near as damn it to one murderer.'

The DCI was tempted but she hesitated. 'I see your point, Rob, but we have a problem. What's happening at the moment is being shadowed by a local reporter. There's a push to get the story spread further – something we don't want to happen just yet.'

'And you're afraid your nick's going to be like a' the rest. Leaky as a sieve?'

Joan Leggatt nodded.

'There is a way round that problem, ma'am.' Both his listeners turned to the DI. 'I could take Rob to my home, saying he's staying with me – which he is most welcome to do. DS Clarke could drive over later, no one knowing where he's going. We would all be able to work through the combined data for as long as it takes.'

'Is there anyone else you'd involve?'

'DC Walsh, ma'am. If he was working on a computer in private here, he could be linked to the one I have at home. Then there's Sergeant Willis.'

'Why?'

'He was in the station at the time, has a very good memory and a very still tongue.'

'Then Sergeant Willis will have to go off duty early with a headache and I don't want any of you back here until this has been properly dealt with.' The DCI turned to McBain. 'How long can you stay?'

'As long as it takes, mam. Peter Anderson, the man accused, was Lorna's teacher and a man well-liked in the district. OK, so maybe there was evidence pointing his way but it wasn't set in concrete. Like you here, there was a push on to get the killer behind bars as fast as possible and Peter Anderson was handy. With forensic evidence seeming to pile up against him, he lost his wife and his family. Peter hadn't been thought of as a risk to himself because he was solid and stable but he hanged himself while on remand. Now you're reviewing your murder and my Chief says we still owe young Lorna and her parents – as well as the Andersons.'

Tyrell leaned across and lifted a sheet of paper from McBain's folder. 'May I? There's something I wanted to check.' He read quickly, then again to be sure. 'I thought so,' he said slowly. 'Simons was certain Carl Miller hadn't left the Forest and couldn't have been responsible for the girl pulled out of the Eden River, yet when Abby Jenkins was murdered, Peter Anderson was already in custody. There's no way he could have committed our crime, so who is the killer?'

Jenny had been warned by a phone call from Keith but the noise in her home surprised her when she unlocked the front door. Coats were drying near a radiator in the hall and from the sitting room voices lobbed ideas and questions at each other. She peered in but was not noticed.

A carefully chosen colour scheme was also ignored, the fire needed more logs and every available surface, including the floor, was strewn with piles of papers, photos, folders. Keith had changed into his old fawn chinos and a green sweater and was sitting at the computer in the corner, occasionally running his hands through his hair as he worked. Brian's broad back she recognized. His jacket must have been tossed somewhere, blue shirt-sleeves were rolled up above his elbows and Jenny guessed his tie was long discarded. Sergeant Willis had shed his uniform and was unfamiliar in a pair of grey slacks and white shirt as he knelt on the floor beside a complete stranger with red hair, both of them engrossed in a file with a Gloucestershire Constabulary logo.

Jenny thought of coffee and crept away. She needed it and it was going to be a long night.

'I thought you could do with this,' she said later as she

carried a tray of steaming mugs into the room full of workers.

With a few quick strides Keith was across the room, kissing her as he took the tray. 'Thank you, darling,' was a whisper only she heard.

Brian grinned and shoved his broad fingers through the cap of black curls as he stretched tight muscles. 'Jenny, love, that smells great. Thanks.'

Roly Willis was more dignified. 'Mrs Tyrell –'

'Jenny, please. I know you like your tea and it won't take a minute.'

'Coffee's fine – and I need to keep my wits about me with these young ones. DS McBain you won't know.'

She shook hands with the young man and saw he was completely at home with his new colleagues. Keith had explained when he called but she could see for herself they all had a common purpose.

'It's real good o' ye, Mrs Tyrell.'

'Jenny.'

The smile was a shy one. 'Aye, Jenny. Your lovely home – it must seem like a madhouse.'

Rob McBain saw Jenny's mischief twinkling in her smile. 'No problem. I spend my days working in a psychiatric clinic.'

She left them to what they must do and returned to her kitchen. Through the open door she heard snatches of discussion when voices were raised in certainty.

'In both cases a knife was used and never found,' came with a Scottish accent.

'Agreed,' was chorused.

'Short-bladed and very sharp,' from Keith. 'Assumption a craft knife of some kind and one which could easily cause damage to the attacker.'

Two or three voices together meant Jenny could hear no individual words and she investigated her fridge and freezer until she heard, 'No semen left behind in either girl, no body fluids of any kind. Condoms used and taken away?'

'And don't forget Lorna's blood as well as Abby's was

130

only found smeared on the frame-up Charley's clothes or gear – not splashed or dropped,' said Rob McBain.

Roly Willis's 'How?' was quiet but it penetrated and there was silence.

'The Joker not only knew where the Charley was, he knew he had time to transfer blood and provide convincing forensic evidence.'

'Keith, how could he be so sure he had time to frame this – Charley – as you call him?'

'There were never any fingerprints,' the Scotsman said.

Keith agreed. 'The Joker could have been wearing gloves,' he suggested.

Brian laughed, a harsh sound. 'They must have been thin ones, then. Thick would have made him clumsy and there's no sign on any of the photos he was that.'

'Anything but,' Roly added. 'He was skilful, very skilful.'

Peas boiled over and Jenny dealt with the temperature of the hotplate and then the mess, before hearing Keith's quiet, incisive tone.

'All the strokes the Joker used were short, shallow and very determined.'

Jenny shivered and turned her attention to laying mats and cutlery on the kitchen table until Roly asked a quiet question.

'Keith, you keep calling him the Joker. Why?'

There was a silence and Jenny guessed her husband was searching for the exact words he needed.

'I can't really explain,' he said at last and Jenny stood unmoving as she waited like the others. 'It's a feeling, really. Tell me I'm mad but I think we've a clever, cunning psychopath who looks for his escape route – and a Charley to take the blame – before he even selects a child.'

'Nothing new there,' said Brian, 'but why "Joker"?'

'It's like moves in a game – a game of chess, for instance. You sense the mind behind the pattern of play.' Jenny barely breathed as she waited for Keith to continue. 'Yes, that's it. It's a game to him, against us and people like us

131

– the power of the law. As far as he's concerned the children are just pawns in his play, expendable and part of the most terrible crimes. Then he wins his game by fooling us all and giving us perfectly innocent men to lock away for good.'

Silence reverberated amongst Keith's listeners, each trying to understand the horror he had glimpsed. The doorbell ringing broke the tension and Jenny heard Keith answer the summons.

'Good to see you. Come on in.'

A man was talking to Keith and she reached for another table setting. A woman's voice was quiet and Jenny opened the cutlery drawer again.

'No, of course you should have come,' Keith insisted. 'We need all the help we can get.'

With the arrival of Rose Walker and Mickey Walsh the meal break took on the semblance of a party. Good food was seasoned with wit and the little beer drunk allowed laughter. Jenny saw the healing release of emotions which had built up through the evening as these people had dealt with evil.

When Keith and Mickey were clearing the kitchen, Jenny and Rose were banished to the sitting room. They stood in the doorway, watching Rob rattle ash in the fire and stack it with fresh logs. Behind him Brian and Roly gathered up the notes littering the floor and small tables, leaving to the last the photos of the two little girls. Gently, reverently, each captured image was handled with care, arranged in its numbered order and stowed away in a folder.

'What have you brought us, Mickey?' Roly asked when they were all assembled.

'Two more certainties, Sarge. The first in the run seems to have been near Peterborough. There's a chap done six years of a life stretch for it but the pattern's more or less the same.' Mickey handed a pile of paper to Roly Willis and Brian Clarke. 'Then there's this one. Village in Kent, near Sandwich. That was after ours. Same MO. The girl was only six.'

'Nothing more since then?'

'Not that came up in answer to a query, no.'

'That's odd,' Keith said as he distributed data around the group. 'The Joker's in the swing of it and then stops?'

'Or goes elsewhere,' Jenny added quietly.

They turned to her.

'Well, he would, surely?' She gestured to the mass of paper. 'You've enough here to hunt him down and put him away for a few lifetimes but he wouldn't stop – he can't. He considers himself much more clever than any police team and he's gambling with his ability to deceive you all. He proves his superiority to himself by having you run in any direction he points – and like any gambler, he's hooked and has to go on.'

'Where?' Rob wanted to know.

Jenny thought for a moment. 'You might say Thailand. It's where many paedophiles go but this man is not necessarily interested in the children. He needs to be where children are prized. He has to be where there are respectable families and, above all, institutions he understands. My bet would be Europe.'

Rob McBain was shaking his head. 'No, we tried Interpol. Nothing.'

'Since the death in Sandwich or before?'

'Before,' Rob said slowly.

There was a stillness, each one in the room facing the idea of these child murders and the injustices they caused spreading like the deadliest of viruses beyond the Channel.

'It's too late to get on to Interpol tonight. In the meantime, let's look at the new material,' Keith decided.

Mickey was hesitant. 'Hope you don't mind, sir, but I rang Peterborough.'

'No problem. Any help?'

'I got through to a DS who worked on the case and we compared the list of what we got from Abby and Lorna with what she had for her dead child. This time the Charley, as you call him, was a postman and the ten-year-old said to have been picked up as he finished his morning round. Her blood was on dustsheets in a lock-up – he had a second job as a painter and decorator. Now he's a lifer and has twice tried suicide. DS Downton would be very glad if you could call her in the morning, sir. Seemed very keen.'

'Thank you, Mickey. Well done. Now, the Kent murder.' In the peace and tranquillity of his home, Keith read out the stark facts. 'Tammy Arnott was eight years old when she was killed, like all the others, slashed across the throat with a very sharp knife – which was never recovered. Her blood was found in a shed belonging to a boatman who was also a valued member of a lifeboat crew. If you could pass the chart you made, Mickey, and the maps . . .'

Paper was distributed, each person reading details too familiar for comfort. In turn they held out a hand and received a map of the Sandwich area.

'No! Christ, it couldn't be!' Rob McBain was on his feet and agitated. 'I'm sorry, Jenny,' he said, contrite because of his outburst, 'but south of where we found wee Lorna is the RAF base at Leuchars. At the time we thought of a serviceman – a flyer, maintenance crewman – and we put 'em a' through the wringer. Nothing. Not one came up dirty – well, no this way, anyway. And now in Kent, another RAF base? It's too much of a coincidence!'

Roly shook his head. 'We've no such base here, in the Forest, nothing since the war. There's been the army at Ashchurch and then there's GCHQ in Cheltenham – maybe there are RAF boys on duty there.' He went on to list every forces establishment in the county he could remember, even as far as, 'RAF Lyneham. It was fully operational five years ago.'

'But it's Wiltshire,' Brian protested. 'Too far away.'

'No.' Rose Walker's quiet voice cut through the discussion. 'No airman being moved around could get as deeply into the community as the Joker did. Take Abby for a start. She was supposed to walk home with friends on a Tuesday

134

after Brownies but she always cut off the last corner and went through a copse to get to her home. Only someone living right in the area could have known that.'

'She wasn't killed there,' Brian protested.

'No, but it's where she went missing.'

'It's a good point, Rose,' Keith said, 'and I've no doubt we'll find similar stories for each abduction.'

Discussions continued long into the evening with everyone contributing. Jenny listened, saying little until there was a brief quiet spell.

'Don't be surprised if, when you find him and he talks, there was nothing sexual in the murders.'

Rob was horrified. 'But each of the girls was raped!'

'Were they?' Jenny had everyone's attention. 'This man is too precise, too careful, too mechanical. I would say it's not normal – or even abnormal – sexual urges driving him. The mutilation of the children may have come so soon after death that any evidence left would make it appear a rape had been committed but not by him, bodily.'

It took time for the idea to be accepted and Jenny went away to make more coffee, breaking open another pack of chocolate biscuits to keep energy levels high.

'There's something else Rose and I noticed from the maps,' she said on her return and when everyone was drinking and eating. 'I don't know about Peterborough, but in every other murder there are quite a few small blue flags. Golf courses. Perhaps that's why the Joker's in a particular part of the country. Could he be a golf pro moving from one club to another? He'd get to know the people in a town or village pretty quickly that way.'

The suggestion was greeted with amusement, then more soberly. 'The argument against that is the choice of Charleys. Teacher, maybe, but a boatman, a postman, a car mechanic? Not the usual types you find at the nineteenth hole.'

Jenny and Rose's ideas joined the others being chewed over as dogs deal with bones, faint hopes being pursued, talked out, discarded. It turned midnight and a mixture of exhaustion and despair silenced them. Keith lay in his chair, his legs stretched towards the fireplace where Rob fought with dying logs and fresh wood. At last flames flickered and as they danced, Keith watched them and let tiredness have its way.

He tried to go back to the beginning and visualize Abby and her killer. Strong hands in thin gloves wielding a short-bladed knife. Almost asleep, Keith frowned. Why did he imagine the Joker holding the knife that way? Surely it was wrong? An indistinct memory slipped its leash of synapses weakened by low blood sugar. It oozed into and merged with the picture in his mind, adding red to the hair and green in the sleeves. The only things which matched were the angle of the knife and the direction of its strokes.

'My God, that's it!'

Jenny and their guests responded slowly to his burst of energy.

'Seen the light, boy?' Roly asked as he rubbed his face with stiff fingers.

'In a way. There's something we've all experienced,' Keith said. 'It's been part of our training, our jobs. Who have we all seen wearing thin gloves and using a very keen knife with great skill?'

Reactions were slower than they would have been earlier in the day.

Brian was startled but unsure. 'You mean Anita McBride – at a PM?'

Rob sat up, suddenly alive. 'It's a doctor – a bloody doctor!'

'Could be an undertaker,' Roly offered, 'but they don't usually travel around that much. Worth checking?'

'No.' Again they turned to Rose and she hesitated, made shy by seeing everyone intent on what she was about to say. She flushed, the warmth in her skin making her look animated. 'Someone was telling me there's such a shortage of GPs in the NHS a good locum can have his – or her – pick of practices. They can go where they want and for as long as they want. The pay's good, too.'

She looked around, waiting for at least one contradiction, then Rob McBain began cursing his stupidity.

'We had a locum. He left the day before Lorna was found. Never thought anything of it because it was known for some time it was when he planned to leave. Strange, looking back, he made sure we did know since the man didn'ae talk much. He was no good wi' people – kept them a' at a distance. Was he laying an alibi ready for us to trip over and get it smacked in our faces?'

'Name?' Keith demanded.

'Mather. Dr Philip Mather. Six one, near enough. Skinny. Curly hair thinning a bit in front. Glasses. A loner. Did everything on his own, even when he played golf . . .' trailed into a stunned silence.

Joan Leggatt listened intently as her DI gave her a brief account of the result of the impromptu think tank.

'You're sure the man we want is this Mather?' she asked.

'As sure as we can be. Of course it's partly guesswork at the moment and we'd never have reached the conclusions we did if it hadn't been for DS McBain's help. Then, when I phoned DS Downton first thing this morning, the data she had ready was almost a replica of ours. She's making enquiries now to see if Mather was a locum there at the time – or just prior to the killing.'

'It's all circumstantial. Has this DS Downton any hope of reliable forensic material?'

'The CID team there is starting to review every detail, ma'am, and Rob McBain's DCI is getting his terriers on the hunt. As for us –'

'We wait for results on those blood spots. What have you arranged for today?'

'Sergeant Willis has a hazy memory of his wife mentioning a young doctor with a name like Mather. He's contacting Mrs Miller's medical practice and asking about locums they've employed.'

The smile was faint and did not warm her eyes. 'Tactfully, I hope.'

'It's why I asked him to do it, ma'am. We can't risk Mather hearing a wisp of a rumour and going to ground. Clarke's on another tack – he's gone to see Mrs Miller and have a cup of tea. With luck, he'll get her talking about the time she had a new hip.'

'Ah! Which of the nurses and doctors visited?'

The DI grinned. 'She'll never guess what he's after. Then there's been a reply from Interpol. They had two deaths which fitted the MO, both in Portugal. The first was just over a year after Abby died. This was a young boy in Oeste, not far from Lisbon and some good golf courses.'

'A boy? Doesn't that make it a whole new ball game?'

'Not necessarily, ma'am, but it could explain why Interpol didn't link it in with the others. The chap I talked to is going over all reports in case any more fit the pattern. It's definitely widespread – he found another in Spain.' He explained his own and Jenny's reactions to the killings and saw his DCI's shock at the concept.

'You're saying this Mather could be murdering children as part of an insane game?'

'Not quite, ma'am. Jenny thinks he sees each incident as a kind of project – a challenge. The children are a means to an end, the way they die in direct opposition to all social mores. The game part is his choice of the other victim each time, the one blamed for his crime.'

'He's out to make us all look stupid?'

Tyrell nodded. 'He's very canny with it and makes sure his part is covert in the extreme.'

Joan Leggatt absorbed the new idea quickly, then braced herself. 'You said Portugal?'

'Six months after the first. Tavira. A girl of eight.'

'And all attacks took place near golf courses?'

'It would appear so, ma'am. It's Mather's only known hobby and he always plays on his own. I've asked Bryony Goddard and Gerry Cross to visit the course near Cinderford, where Mather rented a house. Then there are a couple of other golf clubs very close as well as the St Pierre at

Chepstow and the Celtic Manor one at Newport. Both are excellent and within easy reach.'

'He played on his own, you say? Were there no friends? No relationships?'

'That may transpire later but Rob said the doctor was a loner, the research type rather than a medic interested in people.'

'So, each crime team involved in the past is now alerted to hunt for hard evidence?'

'Yes, ma'am, including one in Spain which is fairly recent. Two months ago.'

Joan Leggatt breathed deeply, forcing herself to subdue all emotion. 'This will have to go up the line, Keith. When it's national and international it'll take a Yard team to have the necessary powers to cope.'

'I understand, ma'am, but I'd have liked to have had a good case ready against Mather for Abby's death.'

'And you'd have liked to arrest him yourself?' she asked quietly, sitting back in her chair and turning it gently as she rested her chin on steepled fingers. 'I suppose we could try and get Carl Miller out on a technicality.'

'That's not good enough, ma'am. If he's freed and comes home that way it'll be assumed it's because we made a hash of things when he was arrested and tried.'

'I see what you mean. Miller would still be believed guilty by the community.'

The DCI swung on her chair which the DI had come to realize was a habit when she was thinking. 'I'll see if it's possible he can be assured, through official channels, that there's hope.'

'Just as it would help Mr and Mrs Jenkins to know we can probably soon name the real killer – and Mrs Miller. The three of them should be told before this hits the headlines.'

Joan Leggatt sighed. 'My God, when Miller's cleared it's going to cost us a pretty penny. There'll be cutbacks to pay for an insurance hike – in addition to all the damages he can be awarded.'

'Then there's Mather, ma'am. It would help to know where he's been employed ever since he qualified.'

'Suggestion, Keith. Go further back. Student days, schooldays. This sort of psychotic tendency starts young and someone may have noticed odd behaviour which could give us a clue.'

'Yes, ma'am.'

'It may take more authority than I've got to prise information from the BMA and GMC but if ACC Hinton stipulated everything possible done, he can involve the Chief Constable. One way or another, Keith, we'll get the answers we need.'

'One thing, ma'am. It would be dangerous if any of the medical people decided to alert Mather we were on to him.'

'The old boy network?'

He nodded.

'Don't worry. I'll warn them if one of them talks too much I'll make it my business to have his – or her – guts for garters!'

Chapter Eight

Tension almost crackled in DCI Leggatt's office.

'Keith! Before I wage war on this damned lab, what's the significance of these blood spots?' ACC Hinton had risen early and was in the mood for battle with someone.

Tyrell rode the storm, briefly explaining the work which had been done and listing for the ACC what remained to be accomplished. Although Hinton might play the big, bluff countryman his mind was clear, his reasoning sharp as he paced the room across the width of the window wall.

'Mm. You're sure about this Mather chap?'

'Since Sergeant Willis reported back this morning, sir. Mather was employed by the surgery caring for Mrs Miller and he left the area, as expected, the day his contract ended and before Abby Jenkins's body was found. He'd visited Mrs Miller at home so knew the layout of the place, and from her records he could have known where to find the key to get in.'

'He could also have thrown blood around the damned bathroom on a normal visit.'

'Agreed, sir, but DS Clarke spent time with Mrs Miller today and got her remembering details. Mather attended her only once and it was when she was recovering from her hip operation. He encouraged her to get out and about more and she told him about the whist drive.'

'Oh, God.' Hinton closed his eyes. 'She handed it to him on a platter – but what about the blood?' he reminded Tyrell.

'Yes, sir, he did visit the bathroom to wash his hands, she

141

remembered that clearly. She told DS Clarke, "Dr Mather was a nice boy, quiet, but like the old doctors he washed his hands before going to the next patient." He couldn't have lost blood on that occasion, she saw no sign of him bleeding when he was checking her blood pressure.'

'Can we prove Mather ever did bleed?'

'Sergeant Willis talked to the practice nurse working on the locum's last day. He had a significant wound inside his left hand which kept opening. She recommended stitches but he was in a hurry and settled for butterfly strips. Said he'd tried to catch a slipping scalpel as he was packing his kit to leave.'

ACC Hinton was a relieved man. 'You've got a good team, Keith. I'll do what I can.'

It had stopped raining and someone opened a window. There was a gush of cool, damp air and it freshened the atmosphere in the CID room, busy with most of its monitors in use. Gerry Cross was on his phone cajoling, persuading, while Bryony Goddard frowned as she cross-checked data in a series of files. In a corner Brian Clarke, shirt-sleeved and earnest, was explaining a situation to Ed Baxter and Rob McBain, the Forester's big hands adding to his description.

Keith Tyrell closed the file he had been reading and added it to those already checked, neatening the pile as his thoughts ranged ahead to what must be done. He had put to one side the hardest task and he faced it now, sliding into his jacket and straightening his tie. He beckoned to Brian Clarke and the two of them were walking towards the door when DCI Leggatt opened it.

'Good, you're all here,' she said, her voice clear, carrying.

There was a general shuffling as bodies followed the heads which had turned at her entrance. Unspoken was the certainty DCI Leggatt had nothing pleasant to say.

'I've just had a call. Because of all the forces involved in the child murders, the Home Office has been notified of the situation.'

'Campbell at it again,' Brian Clarke muttered.

Joan Leggatt ignored the murmuring. 'It's been decided the review and any further investigation here will be handled by a specialist murder unit. This will also be true in the cases of other children in Northampton and Kent.' She looked towards Rob McBain. 'There will be liaison through the Scottish Office with the police in Fife, and in addition two crews are heading for Portugal and Spain to work there. Everything will be supervised by the Criminal Cases Review Commission, jointly with their Scottish equivalent. Fortunately for us, because DI Tyrell and his team have been going over every scrap of evidence, we are ready for inspection of our methods and records.'

There was a restlessness to Tyrell's right. He did not turn his head, merely swivelling his eyes to confirm his suspicions. Dave Beckford.

'When're they coming, mam?' was heard from a desk by the window.

Joan Leggatt turned to the DC asking the question. 'The officers allocated to us are booking into a hotel in Newnham this afternoon, Baxter. ACC Hinton has asked for copies of all relevant files to be delivered there immediately.'

'Just as well it's not the Pinemount,' Clarke whispered to Tyrell, 'or the whole lot could find themselves being done by the tax man.'

The DCI was unaware of the comment, she was too busy allocating despatch duties to Gerry Cross and Ed Baxter.

'Inspector Tyrell,' she called, 'are all current reports ready? You had people out on interview this morning?'

'Yes, ma'am. Sergeant Willis and DS Clarke's accounts are typed up. I'll see copies are made and included.'

Joan Leggatt nodded. 'I'd be grateful.' She turned to the rest of the workers in the room. 'I'd like to thank you all for your co-operation with DI Tyrell. It's never easy to have past efforts which were carried out under extreme pressure, being put under the microscope at a later date. Thanks to the way you responded and all the hard work in the last few days, we already know our weak spots. None of them affect any of you.'

Tension eased and Tyrell was sure he heard Beckford's breath escape in a quiet 'whoosh'. The DCI turned to go, then hesitated. 'Inspector Tyrell, you were going somewhere?'

'Yes, ma'am. DS Clarke and I were on our way to see Abby's parents.'

'Will it help if I come, too?' Joan Leggatt had the rank to reassure the Jenkinses and she had not been in any of the original enquiry teams.

'Yes, ma'am. We'd be grateful,' he said, hoping his relief was not as obvious as had been Dave Beckford's.

It was quiet in the car. Clarke was a good driver and the distance was covered quickly and smoothly. There was no conversation, the grimness of what lay ahead weighing on each traveller. The A48 was busy, huge transporters heading west for the Irish ferries and eastbound tractors servicing farms along its length as they delayed every make of car. Exterior noise lessened when Clarke turned the vehicle to go up into the Forest. This road was narrower, making driving slower, but the closeness of bungalows and houses set in orderly gardens conveyed a measure of the community.

The Jenkinses' home had once been a miner's cottage built, like so many of its neighbours, on a patch of land where a man, his family and friends had toiled through a long night to 'raise the smoke' and have four walls, a roof and a fire ready by first light. The garden which had supplied a wife and children was smaller now, cut by a new roadway as well as extensions to the original building. The house still sat with its back to the Forest and over the years it had become part of the greenery.

'Stay here,' Joan Leggatt said to Clarke. 'Three of us might be a bit intimidating.'

He watched Keith escort her through the gate and along the path to the front door. It seemed a lifetime ago he had gone that route, following DCI Whittaker as he marched towards the unpleasant duty of telling Abby's parents the body of a child had been found and needed to be identified. Don Jenkins had been away from home, searching for his daughter, and his wife guessed their mission. Brian almost wept again as he remembered Molly collapsing against him. He had held her as she screamed and then sobbed uncontrollably, bending to her and soothing her as he would one of his own little daughters.

Brian Clarke sniffed, letting his gaze roam the garden. It was autumn-neat below the closed windows of the house, their blank gaze reminding him of blindness. That awful day the shrubs and borders had been lush with growth and colour, a fitting background to a family blessed with a lovely, merry child. She had been ripped from them and all these years later rage suffused the sergeant. He needed to vent it on the absent Mather but would it change anything? From what he had learned of the so-called man he was a cold fish, his only emotion a hatred of unknown origin which he assuaged by killing small children and seeing decent men jailed.

The door was answered slowly, unwillingly. Molly Jenkins was petite, a once-pretty blonde with hair too long for her chosen style. Tyrell guessed she no longer bothered with regular visits to a hairdresser but he could see her sweater and skirt were clean, of good quality and much laundered. He had stood on so many doorsteps, ready to talk to parents whose lives had been changed for ever by tragedy. As with those other women, old habits of hygiene persisted but Mrs Jenkins's care for herself had died when Abby was lost to her. The woman stood resolute, almost stoic, her feelings hidden behind a mask. Wary eyes followed Joan Leggatt's gestures as she introduced herself and her DI.

'Isn't Sergeant Clarke coming in?'

Both officers heard the hint of pleading.

'He was so kind when . . .'

'Of course, Mrs Jenkins.' The DCI's finger brought

Clarke out of the car. 'It will be good for you to have a familiar face here.'

Don Jenkins hovered in the hall as his wife ushered their guests into the front room of the house. It was a memorial to Abby: framed photos of her were everywhere and in a tiny chair a large teddy bear had pride of place.

'Would you like some tea?' Don Jenkins asked, his skeletal frame bending to the seated DCI.

Clarke remembered him as tall and bony, comfortably fleshed. Now, the man's hair was white, what was left of it, and the lines of his face were deep grooves of past and present agony. Mather should swing for the damage he had done the living as well as the dead, the sergeant decided.

'Perhaps later? We do need to talk,' Joan Leggatt said quietly.

'It's about what Shona McGuire said in the paper, isn't it?' Molly demanded to know, a bright red spot appearing in each cheek.

'In a way, Mrs Jenkins. Because of Mrs Miller's state of health and Miss McGuire's threat to stir up trouble, DI Tyrell was asked to go over your daughter's case. We wanted to make sure nothing had been carried out incorrectly at the time.'

Molly and Don stared at Tyrell, then the mother's eyes swung to Brian Clarke with a silent question. He read her need and nodded. Reassured, she faced Tyrell. 'Are you trying to get him let out? The man who killed her?'

'No, Mrs Jenkins. My job was to see the conviction was sound. It's essential to all of us the man who robbed you of your daughter should receive the maximum punishment the law allows.'

'I'd have strung up the bastard myself!' burst from Abby's father.

'And if Carl Miller was the wrong man?' the DI asked quietly. 'You would now be a murderer.'

The air was still, as unmoved as it had been since the day Abby had gone missing, but today her parents were uneasy with a different fear.

146

'There's something going on here,' her father decided and looked from one senior officer to the other.

They sat relaxed in their chairs and faced his scrutiny. The DCI had taken time to change into civvies but even in her grey flannel suit and high-necked white sweater she was an indomitable woman. DI Tyrell did not look old enough for so much responsibility, the parents thought, but he seemed at ease in their home in spite of the cut of his fine tweed suit and the quality of the pale blue shirt beneath it. Brian Clarke they knew. He was as tall as Tyrell, broader and less careful about what he wore, but they had learned he was strong in the ways which counted.

'Listen to them,' Clarke said quietly to the parents. 'They're good people.' The familiar Forest sound of his voice broke down invisible barriers. 'I'll make some tea,' he said and got up to go to the kitchen. 'I know where everything is,' he assured Molly and she bent her head, remembering how often he had made her tea in the darkest days and nights.

Joan Leggatt inclined her head towards the parents. 'Before I say anything more I need your word – both of you – that what we talk about now remains confidential between us.'

Don and Molly were uneasy, reaching out their hands to each other until the warmth of the grasp brought comfort.

'I can't stop journalists making your life hell but if we can keep all this between us, we can delay the inevitable for a while.' The DCI waited while the parents silently consulted each other and then faced her, nodding. 'Thank you,' she said and they heard her sincerity.

'We've already had one round – a reporter from the local paper,' Don said. 'She wanted to know what we thought about Shona McGuire trying to get Carl Miller freed.'

'What did you tell her?'

'Nothing,' he said firmly.

'Shut the door on her, he did,' his wife added.

Joan Leggatt smiled bleakly. 'I can't promise she won't be back – and others like her. What's about to come to light

147

will be a massive story and your loss of Abby a major part of it.'

Don Jenkins was puzzled. 'I don't understand.'

At a nod from his DCI, Tyrell leaned forward. 'Following direct orders from the Chief Constable we were asked to go back over all the evidence in Carl Miller's trial to see if there was a good reason for an appeal.'

'I thought what came out in court was spot on?'

'So it was, Mr Jenkins. I did find the odd corner shaved a bit but nothing which altered what was found or that Miller was seen near where Abby's body was left.'

'So?'

'It's routine to search for similar incidents in case there are connections.'

'You mean Carl could have done it before?'

'No, Mr Jenkins. There was no doubt Miller had not left the Forest. He was the main carer for his mother and many people could verify he had not left her, not even for a day. At the time it was thought Abby's death was an isolated occurrence.'

'You don't think that now, do you?' Molly Jenkins asked quietly.

The DI was selecting his words carefully and had a breathing space as Clarke carried in a tray, the tea already poured. Tyrell saw Molly Jenkins sip hers. Whatever she tasted it held no surprises and Don Jenkins stirred hard, determined to dissolve all the sugar in the cup. Such little things revealed how deeply Brian Clarke had become engrained in the family at a time when they needed help.

'It was the arrival of a detective from Scotland which changed our thinking,' Tyrell continued. 'Miller could never have killed the girl in Fife but the Scotsman was curious to know if anyone who had murdered the child there could have been here, in Soudley, when Abby was taken from you. We started looking at everything with fresh eyes.'

Molly's cup rattled in her saucer and her eyes were huge

in an ashen face as she stared at the DI. 'Another child?' she whispered.

Tyrell nodded. 'There were others we had to consider, in Northamptonshire and in Kent. After that we learned from Interpol of similar deaths. In Portugal and Spain.'

'But Carl couldn't . . .'

'No, Mrs Jenkins. After each death someone like Carl was found with evidence on their possessions which made them the prime suspect. Nobody linked the murders.'

'Until now,' Joan Leggatt said briskly. She put her empty cup and its saucer on the tray. 'Do you understand now why we need your help? You have every right to know what we have been doing but we must have your silence. This – this man must never get the slightest hint we are on to him. He is extremely clever and he seems to know how we work. Alerted, he could escape to a country with which we have no extradition treaty. I want him,' the DCI said, her features stern with her resolve.

There was no hesitation. 'You have our word,' Don Jenkins assured her and his wife nodded her agreement.

'Tell me,' Molly asked Brian Clarke, 'were they all – raped – like Abby?'

He looked at Keith Tyrell. 'Can't we tell her Jenny's idea?'

Together, the two men sought silent permission from the DCI.

'Go ahead.'

Clarke went to stand behind the Jenkinses and Tyrell crouched in front of them, his eyes on a level with Abby's mother. 'We can't be sure but we've gone over all the evidence again and again.' Hours had been spent gazing at and assessing every pathology photograph and description. 'Abby fought hard and it's possible she injured her attacker. When she did die, it was quick. Very quick. It has been suggested to us that only after she was dead was an attempt made to make it appear she had been raped.'

Molly Jenkins leaned forward and put out her hands to Keith Tyrell. He grasped them, his strength and warmth giving her the courage to voice her thoughts. 'Abby wasn't raped and she never knew what he was doing?' was a whisper.

'No, Mrs Jenkins, I'm sure she did not.' His words, deep and clear, carried conviction.

There was a sob, then tears began to flow. Don Jenkins knelt beside his wife and held her tightly, their faces showing the first relief in years. 'Don! Abby didn't know! She couldn't have suffered – that!'

'You're sure?' Don Jenkins asked the DI.

'As sure as we can be until we arrest the man and persuade him to tell us what happened.'

Don Jenkins had no hesitation. 'Just leave him to the parents – we'd see you got your answers.'

'You've got visitors, mam,' Roly Willis told DCI Leggatt as soon as they returned from Soudley. 'From Newnham – said they couldn't wait till tomorrow.'

It was the smell of cigarette smoke curling from the DCI's office which greeted them first and Joan Leggatt stiffened with annoyance. Seated at her desk was a stocky figure in a black suit, unnaturally red hair in a very expensive cut curving round an oval face with regular features and a pair of very shrewd eyes. The woman remained seated, her hand on an open folder.

'Hope you don't mind us using your office, Chief Inspector, but you were out. I wanted to get on the ground as soon as possible so I got your people to hike the files back and we're camping out here until you can find us a space of our own.'

Joan Leggatt was every inch a DCI as she stared at the invader of her territory. 'I take it you are Detective Inspector Marshall?'

'Carol Marshall.' She pointed to the other two strangers who had had enough courtesy to stand. 'DS Ken Jarvis and the guy in the corner, DC Del Stevenson.'

Graciously, Joan Leggatt acknowledged the other members of the new team under her roof and in turn introduced Keith Tyrell and Brian Clarke. 'Brian, be good enough to show DI Marshall and her colleagues to the office ready for her. I expect Sergeant Willis will provide extra hands to clear away these records.' An elegant hand swept round what had been orderly. 'And DI Marshall, you've clearly been too busy to see all the notices we have around the place. This is a non-smoking work environment. There is a rest room set aside for those who wish to indulge.' She turned away as the woman allowed her annoyance at the reprimand to be seen. 'Keith, I'll leave you to liaise with DI Marshall.'

As Joan Leggatt marched away, the visiting inspector stared up at the resident DI. 'So, you're Tyrell?'

The DI from London was like several of the women he had encountered in his police career. In what had once been a totally male force women had never had it easy. Many like Joan Leggatt used hard work and their wits to get ahead. Others, like Ms Marshall, who must have had difficulty reaching the height limit for entry, had become belligerent, even more so than the worst of her male counterparts. She rose and stood in front of Keith Tyrell, sturdy legs in pricey trousers planted firmly as if for a fight.

'Yes, I'm Tyrell. Can I help you?'

She surveyed him slowly, her mouth's movements making it obvious how much she despised his good tailoring, his grooming, the natural grace of his movements and, above all, his extra inches.

'We were going to come tomorrow but one of your bosses rang and insisted we take over from you, personally, the earliest possible. Seems he doesn't think as highly of you as you do.'

'That would have been a Mr Campbell?' Tyrell failed to hide the slight emphasis on Campbell's lack of rank.

DI Marshall shrugged her shoulders. 'I gather you had a go at reviewing this case – a bit half-assed if you ask me – but then you won't be used to the cutting edge down here. I've got your report and you weren't around when the girl died so I doubt I'll need you now I'm in charge.'

'Of course, I expected nothing less. I would ask you to

be careful with Abby Jenkins's parents and with Mrs Miller. They've been through a difficult few years.'

'Tough! I've a killer to nail.'

Tyrell paused, not allowing himself to be drawn into a retort. 'A killer who took his time bedding into the community to play his chosen game with decent people.'

'I had a quick look at what you wrote in the car coming from Newnham. Far-fetched ideas and nothing to base them on but circumstantial evidence and guesswork.'

He thought of the hours of hard work, the unpaid overtime put in by so many. 'It's an obscene joke the killer's playing and part of it is to go to ground in each community, adjusting his methods to its ways because, as you said, this isn't London.'

'And you'd know, would you?'

'Oh yes,' said Tyrell softly. 'As it happens, I'd know.'

DI Marshall tossed her head defiantly and turned to follow her own ambition. DS Jarvis went after her, dark hair cropped close to his skull, a dark shadow on his cheeks and his black leather jacket almost the uniform of a certain kind of officer clawing his way upwards. Only DC Stevenson was left in his corner, eyes intent on the information being scrolled upwards on the screen facing him.

'Hello, is it Del for Derek?' Tyrell asked.

The young man stood, almost matching the DI in height. He had opted for a suit, its comfortable fit and DC Stevenson's easy manner indicating he was his own man and not worried by the opinions of others. Tyrell had also been scrutinized and earned a grin, wide and friendly in dark skin.

'Delme. My mother's Welsh.'

Tyrell instinctively liked the man. 'We're so near the border you're almost home.'

'I know. My Gran'll kill me if I don't get there before going back to London.'

Tyrell nodded at the screen. 'It should be straightforward.'

'It is – you've a helluva good programmer.'

'The best. I've a feeling HQ would poach him from us if they get half a chance.'

'Forget your HQ,' Del Stevenson said with his big smile. 'Our Madam Marshall will have him if he's useful to her.'

It was Tyrell's turn to grin. 'Won't stand an earthly. We've a very nice PC stationed here and no way will DC Walsh budge from her.' He was walking through the door and towards privacy when DI Marshall appeared and stopped him.

'Sorry, but I'm needed elsewhere.'

'Too bad, Tyrell. I was assured complete co-operation by your ACC and I want answers.'

'You already have a full account of my activities and conclusions –'

'It's this request for blood analysis and what's been done about it. Seems you've not covered enough suspects. You should have realized you needed –'

'The complete list of all visitors to the Miller home is on record. Only one nurse has been missed because she's in Saudi but DC Goddard's due to collect a sample from her mother the day after tomorrow when she returns from a coach trip to Bournemouth. Anything else, ask DS Clarke or Sergeant Willis.'

'Are you trying to tell me there's something more important going on in this neck of the woods? Come on, Tyrell, pull the other one!'

'We might look a peaceful place but crime lurks here, often because the perpetrators think we're too slow and stupid to notice.'

'You really do think a lot of yourself, don't you?' Marshall snapped at him.

The DI checked they were alone. 'No, but while we're clearing the air, I'd like it understood you can say what you like about me whenever and wherever you choose, but the colleagues with whom I've been working are damned good coppers – every one of them. These "half-assed ideas" you've tried to belittle are what caused the Home Office to intervene and get you sent here as part of a complex course of action to find and convict a particularly ruthless criminal.' Tyrell's tone and demeanour had been calm, almost pleasant, but the angle of his features had sharpened and his eyes were cold. 'I would be grateful if you never again attempt to denigrate the men and women of this division who want only the truth of the situation. By doing so we can all then see Abby Jenkins – and Carl Miller – receive the justice each deserves.'

Marshall flushed as she looked intently at the knot of Tyrell's tie. 'If I've caused offence – I'm sorry,' she mumbled.

'Thank you. Now, if you'll excuse me?'

Paperwork was a large and necessary evil part of policing and the DI was finishing off some statistics to be sent up the line.

'Message from Roly,' Brian Clarke said as he came through the door. 'Zinna Richards is downstairs and wants to talk to "that nice Inspector Tyrell".'

The nice inspector threw back his head and groaned. 'What now?'

'She won't say, except to you. Zinna's no fool and knows if she explains to Roly he might deal with whatever she's hung up on today and let you off the hook.'

'Ask Roly to put her somewhere quiet – with a cup of tea – and say I'm in an interview at the moment.'

'OK, but you don't usually resort to white lies so who are you interviewing?'

Tyrell swung his chair, enabling him to avoid charts, numbers. 'You.'

Brian Clarke lifted an eyebrow. 'Honoured, I'm sure.'

'Dave Beckford. Why's he running scared?'

'Is he? I know he's put in his papers for retirement. It was either that or get fit for his next medical and knowing the state Dave's in, that's not an option.'

'Any idea what he did for Simons? He's scared stiff it'll affect his pension.'

Clarke thought hard. 'Nothing I can think of.'

'And we've not turned up anything in the record. Whatever it was couldn't have had any major effect, then or now.'

'Oh well, a month from now he'll be gone, taking his secret with him.'

Tyrell nodded. 'Living out his life as yet another of Pete Simons's victims,' Tyrell murmured.

'Miss Richards.'

Zinna had made an effort to be clean and tidy for her visit to the station. Brushed hair, polished glasses and a red, unspotted sweater the DI had not seen before. Only her trousers were the same, the smudges of grease familiar.

'I've seen it again!'

'Seen what, Miss Richards?'

'The car – this morning when I was riding past on my way to the other shop. The one I don't often use 'cause they charge too much.'

A wrinkled piece of paper was passed to Tyrell. The writing on it was clear, the roundness of the letters and figures those of a careful child. He read an address, a car registration number.

'Are you certain this was the car which you say caused you to fall from your bike?'

Zinna nodded vigorously. 'Positive.'

'Then I will thank you for your assistance.'

'What will you do?' Her eyes were excited behind thick lenses.

'Two of my officers will visit the occupants of this house and question them about the incident.'

Her disappointment was instant and deep. 'Not you?'

'No, I have to stay here and finish other work.'

'Can't you go – and I could come with you?'

'I'm sorry but that's just not possible.'

'They won't be as good as you,' she insisted.

'There I must contradict you, Miss Richards. All the officers on duty here are well trained and efficient. Now, if

155

you really want to help, you'll let them do what they must.'

Zinna sagged in her chair, reminding Tyrell of an elderly puppy who had retrieved a stick and waited in vain for a reward.

'I'll ask Sergeant Willis to get some tea sent in to you before you go home.'

He saw her lips tighten and a frown deepen. 'I want to know what happens! I was the one they left for dead – I should be told!'

'You will, Miss Richards.'

She was cheered by the thought. 'You'll come?'

'I can't promise who will visit you –'

'You'll come,' she told him and there was a firmness about her, suggesting she would accept no one else.

'Anything useful from Zinna?' Clarke asked when he saw the DI return to his office. He was handed the limp paper and read it quickly, raising his eyebrows in a question.

'The car, parked in the driveway of its owner. Who's free?'

'I am – and Bryony.'

'Then I'll leave the two of you to follow through but keep in mind we've no real charges against the driver. All we can manage is a strongly worded reprimand for not taking enough care.'

'No blood and guts, so no real accident, at least that's how the CPS would see it.'

'In which case we can hardly take the driver to court for leaving the scene of one, although we could have him for behaviour likely to cause an accident. See what you can do, Brian.'

'Don't want much, do you? Where will you be?'

'Here – with some of the data which Campbell and his ilk don't understand but which they must have to feel they're doing something useful. It keeps 'em happy.'

'Happy? Wasting good police time more like! No wonder morale's down in every force,' Brian Clarke said as he marched off to deal with Zinna Richards's problem, leaving Tyrell to his analyses.

Satisfying the Campbells of his world took time and patience Keith knew would be better spent on more useful occupations but he persevered. With the final folder closed, the last entry on the computer saved, Tyrell realized he was tired. He closed his eyes for a moment as he summoned up the energy needed to try and get through the handover to Carol Marshall. It was not going to be pleasant and she would be out to score points at every turn. It was exactly what he had explained to Jenny, a good idea going pear-shaped as the ambitious gnawed at hard work done in order to fuel their own promotions.

He leaned back in his chair to ease taut muscles and breathe slowly. It was beginning to work and Keith could feel the breaths becoming slower and more steady, almost of their own accord. Even an image of Marcus Campbell disappeared as does a wisp of mist as the sun rises. Tyrell only turned his head when Brian Clarke came in grinning.

'Hope you didn't have any plans to get home early.'

Tyrell groaned. 'Sleep would be nice.'

'Not for you – yet. You need to visit Zinna.'

There was something in Clarke's look of satisfaction which had the DI sitting up, becoming alert. 'What's happened?'

'I'll tell you on the way. Coming?'

Chapter Nine

It was easy for Jenny to hide her disappointment, talking to Keith by phone. 'I thought you expected to be home early?'

'I did –'

'But something came up. Funny that, when you've been saying all your cases nowadays go on to high-flying squads and leave you high and dry.'

'Most have, darling. This was just an oddity on our patch.'

She stifled a sigh. 'So, when will you be home?'

'An hour – with luck.'

Tyrell closed his mobile and watched the eastern part of Lydney go by as Brian Clarke drove away from the station. After the steep hill levelled, the DI studied his friend and saw lips quirking with a story waiting to be told.

'Well?'

'Zinna Richards had had a lift in and out of Lydney to see you. When she got back home she must have pedalled like a maniac. It didn't take her long to get to the address of the car owner and we were standing at the door, waiting to be let in by this phantom road hog, when Zinna was there behind us. Would she clear off? No way. Fortunately, Bryony's as pig-headed as they come and she held old Zinna at the gate.'

'Was it the car?'

'So Zinna said. I gave it the once-over, looking for any scratches or dents, but nothing. Nor were there any signs of touching up. That bodywork had never come in contact with Zinna's bike.' Clarke was finding it hard to hold back a grin.

'When are you going to tell me what's so hilarious?'

'The guy who's the registered owner was there. The car's been locked in the garage for a while because he's recovering from a heart attack. "Drove himself home when it happened," the wife said. I got as good a statement as I could out of the husband and was ready to come away. He wandered over to the window and peered out. That's when Bryony came knocking at the door, Zinna at her back insisting the husband was the man she'd seen in the car. Not driving – he was in the passenger seat.'

'Who had been at the wheel?'

'His girlfriend. He'd started having bad angina pains when he was in her house –'

'And in her bed?'

'You've got it. Poor sod was in the wrong place at the wrong time. Girlfriend heaved him into the car, struggling to get him home and let the wife call an ambulance. Once outside his own house this guy crawls into the driving seat and wife was fooled – until now. All hell's let loose! If we get a call-out to a murder before morning, don't be surprised.'

'Then why are we going to see Zinna Richards?'

'She loved it. Apparently, she'd heard the car being driven erratically – odd engine noise and gears grating – so she turned her head to look. I've got her to admit that's why she fell of her damned pushbike but she did see matey with his bluish face up against the glass nearest to her. She said he looked as if he was struggling to breathe while someone drove him home.'

'That's still no reason –'

'Wait a minute. Bryony was trying to pacify the old biddy when I heard Zinna say, "At least you're not as rude as that young doctor they sent to see me once. Just as well he went off to God knows where next day."'

Tired as he was, it took a second or two for Tyrell to realize the implication. 'It was Mather! You didn't push her after that?'

'Me? I knew how much you'd enjoy visiting one of your keenest admirers.'

Jenny held his face between her hands and studied him carefully. 'You look more cheerful than you did this morning,' she decided. 'What's happened?'

She was told of a heart attack in the wrong bed. A mistress who was an appalling driver and nosy Zinna falling off a bike. Keith went on to talk of visiting Zinna in her own home, being surprised by the cosy, spotless surroundings and the strong smell of polish for her furniture and brasses, tea in dainty cups and handmade lace on napkins. The statement she had made would guarantee a search warrant for Mather's rented home near Cinderford.

'The day Zinna's talking about, was that the day Abby died?' Jenny wanted to know.

'It was. Roly Willis had already got a list of Mather's appointments from the surgery manager and Brian could recite the times. "Left you at 5.45," he told Zinna – and that's when the fireworks started. Zinna remembered the doctor's visit very well. His rude manners, the way he messed up taking a blood sample. "He was only supposed to check up on my blood pressure," she insisted. After Mather left she cycled to the shop for milk, had a long natter with the owner, rode back home, getting in coal for the evening and wood for the morning. Then she cleaned herself, put supper ready and was drinking tea at six o'clock – the time Mather logged in at the surgery.'

'So he had time . . .'

'To pick up Abby? Yes, and fresh blood from Zinna to prove he'd visited her. With his alibi gone he's fair game and we've done all we can at our end.'

'Brian will be pleased.'

'Over the moon. I left him entering Zinna's statement into records, adding that it had been obtained because of good communication with local officers and useful members of the community.'

'You've always said that's what mattered.'

Keith eased tight muscles in his neck and shoulders. 'It is – and Carol Marshall had better not foul up.'

With the removal to London of all the data and material evidence in the Abby Jenkins/Mather case, Tyrell was left with the task of organizing the copies which Mickey had contrived to make and been careful to keep. Clarke helped and the three men stood and looked at the neat piles of disks and files which had taken a whole day to complete.

Mickey straightened plastic containers of disks into a neat pile. 'Strange to see it all brought to this, sir.'

'You've done everything you could,' Tyrell assured him. 'We all have.'

'But you'd rather have been there at the finish?' Clarke asked the DI.

'Wouldn't you?'

'I don't know. There comes a time to leave it to others – just like charging up the field with a rugby ball. Pass it to the fastest and let them get it over the line.'

'You're right, of course, Brian. Instead of standing here moping I should be polishing the official report for the Chief.'

Brian Clarke's smile was deceptive. 'Reading it'll take his mind off how much Carl Miller can claim off him. Come on, Mickey,' he said, thumping the younger man's shoulder. 'Let's get this lot sealed and labelled so nothing can go walkabout and we can all get an early night for once.'

As soon as the DI walked into his office at the start of shift next morning, Roly Willis was a quiet voice on the internal phone. 'Just to warn you, Mr Hinton's in the building. He's been asking if you're in yet.'

'I wonder what he wants this early in the day?' Tyrell mused aloud.

'Who wants?' Clarke asked as he came into the room and leaned on the DI's monitor.

'The ACC.'

'Hinton? At this hour? Well, it could be a pat on the back for all us yokels wrecking Mather's plans and getting that search warrant for his old home. Poor old Livermore – stamped on by Ms Marshall's size 4s and having an alien forensic crew moving in on him. They'll take everything they can lay their hands on and rush it up the M4.'

'What can they find after all those years in between? There can't be much left – even for the experts going back to the best equipment.'

'Then it could be a "thank you" for you and your snout, passing on data about Brosca Thatcher to the special unit at the Yard.'

'I doubt Hinton even knows.'

Clarke shrugged the bulk of his shoulders. 'Maybe the old boy just wanted to get away from his desk.'

They were not left to their imaginations for long, a summons to the DCI's office coming on the heels of Clarke's last words. Tyrell checked his tie was straight and pulled at the jacket of his suit to let it hang properly. 'And maybe I'll get a rocket for a sin of omission.'

Only Hinton was in Joan Leggatt's office. Restless power encased in an immaculate uniform, the ACC waved Tyrell to a chair. 'Good to see you, Keith.'

Tyrell appeared to be relaxed, at ease, but he had learned to be wary. 'Sir?'

'No, it's not a complaint. You've done some fine work in the last few weeks.'

'I had good people working with me, sir.'

'Yes, you had – and you've the sense to realize it. Now, the identity scam will take a long time to unravel completely and, thank God, we're no longer picking up that tab. As for the Carl Miller review, there's still nothing from the medical pundits or that damned lab and it's all gone up the line anyway. You could have been left hanging about here since crime figures are down at the moment but there's been a request for you to be seconded for a few days. Right up your street, I'd say, and you don't even have to tart yourself up as a yob or a Romanian drug pusher.'

'Glad to hear it, sir. I gather it's a covert operation of some kind?'

'Yes, but I've no idea what. I'm to find some excuse to send you to Gwent HQ as a courier and on your way back from there you're to get a coffee at the Magor service station on the M4. 11.30 on the dot.' The ACC lifted a smallish envelope from the desk and handed it over. 'That's my end done. The rest is up to you and you've no time to hang about. As far as we're concerned, you're cleared to do whatever's asked so, on your way – and good luck.'

A steady drizzle had set in by the time Tyrell reached the turn-off on the M4 leading to the Magor services. It was busy, a phalanx of heavy lorries lining the route to the car park. The DI drove down the slope, hoping to find a space as near to the entrance as possible. The dashboard clock registered 11.15 and he assumed the attitude of a sales rep taking a well-earned break. Locking the car gave him the opportunity to survey the people walking through the lanes of cars as they moved from or towards the building. He joined the latter, seeing nothing out of the ordinary, collected a newspaper from the shop and walked the short distance to the restaurant. Picking up a sandwich he joined the queue waiting for coffee. That transaction complete Tyrell carried his tray as he searched for and found a table in the no-smoking zone where he could sit with his back to the wall. Unwrapping his food, using a knife on his sandwiches, stirring liquid, gave him a chance to look around and then at his watch. It was still a minute or two short of the meeting.

'Keith! I don't believe it – it's great to see you again!'

For a split second the DI froze. Someone who knew him

appearing at exactly the wrong moment was a distinct hazard. He looked up, confirming his recognition of the voice. The broad smile, American accent, large hand extended, were all very familiar. As had happened in Broadway, the clothes jarred with his memories. Today it was baggy chinos which had seen better days, a yellow sweatshirt showing its age and a Yale logo. The eyes were the same as always, intelligent and friendly. Keith reached for the outstretched hand.

'Clay. What are you doing in this neck of the woods?'

'On my way to Chepstow to do some research for the book. Fancied some coffee.'

Tyrell glanced at his watch. 11.29.

'Meeting someone?' Clay deftly poured milk, added sugar, stirred and looked up at his friend with a disarming smile.

'Yes. 11.30.'

'Great. I'm not late.'

Keith did not move. He absorbed the meaning of Clay's words and a few thoughts which had niggled in the past slotted into place. 'You.'

'I requested you not be told who you were to meet. If I'm under surveillance, your surprise was unquestionably genuine. As for you, no one was on your tail – I was watching. We're just two old friends meeting up unexpectedly.'

'And my sneaking suspicion your book was a blind?'

'Never could fool you, could I? Actually, there is a book and I've sheets of it all over the cottage. A would-be Grisham in the embassy sends me chapters now and again. Who knows? The poor dope may really get it published one day.'

'Why Stanton?'

'Where else would a gawping Yankee settle to pen the great American novel but in one of your quaint little villages?' Clay's casual glance accurately assessed their neighbours, his activity covered by a languid yawn.

Keith sipped coffee and gazed at him over the rim of his

cup. 'I had a hunch our meeting in the Lygon was a set-up. Tell me, Clay, what's it all for?'

The American did not lose his amiable expression but his eyes became stern. 'GCHQ.'

'Cheltenham?'

A cheerful nod did nothing to reassure Keith. 'A certain strain of information is being misdirected, shall we say, and it links up with something similar happening in Washington. Since 9/11 the slightest coincidence is treated suspiciously and in this case the stench being given off is nasty and familiar – that's why I was brought in. My boss thinks I'm an expert on English villages, thanks to you and the time we spent in Tolland.'

'It was you asked for me?'

'Why not? Remember, I've seen you at work.'

The two men sipped coffee.

'Two sources of leaks, one here and one in the States,' Keith said after he had laid his cup carefully in its saucer. 'A village, probably in Gloucestershire since my ACC got himself out of bed at the crack of dawn. No apparent rush, yet I'm to be brought in. If you were going the softly, softly route you'd have asked for a specially trained MI5 operative who'd burrow into the community as you've been doing for weeks and be unnoticed as they work. Something's changed.'

Clay grinned. 'Thanks, Keith. You're still the same and reasoning as fast as ever. We need max speed if we're to keep up.'

'With what?'

This time there was no smile and the expression was rueful. 'If you've finished your coffee we'll walk out to the car park.'

A leisurely stroll later, the two men leaned against Clay's Land Rover, suitably aged and dusty for his cover. He aimed his key ring at the dashboard.

'We're OK here,' he said, 'no bugs in the area. Now, all our units in both our agencies are on full alert for terrorism – and I know your views on the guys who play that game. The joy in killing comes first, looking for a cause or religion to hide behind comes second. It's not those individuals we're after.'

The devastation in New York, the recent wars, were hideous memories. 'Not even with the possibility of revenge attacks?' Keith asked.

'They're a major part of the equation,' Clay admitted, 'but other units have that aspect of the situation under control – in spite of all the goddamned politicians and their buddies. No, pressure's suddenly started to build from an unknown source and it's gathering speed.'

'A new faction under way?'

Clay shook his head, smiling broadly for anyone who might be watching. 'Money. Our finance whizz-kids tell us something's up.'

Keith's thoughts raced. 'Cash on the move electronically?'

'Yup. It's not staggering amounts but it's heading towards the suppliers of arms and men. There's no connection to Al Q'aeda or any similar organization. No links with politics, nor with any religion, established or otherwise. The only explanation making any sense is that terrorist attacks are being planned to cause havoc in the money markets – remember what happened after 9/11?'

'Too well.'

'Shares going up and down like yo-yos and some finishing up on the floor.'

'Are you saying this new player wants a repeat performance?'

Clay nodded. 'The most likely targets are in Wall Street. Imagine it – if even a small part of the Dow Jones is suddenly going to go haywire, it can pay well to know in advance. This guy behind it all needs to be sure when it's the exact moment to shake up the money men, and that's why Washington and GCHQ are possibly being milked for useful information.'

Keith was shocked. 'Someone's planning to initiate and orchestrate terror to influence specific financial markets and cash in? It's obscene!'

The American nodded, his expression grim. 'And imminent. As you guessed, I've been based in the target zone for a few weeks. Since then, increased funds have started going to suppliers who like cash up front. Our experts have been tracing the money back to source and that's where I come in because the track ends somewhere in your county.'

A shudder of fear was suppressed. 'Where's the terrorism going to break out?'

'The US. There's no doubt at all on that point. All the organization is happening Stateside – not here. That's what's so damned clever about the plan. The main man is tucked up thousands of miles away from the action and apparently leading a quiet, blameless life. Whoever he is – I tell you, Keith, his cover's faultless.'

'But why involve me? I mean, Clay, with all the electronic wizardry at your disposal, I'd guess every resident, or even visitor, in the entire county has been put through the wringer several times over and they won't have any idea it's happening.'

'You're absolutely right. What we already know you wouldn't believe. Between Stanton and Broadway, for instance, we've pinpointed one very respectable matron who started out as a fella, three bigamists, a handful of individuals who've served time and kept it under wraps and a few potential paedophiles. Oh yes, we know all that sort of thing and we can make good guesses but we're nowhere near proving one hundred per cent who's the slimeball behind the money movements. Believe me, we're running out of time.'

Keith let his thoughts work out the parameters of the problem. 'There can't be many with the cash background to make them likely suspects.'

'Don't you believe it! We've homed in on area south of Broadway where it costs a small fortune just to live like an ordinary villager. As for ye olde worlde mansions, large and small, there's many made their stash and live in state in them. Besides, our man may only be relatively wealthy and relying on this plan of his to really make it big for him. I need your instincts with village people to get to him. He may be a newcomer or have been born there – could even have moved in years ago. One way and another, we've narrowed the search down to one of three villages in your county. Buckland, Laverton, Stanton. We don't know which one and there's no time to be sure the covert way. Will you help me?'

Keith knew the area well, loved it and its people and wanted it left untouched by outsiders, certainly undamaged, but he was under no illusions. In the defence of their own homeland, Americans were quietly at work in the county and they needed a local officer as a liaison who would work with them and give them an essential credibility. 'Of course I'll help – if it's possible.'

'In this emergency, you're the only one who can help. You've the contacts in Laverton and villagers won't be surprised to see you wandering round.'

A startled Keith realized how far the undercover operation had already progressed. 'My God, Clay! You've done your homework but you've forgotten I'm known there as a copper. What's my excuse for staying in that part of the county when I should be on duty?'

The American brightened. 'No problem. Your aunt, Mrs Astley, lives in a very nice house on the edge of Laverton.'

'Aunt Sophie!'

'A great lady. She's with your parents in London. Tonight she'll have a fall and damage her ankle.'

Keith was instantly furious. 'No! I won't have her being hurt.'

'Cool it, Keith. All she'll get is a bandage and a limp. It does mean she'll need someone to stay with her when, against all medical advice, she insists on going back to her own home.'

Unable to believe what he was hearing, Keith shook his head in amazement. 'She's already agreed to this?'

'Sure. Says she hasn't had so much fun in ages.'

'You're telling me it's all set up? Every last detail?'

'Yup. I just need your agreement.'

Keith had learned to trust the American, to respect his

integrity, and there was no doubt his friend was desperate. 'I suppose I'm due some leave?'

'And Jenny.'

'You've thought of everything,' Keith said bitterly, not pleased his family was being used so ruthlessly, but he had seen in Clay's eyes resolution covering the edge of fear. 'Are the villagers in any danger?'

'Absolutely not. Unwittingly, they're providing cover for this bastard. My guess is he's chosen to retire and live there permanently so he's hardly likely to arrange to be blown up in his own bed. As for us, once we're certain of his identity, we just want him winkled out and away.'

'Where to?'

Clay shrugged his shoulders and Keith guessed the real action would be away from his beloved corner of Gloucestershire, probably off the British mainland altogether.

The world had changed when Bin Laden sent his men to their deaths with thousands of others in New York and Washington. The work of Clay and so many like him was necessary to protect ordinary citizens intent on leading a normal, peaceful life. Keith knew if he was to be part of this operation, the only outcome with which he could live would be that he had personally ensured the right man was delivered to the covert forces for justice to be served silently, distantly.

'What do I do now?'

Clay was obviously relieved. 'Go back to Lydney, then wait to hear from your mother. She'll drive your aunt back to Laverton as soon as you and Jenny are ready to move.'

The journey was a silent one. For the first half-hour Jenny was tense, her breathing shallow as she worked hard to assimilate all she had learned. Racing home after the clinic's director had given her 'as long as necessary' to help her husband with a family emergency, she was at first furious at all the fuss being made of a sprained ankle. Once Keith could persuade her to listen calmly, he explained his secondment at Clay's request, the urgency of the task awaiting him and the need for a cover story which could be put in place at once. The horror and destruction which would result from failure he kept from her.

Keith had time to recall his last conversation with Brian Clarke, just before he left Lydney.

'What's up?' Brian had asked. 'Your father rang. Is anything wrong?'

'No, he's fine and sends you his regards,' Keith said, grateful for his friend's concern. 'It's my aunt. She's been staying with my parents in Town and tripped on the steps into the house. Result – one badly sprained ankle.'

'Sorry to hear it. Is it a problem?'

'The ankle? Not really. It's heavily bandaged and Aunt Sophie's insisting on going back to her own home. My parents are due to fly out to The Hague the day after tomorrow and she doesn't want them to miss out.'

Brian Clarke had been a detective a long time and his instincts were alerted. Keith was an astute devil but something was making him uneasy. Whatever orders Hinton had issued, it was obvious Keith had been told they must be kept to himself.

'I've leave due so I'll stay with Aunt Sophie – Jenny too, if she can swing it.'

Definitely something up, the sergeant decided, but he made no comment until, 'That's a bit rough, looking after the elderly when you should be slaving over a hot beach somewhere.'

'You don't know Aunt Sophie. She's great company and her house is a delight. A few days in a quiet Cotswold village, what could be better after all we've been up to in the last few weeks?'

Keith was returned to the present as Jenny stirred. Her chin was up, her mouth resolute, and he realized she had come to terms with all that lay ahead.

'You don't mind coming with me?' he asked.

She shook her head, the dark silk of her hair swinging round the calm oval of her face adding emphasis. 'I'd be severely annoyed if anyone else was providing you with credible cover. Besides, looking after Aunt Sophie when there's nothing actually wrong with her should be a doddle.'

Keith said nothing, hoping Clay's expectations materialized. The first approach had been made to his father and Keith was certain only a member of Special Branch or MI5 with considerable clout could have persuaded Sir John Tyrell into allowing any member of his family to be involved in a foray against terrorism.

For some reason there was a cold spot between his shoulders which the warmth of the car could not dispel. Keith kept his eyes on the road as he silently told himself it was merely the adrenalin high at the start of an undercover operation. He had experienced it often enough in the Met, and some of the back streets and deserted wharves and warehouses on the banks of the Thames were far more dangerous than a stretch of familiar open country.

'How much longer?' Jenny asked.

'Twenty minutes – half an hour. Hungry?'

'Getting there. Do I cook or are there takeaways at the end of the phone?'

'Neither. My mother said Aunt Sophie went mad in Fortnum's when she knew she was to have a large bandage. I know what she's like in that mood. It'll take us days to eat through what she laughingly calls her luggage.'

The car was comfortable, background music low and pleasant, hunger pangs assuaged by promise of food, and Jenny's thoughts flew ahead. Bowman's was a gracious house, beginning as a cottage tucked in a fold of the hills. Legends told of an archer returning from battle with a pouch of silver lifted from fallen enemies. He had bought land away from the heart of the small village, built his homestead and cultivated his soil to feed a growing family. Through the generations, Keith had told her, extra rooms had been added to the main building until the house was long and low. The flush of Cotswold stone had darkened over the ages until it blended into the hillside, the house protected by a garden amply bounded by shrubs and trees

171

amongst which small children could run and live out their dreams.

'You know,' Keith said softly, 'when Jeremy and I cycled this way it seemed to take for ever to get from the village to the house.'

A few minutes later Keith slowed the car, driving between imposing stone posts, the gates hanging wide in welcome. Bowman's lay in front of them, lights in the small-paned windows giving a sense of homecoming, of safety. Gravel scrunched under their wheels and Keith parked next to his mother's car.

Their arrival had been awaited and was heard, the oak door opened and his mother's smile was for both of them. 'Jenny!' was kissed and hugged, then her arms opened for her son. He bent and kissed the fragrant cheeks gently. 'Thanks, Mum.'

'No need. Your aunt thinks it'll be a great game and your father has no problem with whatever it is you're doing.'

'But you're worried.'

'Darling, I'm your mother. What do you expect me to do?'

Later, he stood with Jenny at the front door and waved his mother away. Her concern had made him feel again the chill below the base of his neck. Perhaps it was wise to have such a spot, a constant reminder to take care.

'Time for G and Ts, Keith,' Aunt Sophie decided, comfortable with her bandaged ankle on an embroidered footstool. The chairs and couches in the room were large, their upholstery soft with use and the covers of rose-flung chintz gentled by wear and washing. Lamps aimed a golden pool of light at each seat and the deep pink of the walls was spiced by jade green velvet curtains keeping away the night and the cold. Glass fronts of bookcases gleamed in dark wood while newspapers and magazines spilled across a large, low table in front of an open fire of logs bordered by the dull gleam of firedogs.

As Keith bent to a trolley in the corner, Jenny heard the

clink of glasses. Aunt Sophie rose and walked swiftly to the kitchen, returning with a bucket of ice cubes. The doorbell rang, startling all three of them. Jenny grabbed the ice and Aunt Sophie arranged herself artistically in her chair, her bandage once more displayed to effect on the footstool. She nodded and Keith went to answer the summons. The two women heard his deep, calm tones and the noises made by a shrill, forceful woman.

Aunt Sophie closed her eyes in despair. 'Oh, no! It's that ghastly female!'

'Who?' Jenny wanted to know.

'Gwynneth Addiscombe. I can't stand her but she works like a Trojan for any charity daring to poke its head above the parapet. The village owes so much to her for her fundraising efforts but I can only face her . . .'

'In small doses and at a distance,' Jenny said and chuckled.

'Exactly. Save me, darling Jenny. Please!'

Into the room strode a bosomy woman with a plain face and grey hair. She was of medium height and like all those who aspired to and wished to conform to a lofty social circle, she was clad in a sensible corduroy skirt, dull green cashmere sweater and obligatory pearls. From her low-heeled navy loafers and navy stockings to hair coiffed and ready for a headscarf or a tiara, Jenny instantly recognized Gwynneth Addiscombe as a type found in Cheltenham and all points south and east.

Aunt Sophie greeted her unwelcome visitor with a charming smile and polite introductions. She fended off insistent offers of help, gesturing Mrs Addiscombe to a chair and Keith to provide her with a glass of her favourite tipple.

'I came as soon as I heard. How dreadful for you to have to come home and be on your own! I immediately told Gerald he must look after himself while I am here to see you have all you need.' Mrs Addiscombe perched on the edge of her chair, ready to rise and give orders.

'How very kind of you but as you see, my nephew and

his wife are staying for a few days and will be my legs for me.'

'And when they've gone home? I'm sure they have very responsible jobs to keep them busy?'

Bold eyes stared at Jenny and then Keith, waiting for them to bluster an explanation of their daily lives. Neither obliged, settling in their chairs and patently quite at home.

'Fortunately, I've had expert treatment in Town,' Aunt Sophie said. 'A charming doctor assured me if I stayed in my own surroundings for a few days, my ankle will heal rapidly. It will bear my weight easily when these two young people must return home.'

'Do you live far?' Keith was asked.

'Not very,' he said and smiled at the woman, thinking Mickey Walsh would describe her as a 'right nosy old bat'. 'Can I refresh your drink, Mrs Addiscombe?'

She waved away his offer and leaned towards Aunt Sophie. 'The coffee morning tomorrow, Mrs Astley. What a pity you'll have to miss it.'

'Yes, it is, but perhaps my nephew and his wife can take my place? After all, it will help the funds if they do. At Mrs Savage's, isn't it?'

Protruding eyes glistened. 'That will leave you on your own.'

'Not at all. Nanny Bowler's coming after breakfast. She's getting lunch ready for us all.'

Thwarted, Mrs Addiscombe drained her glass, plonked it on an antique piecrust table and took her leave of them. Keith saw her out, thankfully locking the door behind her.

'I see what you mean. Not good with the word "no",' Jenny decided.

'But you can understand why people give so willingly to her charities. It's the only way to get peace and quiet,' Aunt Sophie explained.

Keith stood in the doorway and Jenny realized how much he was at ease in his surroundings. Even in a sweater and jeans he was part of the ancient, graceful room.

'Why did you get us invited to meet this Mrs Savage?' he asked his aunt.

'Simple, darling. Auriole Savage is charming and her get-togethers are always well supported. This one's for water in Africa – I think. Anyway, it's a deserving cause and you have a perfect entrée into a great chunk of locals. That's the morning taken care of and Nanny Bowler to talk to all afternoon.'

'Very neatly done,' Keith admitted.

'An army wife all those years, what do you expect? By the way I have something for you from that charming American.' From under a cushion she retrieved a mobile phone. 'It's one which works on those card thingies. Major Gifford said you'd understand why – and why it's bulkier than usual. His number's taped on to it and will you call him in the morning, 8.30 on the dot. Now may I have another G and T and this time, Keith, plenty of gin and go very easy on the tonic.'

By 8.30 next morning Keith had walked across the garden which had been a playground when he was a child. He hefted the phone Clay had left for him, calls untraceable by normal means and a scrambler device weighting the instrument and ensuring privacy. Keith switched on the scrambler, punched in Clay's number and it was answered immediately.

'Hi!' Clay's delight echoed in Keith's ear. 'I knew you were the right guy for the job.'

'I'm still not totally convinced.'

'Why not? You're on leave and so well known you're almost a chameleon, disappearing into the hedgerows. You only got to Bowman's at 7.15 last night and already you've established your cover story and got yourself invited out this morning to where you may have a target or two under the same roof.'

'That was Aunt Sophie's doing.'

'She's a terrific lady, very quick-witted and daring. She'd have been good in your SAS.'

'Her husband was for a while,' Keith said quietly.

'It's as I told you, you've got the right connections.'

Keith was silent, still not completely happy with the situation. 'You still won't give me a clue as to who I'm supposed to look for?'

'No. We do have our ideas but we want you to draw your conclusions independently. It's important,' Clay said, urgency reverberating through his words.

Keith suppressed a shiver as he began the walk back to the house. It was cold in the garden, he told himself, the air damp and clammy, air shared by the prey he must help hunt down. He looked up at the trees he had climbed so often with his cousins, and with Jeremy and Ben. From up there he had treasured all he could see of this part of the county. It attracted many, pensioners settling into old bones in tiny cottages, the new rich in creaking mansions as they used money to restore a level of grandeur they would have liked to have known all their lives. Scattered around were those whose ancestors had been buried, generation after generation in the churchyards of Stanton and Buckland.

This was a countryside rich in tradition, its yeomen and women breeding life which carried those traditions worldwide. The peace and beauty had tempted someone, allowing them to believe they could rely on such dreaming perfection to insert themselves into a community, a blanket of respectability as a cover while they made plans to murder indiscriminately. A hollowness in his stomach made Keith doubt his ability. 'A week at the most if we're lucky,' Clay had told him, 'and then we can all go back to normal.'

Normal? He thought of ideas he had talked over with Brian. They had agreed present-day law enforcement was in a state of flux as victims lost out in offences committed and in the courts. In addition it was a new century with more modern crimes to be dealt with by outdated statutes.

176

A sense of helpless urgency flooded Keith and he fought it, striding back to the house and breakfast in an attempt to disperse the rush of adrenalin he had endured. The 'fight or flight' hormone, adrenalin was called. For him there could be no choice.

This was his territory. If necessary it had to be a fight to the end.

Chapter Ten

'Your father's right,' Keith said, shortening his stride to match Jenny's.

'Hell is being shut in a room full of people you can't stand?' she said and was heartened by his quick grin.

They were walking towards the cluster of houses that was Laverton, their instructions that Auriole Savage's home had been created from a barn not far from the old village school. As they neared the conversion they could see that stones weathered by centuries had been matched exactly by contemporary masons and new wood was as good and thick as the day the first farmer had seen the barn erected. Keith guessed a first-class architect had blended ancient and modern so seamlessly and he was not surprised by an immaculate façade with its deep-set windows and iron-studded door, the whole covered and protected by a roof tiled to echo the oldest houses in the village.

It had not been a long walk from Bowman's and it was not raining although clouds threatened. Mrs Addiscombe had seen them coming through what had been a farmyard, translated into a patio with slabs and pots of late-flowering plants.

'How good of you to come!' she called. 'Hurry up and get in the warm.' There was no time for more as the woman hurried out of sight.

Inside the house Auriole Savage was a charming version of a newcomer to Laverton. Her fawn wool trouser suit was perfectly tailored to fit her slim figure and the copper-coloured scarf at her throat emphasized the natural auburn in the silver of her hair. 'Do forgive the noise – but the coffee's quite good.'

Gwynneth Addiscombe bustled up, stripped Jenny of her jacket and held out a hand for Keith's waterproof. As she went to stow them in a closet, they turned to face the crowd, the source of the din resolving itself into a mass of bodies. Most were female, the few men present elderly and clad in cavalry twill trousers, blue blazers over check wool shirts and an obligatory silk cravat at the neck.

Jenny, like Keith, was comfortable in her normal, casual clothes. 'Does everyone here live in Laverton?' she asked.

'Gracious, no,' said Mrs Savage with a laugh. 'I don't know where Gwynneth gets them all from but they appear when she puts out the word and buy lots of raffle tickets. It's worth having so many when it means a good return for coffee and a few packets of biscuits.'

Keith had been dragooned by Mrs Addiscombe and was being relentlessly introduced to people she thought mattered. Mrs Savage took Jenny's arm. 'Come and meet Jane Scholes. She's the reason I'm doing this.'

It was a small, dainty woman with grey hair, her skin the fine-lined suede of age, who turned to watch their approach. As did Auriole Savage, Jane Scholes dressed to please herself and was from another era in her tailored grey skirt and plain white shirt held at the throat by a silver filigree brooch, her cardigan hand-knitted from soft lilac wool. Jenny liked her, saw the humanity in the faded blue eyes, and they chatted of life in Kenya before Mau Mau tore the heart out of a country.

'Do you go back often?' Jenny asked.

'Not as I'd like but the debt I owe my friends will take a long time to repay.'

'They're still there?'

'Of course,' Mrs Scholes said softly, 'they're Kikuyu – part of the land.'

'But I thought the Kikuyu . . .'

'Were Mau Mau adherents? Not all of them, my dear. One had grown up with my father and when it was

179

whispered our farm was to be attacked, we were warned and led into hiding.'

Jenny realized the woman was reliving her flight through the bush.

'Fire,' Jane Scholes said quietly, 'it takes no prisoners. Fortunately for us it was assumed we had all died in the flames and the wild men with their pangas were too busy running off cattle to hunt for mere corpses.'

'You returned to help your Kikuyu friends rebuild?'

'More than that. There's a clinic now – and a school. I can't nurse or teach but I can come to mornings like this and help pay the way of those who are of use to that township in the sun.'

'This morning?'

'It will help towards another teacher. The children from the school do well but they're avid for even more knowledge.'

A young woman in jeans and a large Fair Isle sweater joined them. 'A good turn-out, Aunt Jane.'

'Indeed it is. Have you met Mrs Tyrell?'

A shake of blonde curls and Jenny was introduced to Megan Baverstock, green eyes in a round face assessing Jenny. 'Your first time at this sort of shindig?'

Jenny chuckled. 'Railroaded into it within twenty minutes of parking the car.'

'You were lucky you had time to draw breath. I mostly cheat and use the excuse of my children quite shamelessly. As for Aunt Jane, she scarpers off to Kenya at every opportunity.'

Jane Scholes wagged her head reprovingly at Megan. 'Quite untrue, dear. I never "scarper".'

'Escape, then?' Megan offered and the older woman's smile was gentle.

'How often do you have these fundraisers?' Jenny wanted to know.

Mrs Scholes shrugged her shoulders but Megan had no doubts. 'Too often, which is why the Addiscombe has to sweep the highways and byways to find her prey. Most of the villagers give her a wide berth and I only come if it means I can help Aunt Jane.'

'Megan's parents have lived in Laverton all their lives and were very kind to me. Then, Mrs Addiscombe does work unceasingly for her charities,' Mrs Scholes told Jenny.

'Her poor husband must see very little of her – I presume there is a Mr Addiscombe?' Jenny asked, her eyes innocently wide.

Megan reached for a biscuit and Mrs Scholes lowered her eyes, inspected her cup, then sipped at the liquid cooling there. They were not left in peace for long, Mrs Addiscombe pushing her way towards them.

'Jane! No hiding in a corner! Megan, you really should let dear Jenny circulate and Jane must meet the Wilkinsons. They're new and want to hear all about Kenya.'

She was unstoppable and Jenny was left standing with Megan. 'Is this the only social life in the village?'

'Heavens, no! And this has nothing to do with the village proper.'

'So, what do you all do?'

Jenny was told of playgroups and rotas giving young mothers the chance to talk, stay sane, as well as working couples meeting in small parties to dine out at restaurants or in each other's houses. She heard of older members of the community helping each other with library books, shopping, cooking and of the regular whist drives for the real villagers, most of the newer variety preferring to be seen playing bridge, Jenny was informed.

'Then there's music. If you can make it, there's a concert in the church tomorrow night. A guy who lives in Buckland sings with a choir in Cheltenham – only a small one. I heard them last time he brought them over and they're really very good.'

Jenny's spirits rose. 'I'd like to hear them but it depends on my husband's aunt.'

'How is her leg? I heard she'd broken it and would be laid up for weeks. Don't worry, we'll all rally round and make sure she's not neglected when you go back to work – in a hospital, we were told?'

Jenny marvelled at the efficiency of the local grapevine and wondered how shocked everyone would be at the speed of Aunt Sophie's complete recovery. The noisy mass moved, engulfed, absorbed, and Jenny was bombarded with questions boomed at her from every direction as well as comments on life in this quiet corner of Gloucestershire.

'Such a relief to get out of the city,' she was told in a variety of accents from Coventry, Birmingham, London.

She watched Keith when she could and occasionally caught a fleeting smile from him, the special warmth in it heartening. He was doing very little talking but she knew from the angle of his head, his body, he was listening intently, not so much to words as to nuances of tone. This was Keith at work and Jenny turned her attention to a fat little woman addicted to gold chains. She must be very new to the district, Mrs Addiscombe not yet having time to get her into the local uniform of the 'right kind of people'.

'That was a wasted morning,' Jenny said ruefully as she and Keith tramped their way back to Bowman's.

'Was it?'

He caught her hand and they walked the rest of the way back in companionable silence.

It was pleasant to gather around the big table in Bowman's kitchen. There was laughter and a sense of companionship, blessings on the work which remained to be done. Aunt Sophie sat in state, while Jenny helped Nanny Bowler transfer dishes from the Aga and Keith poured wine. As the meal progressed Jenny entertained with gentle assessments of the individuals she had met that morning.

'That was great, Nanny,' Keith said when they had eaten their fill of a savoury casserole and fresh, colourful vegetables.

'Liver and bacon, Keith. One of your favourites, as I remember.'

Nanny Bowler might be solidly boned, her grey hair high on her head in a bun, but the wrinkles around her eyes had been deepened by years of understanding and kindness.

Jenny kept a straight face as she looked at Nanny Bowler. 'Do you remember all his weaknesses?'

The old woman's chuckle was rich with memories. 'Only the ones he's let me see over the years. Now, young Peter and James. That's a different matter.'

Aunt Sophie tried to look horrified. 'Are you trying to tell me my sons have secrets hidden from me?'

Nanny tidied her knife and fork, placing them carefully at the angle decreed to show she had finished eating. 'You know them best of all, madam, but they are grown men now,' she gently chided.

Emptied plates were being cleared away when Aunt Sophie asked if the coffee morning had proved useful.

'Hard work,' was Jenny's contribution but Keith hesitated. Clay had been so pleased they were to be there but nothing much had surfaced. He had picked up the odd hint of mutual dislike, even a suggestion when reading body language. He had noticed a dapper Midlander, clearly not short of cash, who had some sort of arrangement with a gamey blonde tired of a bumbling husband. What had been most obvious was the boredom of men and women who had moved away from their roots and had no real aim in life, frittering away a few hours in a house they wished they owned.

'Have you ever had one of Mrs Addiscombe's rituals here?' he asked his aunt.

That lady regarded him calmly, her eyes with unaccustomed chill. 'Never!'

'Anything to raise money to help others, we do all the work ourselves,' Nanny said, her lips firm.

'Why does she go to all this effort?' Keith wanted to know. 'Doesn't her husband have any say in what she does?'

Aunt Sophie concentrated on her silver napkin ring, while Nanny folded her damask square with great precision.

'I thought so,' Jenny said. 'He's got a girlfriend, hasn't he?'

Two pairs of knowing eyes stared at her. Aunt Sophie shrugged her shoulders and Nanny became prim. 'He often works late at night, so we're told, but his office is usually shut up then.'

'Does everybody know?' Keith asked.

His aunt seemed surprised by his question. 'Darling, this is a village, for heaven's sake.'

Jenny was finding it hard to be serious. 'How about his wife?'

'Silly woman hasn't the faintest idea,' Nanny said, her mouth tightening in a firm line. 'She thinks she's really got him under her thumb while she's out ferreting around in other people's lives and organizing parties, as she calls them, in their houses.'

'Does she never feed them in her own home?' Keith wanted to know.

'No room. She lives in one of the tiny terraced cottages in Buckland. I think she just adores taking over a desirable residence and pretending it's hers for a day or two.' Aunt Sophie could be very matter-of-fact.

'She doesn't get a chance here,' Nanny added, 'but the house she's really aiming for is Jack Weston's. She won't have much luck there either. Fortified gates, he's got, and dogs. Even the postman is made to wait out in the road if there's anything to be signed for.'

Dishes with light-as-air rhubarb fool tempted and there were thin rounds of shortbread piled high in the centre of the table.

'Nanny, this foot of mine will have to heal fast or I'll be as round as a dumpling.'

'Nonsense, madam. You'll soon run off the extra weight when you've mended.'

Keith made inroads into the shortbread. 'Jack Weston, who is he?'

'Our very own millionaire, darling. He lives in Perrot's old farm, across the main road and down one of the lanes which end up in Childswickham. Do you remember the Perrots' place? It was a fine old house going to pieces when old Joe Perrot was there. Plenty of money's been spent on it recently but Weston brought in builders from London.'

'With all the good craftsmen we've got round here it upset a few, I can tell you,' said Nanny as she tried to persuade Jenny to another helping of the fool.

'Rumours have flown, as you can imagine, but there's no doubt he's very security-conscious.' Aunt Sophie nibbled carefully at her one piece of shortbread. 'There's talk of fabulous antiques but no one's ever seen them. What other reason could a man have to protect his home so tightly?'

'Yes, one does wonder,' Keith said slowly and Jenny understood what he was thinking. 'Who is he?'

'Gracious now, there's no mystery.' Nanny pushed the shortbread at Jenny and Keith in turn but there were no takers. 'I remember his father taking the whole family away after the war. Young Jack was mixing with the wrong crowd and Childswickham was too small a place to let him get away with it. Canada did the trick, we heard. Sammy Weston, the dad, started as a labourer and then had his own plumbing business. Young Jack began buying houses in a bad state. He worked on them, then sold on. It wasn't long before he became a property developer.'

'You knew him well?' Jenny asked.

'No, but his auntie, Sammy's sister Jessie, was a friend of mine and living in Evesham. She passed away five years ago.'

'Was that when Jack returned?'

'Not long after. His wife had died so he brought his son here, although there're no other Westons left now. Jack's kept himself to himself but all the Westons were like that.' Nanny stared at the tablecloth, thinking of good times with a friend. 'Good-looking as a boy, he was. Fair hair and blue eyes but one had a brown fleck in it.'

Aunt Sophie turned to Keith. 'Remember your mother

talking of the Musgraves? One of their sons had the same thing. His one eye wasn't really brown, more a wishy-washy hazel, but it still didn't stop him being teased unmercifully at school.'

Jenny was thoughtful. 'Perhaps that's why the young Jack Weston kept getting into trouble when he was a boy.'

Keith's mobile began to vibrate and then ring. 'Sorry, I'll take it in the hall.' As he left the room he could hear Nanny decrying all the goods Weston had bought in London and ferried down at great expense to the new-old house near Childswickham.

'Keith, you OK?'

'Brian! Good to hear you. How's it all going?'

'Fine. Mickey's still getting information on cases where identity may have been stolen. He passes on what he considers Morrison should have.'

'Anything more on Mather?'

'In custody. He was picked up in Pembrokeshire – plenty of good golf courses. At the moment he's in a secure station and that's all we've been told. The Scots boys want first crack at him so there're high-level discussions going on.'

'Any idea yet as to motive?'

'Nothing concrete but his father's a retired police sergeant somewhere north of Sheffield.'

'That explains why he knew how we worked.'

'Not quite. There's another Mather in the police. This one's younger, a graduate and rising rapidly up the ranks. Good-looking and a nice chap, by all accounts. He's very well liked.'

'God, sibling rivalry gone mad?'

'It's the logical explanation. By the way, how's your aunt's ankle?'

'Not too bad but she's not happy sitting still.' The line was silent for a long moment. 'What is it, Brian?'

'I can't talk now, something's come up. You've got my mobile number, haven't you?'

'Of course I have.'

'Well, give me a ring on it – when you're free.'

A click and the connection was broken but Keith did not hesitate. He picked up the mobile Clay had provided before he walked into the garden, appreciating the beauty of it as he stood under the old cedar tree and dialled a familiar number.

'Brian, what's wrong?'

'I'm glad you understood the Sherlock approach but I don't know what the hell's going on. I was hoping you would.'

'Something's happened?'

'I've just had a phone call, direct to the CID office and specifically asking for me. It was a DCI Stephen Childs from the Met. He said he'd been trying to get hold of you and did I know where you were? I told him about your aunt and your leave and he was very grateful. The only trouble is I've met Stephen Childs, remember? It was at your place. Very distinctive voice, the Stephen I talked to that night. Not a bit like the one I've just listened to.'

When Brian was reassured that Aunt Sophie was indeed making progress and her bandaged ankle there for all to see, Keith contacted Stephen Childs at Scotland Yard. It took some time, DCI Childs having been called to the Home Office, a clipped voice insisted. There must have been a sense of urgency in Keith's appeal because his informant broke into a meeting of politicians and policemen to hurry Stephen to a phone.

'Are you working on something significant?' he asked when he reached Keith.

'Not me personally. I didn't think I was anything but a minnow on the edge of a shoal of sharks.' Keith explained what he could, knowing his friend had the experience to understand the pattern.

'You'd better think again,' Stephen warned. 'I'll do what I can this end to find out who's been asking questions. Don't worry, I'll be discreet but if they've penetrated us at the Yard, they've got money to toss around. Just take care.'

Clay Gifford was the next one contacted, delighted by what had happened. 'Great! They're moving.'

'Is that what you wanted?'

'Sure – remember this is hunting country. Which is easier to spot, a fox running or one gone to ground?'

'I get your point.'

'Listen, taking you out wouldn't help them, so they won't risk breaking cover to harm you in any way.'

'Gee, thanks!' was Keith's passable imitation of Clay's accent.

'You know I'm right. This morning you went off to the coffee morning. Anything?'

Very briefly Keith described the noise and the boredom, the new villagers drifting like tumbleweed. 'But the coffee was good,' he added.

'You've had time to feel your way around. Any names floating up?'

'Gwynneth Addiscombe. My idea of the worst kind of prison wardress.'

'She's not a problem. No record and husband's a mouse who works in Cheltenham in insurance. He makes a habit of staying late at the office – and who can blame him?'

'He's not in the office when he's working late.'

'The hell he's not?' Clay was astounded. 'A woman?'

'It's assumed so. As for the biscuit munchers I met this morning, most of them I wouldn't trust to run a bus, let alone anything covert. There were no real personalities and Stephen implied it would take someone with a lot of clout to get past the Yard's security.'

'Or cash.'

'As you say. One name's come up locally as being loaded, as well as being in a house alarmed to the rafters. Jack Weston.'

'Checks out clean. Canadian national of fifty years. Background of a hard-working money-maker. Devastated when his wife died so moved himself and his son back to England and there've been no major changes in the way he handles his bank accounts over the last twenty, thirty years.'

188

'Then I'm sorry. Nothing else.'

'Who do you propose to pump next?'

'Nanny Bowler. She was born here and has a memory to outdo an encyclopedia.'

'And as she's known you all your life she'll unwind to you fast.'

'Clay, you're a devious bastard!'

'One of the survival techniques. Any more invites?'

'Jenny mentioned a concert in the church tomorrow. She'd like to go.'

'Then I'll see you there – and act surprised.'

Aunt Sophie declared herself tired. 'I'll take myself off to the study, the day bed there's very comfortable.'

She limped away and Keith exchanged smiles with Nanny Bowler. There was also a TV in the study and racing was due to start in five minutes.

'I'll clear away, Nanny,' Keith said. 'You and Jenny get warm in the drawing room.'

'Nonsense!' Nanny declared but she had not encountered Jenny in action. Quietly, the old lady was ushered to a seat by the fire and Jenny sat facing her.

'Aunt Sophie told me you've always lived in Laverton.'

'Indeed I have, my dear, although it was a very different place before the war.'

'You'll have seen some changes.'

It was almost a question hanging in the air and Nanny was content to talk, feeling no sense of enquiry or compulsion. She barely noticed Keith carry in a tray of cups and saucers, accepting her tea and sipping appreciatively.

'Changes? You've no idea! Why, when I was a girl, before that madman Hitler got so greedy, every day seemed the same and nothing happened. There was no TV of course, and not everyone had a radio, even fewer had electricity. Candles in the bedrooms, gas in the kitchen and parlour, if you were lucky. Most folk still had oil lamps but nobody minded. The school was busy then and you saw people about the village. Pushbikes, the odd pony and trap, and once in a while a motor car. Women scrubbed their front step of a morning and we little ones were welcomed in any kitchen with a smile and a cup of milk.'

Nanny settled deeper into the softness of her chair, her eyes unseeing, her mind in the past with its kindnesses.

'Not a large cup, mind you,' she told Jenny, 'times were hard. Oh, there was the odd party. An old couple living near the schoolhouse saw in their diamond wedding, bless 'em. What a day that was!'

Jenny could see from the inward smile how exciting it must have been for the children as they ran in a roadway empty of vehicles, with cakes and pies and sandwiches by the handful.

'Not many lived that long, I can tell you, doctors not having the medicines they do today. There were a lot of widows,' she said so quietly Jenny barely heard her.

'When I first walked through Laverton I saw the name "Grimmitt's Orchard",' Jenny said after a while.

'Dear soul! The Grimmitts, they were everywhere at one time. My Dad remembered the church choir was all Grimmitt boys – and the local cricket team. There were two cousins lived up opposite the school, Alfred and Arthur, master carpenters the pair of them, though Fred was the postmaster as well. The 1918 'flu got him and his widow started up a shop in the house. It's been there ever since. Arthur lived next door – well, it was next door until his daughter built a bungalow in between – but that was years later.'

'The orchard?' Jenny reminded gently.

Nanny nodded. 'That was Fred's son, Pat. His proper name was Martin but he was always called Pat, like his brother Guy was always Gunner. I don't know why.' She sighed. 'They're all gone.'

'Was it after the war the newcomers came?'

'No, it started long before that. A couple of old cottages falling down near the new main road were bought up by folks from Coventry, I think it was. They had 'em put right, doing most of the work themselves, and came here at

190

weekends. That was before the war and that was the start.'

Memories held Nanny and she was silent for a spell but Keith knew Jenny spent her days relieving tortured souls of their mental festers. At least Nanny Bowler's reminiscences would make for a more cheerful experience. As he sat in his corner, the gentle old voice with its faint Cotswold burr told of strangers moving to the isolated peace of a country urgently threatened by war. Unfortunately, they brought with them not only enough money to buy out the villagers but the suspicions and locked doors of town dwellers.

When war came Buckland Manor had been turned into a nursing home for wounded officers and there was work on offer as well as beds needed for nurses coming off long shifts. It did mean extra money in the pockets of families bereft of wage earners. Not all loved ones had returned, their graves scattered worldwide. Keith and Jenny heard of cottages left empty, then rented or bought by incomers yearning for beauty and stillness the horrors of war had denied them.

'Trouble was,' said Nanny, 'they wanted to be part of the village but their way, not ours.' Gradually, the community she knew and loved had died, she told them, its skeleton the ancient houses of Cotswold stone strung like the jewels of a necklace from Broadway. There had been no vacuum. Buildings had been enlarged, improved, but there were too few children for the schools in Laverton and Stanton and the spirit of the villages had not been reborn.

The woman who had seen so much mourned the old days until Jenny judged the moment right and led talk to the present-day inhabitants. Keith rose and went to pour drinks, sherry for Nanny, soda with ice and lemon for Jenny. He took a large glass of gin and tonic to his aunt happily esconced and cheering on the horses, then he returned to the drawing room to sit out of Nanny's line of sight, shielding her from his notebook. There was no need for maps. Clay and his associates had every house and caravan for miles labelled with their occupants.

Nanny sipped her sherry, looking at Jenny, then at Keith, with eyes suddenly sharp, shrewd. 'That was a nice wander down memory lane but it's not why you're here, is it?' The sherry glass was placed carefully on a nearby table. 'I'm not so much green as I'm cabbage-looking, Master Keith,' she said, returning to the discipline of Bowman's nursery. 'I've cared for too many souls with sprained ankles to be fooled by Mrs Astley, although she's making a good job of it, all things said and done. She doesn't need nursing, so what is it you want from me?'

Keith did not hesitate. 'It's vital, Nanny, that's all I can really say, and it's not up to me to tell you why. As quickly and as quietly as possible I have to find out all I can about the people living in the three villages.'

'Not just Laverton?'

'No, Buckland and Stanton, too.'

'What for?' she wanted to know and Keith looked at Jenny. Slowly she bent her head and he was relieved.

'Someone is using the normal life of these communities as a cover. They may have recently moved in or they may have been here for years, but we need to look for a pattern – fast.'

The old woman who had watched him grow, studied the man. She had no need of spectacles to help her judge what she saw in him. 'What is it you have to find out?'

It took time, Jenny going unnoticed to make sandwiches, look for cake, brew tea, as Keith asked questions, his knowledge of the area saving hours.

'Why not Broadway?' Nanny asked at one point.

'Good question. Technology being used says no, but I think it's because there's too much of a town atmosphere there. Our target needs to be clearly seen as part of one of the communities with nothing apparently hidden.'

It made sense to the elderly woman and she poured out information gathered over so many years. The racing over, Aunt Sophie joined them, offering details and fleshing out characters, lifestyles, to add to those of a woman who had been her steadfast friend for a lifetime. When she saw exhaustion draining the aged face she called a halt.

192

'We're all numb, darling,' she told her nephew. 'Why don't we ask Nanny to stay the night?'

'No, thank you, madam, I need my own bed but I'll do what Jenny suggested and keep paper and pencil with me. Now so many memories have been set running, I may recall an odd fact or two.'

She did agree to Keith running her home. The drive to Nanny's cottage was short and she was silent in her fatigue but she roused when the car stopped. Keith helped her from the car, saw her into her little house, each room shining and fragrant with polish and the scent of lavender. He checked doors and windows and kissed her goodnight.

Nanny laid a warm hand on his cheek. 'It's important what you're doing?'

'Yes, Nanny, very. Many, many lives depend upon it.'

'And someone who's here among us could take those lives?'

'Not on their own. They'll be in the background of events, organizing and making sure there's money for arms and explosives to be used where there are a great many people.'

She shivered. 'When you were a little boy you were the one who watched what was happening as you all played. You've not changed, young Keith. I'll thank God for that tonight – and I'll ask Him to keep you and your Jenny safe.'

Keith sat in the car when he returned to Bowman's. It was late but Clay answered the call immediately.

'Anything?'

'I've the complete list of who works at GCHQ or is related, one way or another, to someone who does.' Keith rattled off the names.

'That agrees with our data and they all come up squeaky clean when checked out. There must be a link somewhere! Did anything cross your mind as she talked?'

'What you're really after is a money man, one whose

financial activities are big and complex enough to hide transfers to odd places.'

'And you thought of Jack Weston. Well, I told you we did too. Our boys in Canada have crawled over every inch of his past and there's nothing but good guy at every turn. His money's been soundly made and all accounted for – even their IRS is happy with him. He's rich but not all that rich. Not enough to fund terrorists and buy missiles from Russia.'

'He still smells right to me,' Keith insisted. 'Since coming here five years ago, Weston's turned himself into a hermit. The son has a flat he uses in London when he's working – something to do with computers, Nanny thought. There are no known visitors, not even the postman's allowed through the gate. The only exception is a chap from Buckland who does a lot of cycling – and then only when no one's likely to see him going in. Tony Petherbridge.'

Keith could hear rustling.

'Accountant. One-man show with an office in Cheltenham. He came out Simon Pure as well,' Clay said at last.

'Nanny Bowler's going to keep thinking, so is Aunt Sophie. They may have something for us in the morning.'

'I hope to God they do. Time's getting short.'

'What have you heard?'

'Money's appeared in an account our Washington friends have under surveillance. It's linked to a couple of stockbrokers and whoever's transferred it must be getting ready to buy great tranches of shares for peanuts, maybe giving him control of some useful corporations.'

Keith held in his disgust. 'With widespread massacres to achieve it for him? The man's insane!'

'I doubt it,' was Clay's answer. 'He's too cold and calculating for that excuse. Don't forget, the seconds are ticking, Keith.'

'I know – and we've promised to go to that damned concert tomorrow.'

194

Chapter Eleven

Breakfast was crumbs and an empty coffee pot when Nanny Bowler arrived. As he was the only one dressed, Keith unlocked the front door and led her through to the large kitchen warmed by its Aga. Jenny was still drowsy, her emerald velvet dressing gown adding to her elfin look as she smiled at the newcomer and wished her good morning.

'Did you sleep at all, Nanny? Or did you stay awake going over all the old scandals?' Aunt Sophie asked.

Nanny recognized the housecoat worn by her mistress. It always came out of the wardrobe when she was ready for a long session with a sick child. Attractive, although the pink wool was faded, it was practical and still reassured.

From her large handbag, Nanny drew out a notepad. 'I thought of one or two more snippets which might come in handy.'

Jenny left them to it, making fresh coffee as well as a small pot of tea for Nanny Bowler. Unnoticed, she cleared the table, stacked the dishwasher and went quietly away to shower and dress.

The other three were still intent on each inhabitant of the area when Jenny returned to the kitchen. Keith would have risen from his chair but her hand on his shoulder stopped him. She smiled and took away the empty cups, leaving more space for papers and rough maps to be spread on the wiped pine.

'You can add the Bugginses to your list of genuine ones,' Nanny advised Keith. 'They've been living in Stanton for at least five years, maybe more. Cheltenham, they came from. Said they knew some of the Proles who ran the post office in Stanton in the old days. Nice people, Ruby Prole and her family.'

Jenny went away to the long, low-ceilinged drawing room, plumping up cushions and stacking papers and magazines. Flowers needed water and she made her way to the scullery with its deep stone sink and old-fashioned taps. It was satisfying to refresh the blooms and when she had finished, Jenny knelt on the wide window seat of the drawing room, its cushions bearing witness to the children who had dreamed there.

The garden stretched in front of her, grass at its winter length. Some shrubs and trees were dark with the fullness of evergreen while others had the bare branches which reminded Jenny of Japanese paintings. In the morning stillness her thoughts roamed back to the first garden carved from the hillside by a battle-weary archer. Autumn would have seen crops harvested in abundance and stored for hard winters. Onions, cabbages, leeks, peas, she decided. Only after Raleigh had brought them back from the Americas would potatoes have become fashionable and then plentiful enough to feed hungry children.

These days the garden was for pleasure, she mused, then frowned. Just that? More than pleasure, it gave a sense of peace and order, of timelessness and the bounty of nature. Was that what Colonel Astley had needed from his home? Nourishment of the mind and soul to be bequeathed to his wife and sons? Jenny stirred herself. There was work to be done and by the time she returned to the warmth and early morning kitchen smells, Keith had a series of lists in front of him.

'Progress?' she asked.

He nodded. 'With the help of these two ladies I've discovered no one has breathed or coughed in the three villages without being noticed by them.'

'Technically, darling, there are only two villages,' his aunt said, 'Stanton and Buckland. Laverton has no church of its own.'

'But it's large enough, it does have a shop and it did

have a school,' he said and smiled at Aunt Sophie. 'I'd like to hear you argue the point with your neighbours. Mrs Addiscombe, for example.'

As Aunt Sophie and Nanny conspired to defeat Keith's reasons, Jenny reached for the coffee pot keeping warm at the side of the Aga and Keith made his excuses, strolling towards the dampness of the garden. He switched on the scrambler system as soon as he had punched in Clay's number. 'I can assure you I've the most comprehensive list imaginable. Getting Nanny Bowler on side was a boon. Between them, she and my aunt haven't missed a thing in the last half-century.'

Clay was cautious. 'This Nanny Bowler can be trusted?'

'Totally. I've known her all my life and she can keep a secret better than anyone, thank God! She's saved my hide that way on the odd occasion.'

'OK. What's your gut instinct?'

'Weston – but I've no real clue how he's getting his local information.'

'What happened to make you so sure?'

'Two things. We've covered every person who lives here and he's still the most likely. Then there's Nanny. It's not what she's said about him, she's been too quiet there. I don't think she's sure of him.'

'That's what I've been hoping for,' Clay said cheerfully. 'You picking up on subtleties other agents would never notice in a million years. What is it she does say about Weston?'

'She's mentioned him being visited by Tony Petherbridge, the accountant living in Buckland.'

'He's the only one you said was seen going into the Westons'. Something odd about the visits?'

'Petherbridge only appears there when no one else is around and he's let in without having to wait.'

'How the hell can she know that?'

'A friend of hers whose farm marches with Weston's land. Quiet chap, a loner. He keeps sheep and walks through them at odd times looking for pests in the wool and keeping an eye open for rustlers.'

'Rustlers! You can't be serious?'

'Very. Good fat lambs, Birmingham and Coventry just up the road.'

'You always say Gloucestershire has everything! Is that why this chap comes and goes without Weston and Petherbridge seeing him? He's tucked away in the shadows?'

'More like part of the landscape. Neither the Westons nor Petherbridge would notice him.' Keith waited for Clay to digest the information. 'Are you really sure it's this area?'

'As we can be. Some interesting messages being passed and satellite positioning homed in on the possible source.'

'Surely the exact house can be pinpointed?'

'A fact known to too many people. It's why the target only relays orders when on the move and possibly with an untraceable mobile phone. Statistically, the road used most often is the stretch between the Stanton turn and the Buckland turn on the B4632. We've had surveillance along it and at either end but there's no pattern to the vehicles going along it either to or from Broadway or back towards Toddington.'

Keith was stunned into momentary silence. 'That's all you have to go on?'

'It's enough – considering the time we haven't got.'

Before Domesday there had been a holy site on the knoll at the foot of the hill in Buckland, the church now standing there having held the prayers and banners of far too many wars. Smooth grass surrounding the grey building was filled to capacity with graves and headstones, the new graveyard separated from the old one by a road and a stream.

A fussy woman in a swirling purple cape took their money at the door and nodded them inside, her white curls bobbing. An organist was above them in the loft, the music emanating from the pipes gentle and welcoming. All Keith could see of the organist playing was a man's narrow back in dark suiting and with carefully combed hair. A childhood memory floated up, a moving female figure and firm, regular notes. 'Jo is a boy's name,' he had insisted to his mother and Aunt Sophie had smiled.

Mrs Addiscombe came bustling importantly and tried to drag them to a pew near the front but Jenny loved music and knew where best to sit and hear a choir in such a small space. To their right and behind them in the south-west corner, women organized plates of sandwiches and cakes sealed under plastic, their movements quiet, efficient, as they arranged crockery and napkins.

Familiar faces smiled at Keith and told him they were glad he was with them as they sized up Jenny, approved, and included her in their welcome. It surprised him how many of the older villagers he remembered and could speak to by name, asking after grown-up children and being told with pride of good jobs, large houses and grandchildren. Keith was gratified, yet humbled they all seemed pleased to see him there.

'Have we got to eat?' he whispered as they settled in their pew.

Jenny shook her head and grinned. 'Choir supper.' She wriggled, sighed, was content.

Keith had a moment of contrition. He knew Jenny adored live music but because of his job they could seldom get to concerts of any kind. Even tonight he had begrudged the outing, preferring to have stayed at Bowman's and carry on working. Only the thought that he could spend an hour or two mentally reviewing all they had so far accomplished had brought him with any willingness.

He looked around the church, remembering his uncle's funeral when the nave was filled with scaffolding. Somehow it had seemed appropriate for a soldier. There had been other times when he had roamed with Jeremy and his cousins and on one occasion scoffed at Imogen as she found a 'G' carved into the end of each pew. The Grimmitt family making and carving church furniture, filling its choir stalls and its graveyards.

'Jenny! Keith!'

They looked up, Jenny genuinely startled to see Emma and Clay Gifford. Keith feigned surprise and hoped he was not over-acting. It helped that Emma was dressed appropriately in peasant blouse and skirt under a multi-coloured knitted coat, narrow scarves knotted around her neck instead of a necklace. With her reddish fair hair gelled to stand in peaks she personified the scatty wife of a yet to be published author. Clay was tidier than Keith had feared in a crumpled linen suit and black polo neck sweater, but he was still far more casually dressed than the rest of the audience.

'You must come and see us,' Jenny was insisting. 'Keith's aunt would love the diversion and you would enjoy her company. The garden's lovely, even at this time of year.'

A grey man in a grey suit approached, shushing them and pointing at a choir beginning to assemble. Watched by the rest of the audience, Emma and Clay were taking their seats when the main door opened and a slim man in late middle age walked in. Every head turned to him and there was a susurrus of whispers.

'Who's that?' Jenny asked quietly after he had walked past their pew.

Keith had only seen photographs but the man being helped out of the silky black coat could be identified. 'That's Jack Weston. I guess, from Mrs Addiscombe's description of him, the young man with him is his son.'

'Must take after his mother, then,' Jenny decided as the boy followed his father to a pew below the pulpit. Anyone already there was persuaded to move up or move out so Mr Weston could have pride of place. 'Sponsor of this concert is Mr Jack Weston,' she read from the programme.

Behind them a man and woman were murmuring and they gathered that Weston's presence was a very unusual occurrence. 'Usually just gives money. Never comes himself,' was heard whispered.

Keith was intrigued, hearing bouts of hushed voices and seeing nodding throughout the pews.

'Something's up,' he whispered to Jenny. 'Change of behaviour patterns,' he added as the basses and tenors filed along the nave.

When the choir had assembled and was grouped gracefully in the chancel, everyone was welcomed by a curate deputizing for the rector. The conductor was introduced, the accompanist at the organ acknowledged and the concert began.

Jenny was enthralled by the voices and their harmony. 'They're good,' she said amidst the applause at the end of the first item. 'That conductor has them all feeling as Mozart would have wanted.'

Keith took her word for it and let his mind wander, precise diction and clarity of notes helping lateral thoughts. 'Brenda and Brian would have loved this,' he told his wife in the next round of clapping.

Bach. A series of motets. There was an order, a logic in the composer's use of notes. Mickey would appreciate that much, even if he groaned at the sounds that resulted. Mickey. The search for other victims like Harding. Dead ones surfaced and could be seen but knowing the live ones would give the pattern of the conspiracy of which Brosca Thatcher was a major player. How could dead victims be of any use to an identity scam?

More clapping and a change to modern works, intricate rhythms expertly sung. The music was exciting and every member of the choir alert, intent on the conductor's slightest movement. 'Smoke gets in your eyes', Keith read from his programme and listened to it carefully, the throb of the accompaniment linking ideas he had never before connected. He must get Clay on his own as soon as possible.

'You enjoyed that,' Jenny said as she smiled.

He caught her hand, grateful for the being which was Jenny. Throughout the day she had been vigilant, seeing to it the older women were rested, fed hot food or received an unending supply of daintily laid trays which allowed the stateliness of the British tea ceremony to calm as much as did the brew in the silver pot. For Keith it had added a surreal dimension, the deliberate serenity emphasizing by contrast the desperate need for haste and the images of failure.

Try as he might to widen the scope of the investigation, no one else filled Clay's requirements as well as Jack Weston, yet the boy from Childswickham Nanny had known could never have been a potential mass murderer. 'Got into trouble,' she had said, but when she was asked to explain it became the exploits of a teenager high on local cider. Fences had been wrecked, an irate father had threatened him with a shotgun but no girl had been left weeping or pregnant, and Sam Weston, with his son's help, had repaired for free any damage young Jack and his cronies caused.

Keith had the height to see Weston in the front pew. Faded fair hair was held smooth and gleaming with a discreet dressing; beside him his son Jason was as dark almost as a Spaniard. After studying the two heads and searching for any similarity, Keith could only assume the mother's genes had been dominant when the boy was created. It would be easy to say they were impostors but there was evidence from Weston's friends in Canada that they were the father and son seen off on a plane from Toronto. The two Westons in the church were certainly the ones driven years ago from the airport to Childswickham.

A soloist was introduced to a polite round of clapping. She was a lady of girth and plenty of years, her voice surprisingly sweet. Keith let the melodies she sang pass him by, all attention given to the problem he shared with Clay. Choristers were seated in the choir stalls, a few perching on the steps of the pulpit. Foremost was one of the tenors who seemed quite at home in the church and Keith realized he must be the Buckland man of whom Nanny had spoken. Tony Petherbridge. What was it Nanny said of him? 'The only one to visit Jack Weston.' The old lady had not been surprised. 'Accountant he is, after all. Stands to reason he and Jack would see things the same way. Money.'

Was Petherbridge involved? Tall and slender, he had greying hair which shone in the light from candles and wall lamps. Distinguished, he could be described as, Keith decided, but was it only because he was wearing the choir's uniform of black dinner jacket and bow tie? The man did seem more comfortable in his official suit for singing than did some of the tenors and basses. Keith was puzzled. Petherbridge's secret visits, the Westons' hermit-like existence, yet all three were here together. Why? What would drive them to gather in the church? He thought of Clay's hunting comparison. Breaking cover? It made no sense.

The soprano disappeared after enthusiastic applause and the choir continued their schedule. Keith hardly heard them, trying to picture Petherbridge as part of a group organizing mass murder. The very idea seemed incongruous.

The last item was being sung, an early Rutter composition. 'The Clare Blessing' gently ended the evening and as the curate waited for the plaudits to die down, Keith caught a movement at the door. A young woman was slipping away, her body bent with the tension of an anxious mother. The door closed and Keith swung his head round in time to see a bouquet appearing for the soloist, buttonholes for the conductor and accompanist. In the general fidgeting after all the thanks and extra applause, Keith noticed the heavy door being pushed wide.

'It's Megan – Megan Baverstock,' Jenny whispered urgently. 'Something's wrong!'

The young mother had returned and was in a state of severe shock. Curls draggled either side of an ashen face and Keith strode to her, Clay following.

'Mrs Baverstock – Megan, can I help?'

The timbre of his deep voice, the curve of his body as he bent to shield her from the gawping stares of the audience helped her struggle to shape words.

'I didn't hit him! He was just lying there.'

'Who?'

'I don't know.'

Keith led her out into the church porch and Clay closed the door behind them, hanging on to the latch so no one could interrupt.

'I wanted to go home quickly so I had to get the car away before there was an awful scrum. It was when I was driving over the verge to get away. He was there, in the headlights. Just lying so still.' She gulped nervously, swallowing air. 'If someone hit him, it wasn't me!' Megan sniffed, delved into a pocket of her jacket and dragged out a tissue. After blowing her nose she was able to straighten up, gain control. 'This side of the manor drive.'

Keith was well aware Buckland Manor had been turned into a prestigious hotel, indeed he had dined there in the past with Aunt Sophie. 'You stay here, Megan. Clay, can you get Emma?'

The American opened the door a few inches and found his wife waiting.

'Can I help?' It was not the voice of a dippy wife but the calm assurance of the excellent police officer she had been.

'Look after Megan. I think I saw someone sitting at the back who could be of use to us.'

It did not take long for Keith to beckon out a tall, burly individual with an almost bald head and an impressive moustache. 'Sergeant Booth, I thought I saw you. Possible suspicious death just down the road. With parking as it is, it's essential no cars are moved until we have the basic facts at least. Can you keep everyone inside? Get the church ladies to feed the choir and anyone else who's desperate. Mrs Gifford will help you collect names and addresses of choir and audience. Pew by pew would be easiest.'

'Yes, sir. Glad you're here tonight. On leave, I believe.' Retired to Toddington from the county force, John Booth had been stationed at HQ and an asset to the police choir. 'Any idea who's dead?'

'Not yet. I've a torch in my car and Mr Gifford will come with me.' Keith saw Booth's unspoken question. 'He knows what he's doing and he always has a notebook on him. He's a writer,' he explained and Sergeant Booth relaxed, closing the door behind him.

'Will you be OK to show us the body?' Clay asked Megan.

With the first shock receding, her natural resilience emerged. 'Of course.'

'Right, Inspector Tyrell, we'll take over now.'

DCI Ian Creed was solid, frowning darkly, and obviously not willing to have his territory taken over by a visiting DI, however many locals were his relations.

'Naturally, sir. We'll go back to the church. I'm assuming you'll let us know when we can all go home?'

'You've kept everybody there?'

'Yes, sir. It was Mrs Baverstock, attempting to leave before the rush, who found the man. Once the church empties, this road will be like a racetrack, parking being as tricky as it is for any function here. Not everyone can turn easily, sir, and I guessed whoever was in charge wouldn't want the scene contaminated.'

Creed said nothing but his full red mouth narrowed, tightened.

'What about me?' Megan Baverstock demanded. She was standing by her car, ready to drive away as fast as possible. 'Can I go home now? My children —'

'No, madam.' Creed was determined to have someone sticking to his rules. 'I'm sorry but we have to leave things as they are until all necessary evidence has been collected.'

Megan had had a stressful end to her evening and wanted to return to her family. She bridled at the man's tone. 'I am not an idiot – nor am I a naughty schoolgirl – so don't patronize me! If I hadn't tried to leave when I did, you'd have had the wheels of half the county going backwards and forwards and that poor soul could have been run over a dozen times. Besides, I promised my husband I wouldn't be late and I keep my word!'

Keith stepped towards her, ready to intervene. 'May

I make a suggestion, sir? My car is parked further down the road. With your permission, Mr Gifford could see Mrs Baverstock reaches home safely.'

'I've a better idea, Tyrell. You can both take her. Sergeant Paxton!' he called and a tired blonde walked into the circle of light thrown by headlights and torches. 'Get to the church and keep it secure till I say otherwise.'

With Megan Baverstock safely delivered, Keith turned the car towards Buckland.

'OK. When you called in it wasn't the usual, "My name is Tyrell and there's a dead guy in Buckland." What went on?' Clay wanted to know.

'I called HQ direct. Technically, Buckland is in Gloucestershire but its postal address and nearest town is Broadway – Worcestershire. There's a good working relationship but I wanted to make sure any investigation started out through us.'

'Easier to keep up with any useful information?'

A curt nod and Keith signalled the turn off the main road, waiting for a car to screech its way towards Buckland and the church.

'So you do think this dead guy's linked into our little problem?'

'Don't you?'

Parking the car near the old forge took little time but Clay stopped Keith opening his door. 'You don't believe in coincidence?'

'Face it, Clay, the Westons are in church – a very unusual event and they sit where they can be seen by the maximum number of witnesses. Petherbridge is in full view for the entire concert. It's a cold night but when I got to the body it was still warm. That man was killed while we were listening to some very good music.'

'What else did you notice?'

'Angle of the head. I'd guess a broken neck. No obvious signs of bruising so it may have been a clean kill. Position of torso and limbs as if he's been tossed there.'

'Dumped where someone leaving the church was bound to notice him.'

'A lot of trouble to go to for our benefit.'

'Ours?'

''Fraid so. Gathered together were the Westons, father, son, and an unholy ghost by the name of Petherbridge – a satanic trio if ever there was one.'

'With you and me giving them watertight alibis.' Clay groaned. 'Keith, why do I get the feeling we've just seen a damned great wrench lobbed into the equation and that we're right out of time?'

'The real puzzle is why this chap is lying dead up there – and who the hell is he?'

There was an uneasy atmosphere in the church, several of the older men desperate to get out and the strident voices of women not allowed to go where they pleased, adding to the noise. DS Paxton was doing her best, relieved when she saw the tall figure of a DI she knew by repute.

'Can you do anything, sir? You're known around here so they might take it better from you.'

'I'll do my best. Can you go and ask DCI Creed if we can let these people go? As we walked past the end of the manor drive the crime scene was taped off. There seemed to be enough uniformed officers there to get the road cleared and until that happens no one can find out if the vehicle the man arrived in is still in Buckland.'

The exhausted woman straightened, ready to face DCI Creed as ex-Sergeant Booth approached.

'Just the man, Sergeant. Can you supervise a relief party for me?' Keith nodded towards the elderly men grouped by the door.

'See what you mean. Want 'em back in afterwards?'

'Please – until DCI Creed gives the all-clear.'

'Don't hold your breath,' Booth muttered and marched away to do what he could.

Vociferous women objected strongly at what was happening but Emma calmed them and Keith looked for

Jenny. She was helping the church ladies busy with a tea urn. As she offered sandwiches and cakes, her smile and cheerfulness gave the darker corners the air of a subdued party. From there could be heard appreciation of excellent cooking as well as occasional laughter. He thought how once again food and hot drinks could have the effect of smoothing the course of an enquiry.

'Mr Tyrell, or should I say Inspector?'

Jack Weston was taller than Keith had first thought. 'I'm on leave, sir, and not officially on duty, but can I be of assistance?'

'It's all these flowers in an enclosed space. Allergy, I'm afraid. I've been sneezing my head off. When can we go home? I'd like an idea so my driver can be called.'

'You didn't park your car here, sir?'

A frosty smile warmed the blue eyes very slightly. 'No.'

'If you could be patient, sir, Sergeant Paxton has gone to see if the roadway can be used again.'

It was almost an hour before the church was finally cleared and the door locked, the last to leave the stalwarts who had calmly catered through the crisis and were in charge of the massive key. Emma and Jenny led the way down the path and began to walk through the village, quiet enough now for them to hear the gurgling of the small stream running alongside the road.

'Clay, can you get hold of your people tonight?'

The American stopped and looked hard at his friend. 'Sure. Something happened?'

'Weston. Nanny Bowler told me about the brown fleck he had in one eye. When he came into church this evening I automatically looked for it. Instinct, I suppose.'

'Wasn't it there?'

'Oh, yes. Even at a distance I could see it. Unfortunately for him he's since done a lot of sneezing and nose blowing.'

'So?'

'The brown patch has moved through more than ninety degrees. It's on a contact lens and I doubt he's the original Jack Weston who left Childswickham as a boy, or who boarded the flight which landed at Heathrow.'

Clay was stunned into silence but not Emma. 'We can soon find out who he is,' she said, deceptively innocent.

'How?' Keith and Clay chorused.

Emma took from a large pocket in her coat something wrapped in one of her scarves, unfolding the silk to reveal a cup and then a saucer. 'Jack Weston's. It was Jenny's idea.'

From her jacket Jenny drew out her hands, each holding tissue-wrapped objects. 'And I've got his son's.'

Chapter Twelve

They found a quiet corner in the cafeteria at a busy round-about. It was mid-morning and the dining area not too crowded. Keith and Clay stirred coffee and watched juggernauts thunder past, heading for the maze of roads around Birmingham. A tall, dark man with broad shoulders and keen eyes was anonymous in a dark blue jacket and jeans as he carried a tray with a steaming mug and a plastic-wrapped sandwich. He glanced at the two friends, gave a slight nod and settled at the next table, spreading and reading a newspaper. Ensuring he had no companions, the man also isolated Keith and Clay from eavesdroppers.

'His driver,' Keith said. 'The boss must be waiting until no one will notice him.'

'Too well known in this neck of the woods?' Clay asked with a grin.

'Well, he is the very public face of the force.'

The man for whom they waited came in at a leisurely pace. ACC Hinton was dressed in a zipped windcheater and slacks as if for a round of golf. He was almost un-recognizable without his uniform, his grey curls a halo instead of being gelled into submission. Hinton raised an eyebrow at his driver, received some kind of acknowl-edgement in return and slid into the seat next to Keith with a smoothness belying his years and bulk, clearing the tray he carried of coffee and a plate of doughnuts.

'The link with your GCHQ's been found,' Clay told him in a quiet voice.

The ACC's expression did not change. 'So I gather. How did you get on to it?'

'A piece of gossip from one of Keith's informants. A man was followed last night to his girlfriend's flat and she was checked out. Works in a decoding section at the centre.'

'Direct links to your project?'

'Very direct, sir. The flat used by the couple was one above an office in Cheltenham, the occupant of the office, an accountant who lives in Buckland.'

'Name?' Hinton queried.

'Petherbridge, and the wandering husband is Petherbridge's next-door neighbour, Gerald Addiscombe,' Keith added. 'Last night he made the most of his wife being busy at the concert in the church.'

'And this Addiscombe has a rock solid alibi for the murder?'

'Agents at all exits can verify that, sir,' Clay said.

'Addiscombe must have been being blackmailed by Petherbridge,' Keith suggested, 'the payment being information supplied by his mistress. It still doesn't explain the body in Buckland.'

The ACC unzipped his jacket and with enviable sleight of hand passed a folded envelope to Keith. 'All you asked for from last night – and as up to date as I could get it.'

'Thank you, sir. Any identity for the man found dead?'

'Nothing confirmed but you'll see a report of a fire in Cheltenham last night. Small shop and flat above. Nothing out of the ordinary, except the missing tenant fits the description of your corpse – who had a broken neck, as you suspected. The MO's been checked out and so far fits a killer for hire, nickname "Cracker". One twist . . .' Hinton's craggy features seemed carved from stone. 'Real name Michael Devlin, who always has an impeccable alibi.'

Clay was puzzled and leaned towards the ACC. 'You said a shop in Cheltenham. What kind of shop, sir?'

'More a depot, really,' Hinton replied. 'This chap repaired computers for a living, although he did sell off

211

spare parts he'd stripped from defunct machines. Name of Paul Giles. Neighbours had the notion he had a mother living in Carterton.'

Keith was shocked. 'But that's near –'

'Brize Norton.' Hinton's expression was grim. 'I hope to God we're not in the middle of the biggest mess ever.'

'I doubt it, sir,' Clay said evenly. 'The fact this guy, Giles, was killed and dumped where he was confirms the possible terrorist targets are, as we thought, nowhere near this county and not even in the UK.'

'Giles and computers,' Keith said slowly. 'Chances are Giles has been muscling in where he's not wanted. Weston's son is a computer whizz-kid and bases his activities in London. I doubt he'd use an obscure mechanic in Cheltenham. No, Petherbridge may have been putting the squeeze on Addiscombe for information but was Giles, in turn, trying to blackmail Petherbridge for cash – to keep quiet about data he'd found on a hard drive?'

Clay grinned. 'Catches on fast, doesn't he, sir?'

The ACC was not a happy man. 'Yes, he does, and I want him back on duty as soon as possible. Surely he's done what you wanted?'

'Yes, he has, but we'd like to keep a lid on everything for twenty-four hours.'

'Why?'

'I'll make a guess there's not a scrap of evidence to link the Westons or Petherbridge to Giles's murder. Wait until the woman's been arrested at GCHQ. You can pick up Addiscombe at the same time and he'll probably sing like a canary.'

Hinton was not convinced. 'What about Addiscombe's wife?'

Keith shook his head. 'I'd be surprised if she knows anything.'

'And I'd agree,' Clay said. 'That woman couldn't keep a secret if her life depended on it but her husband'll give you Petherbridge on a plate.'

'Won't that upset your plans, Major?'

'Not at all, sir,' said Clay. 'Events were already coming to a head and after last night and the appearance Weston made, I'd say he's changed his retirement plan and is ready to move on within hours.'

'Whoever Weston is,' Keith added.

Clay said nothing and Keith looked hard at his friend, raising a questioning eyebrow.

'OK. The girls got us prints last night and I sent them off on a rush job,' the American explained to Hinton. 'Weston's from Miami. There, he was Vincente Romano. It's probably not his original name and he may even be English but he appeared first in New York. It wasn't long before he fancied the lifestyle of the Mob and became of "Italian extraction" – with an appropriate name to go with it. As Romano, he liked to think himself as socially a cut above the other hoodlums which is why he headed for Miami and then set up this caper, probably on his own. Jason Weston was born Salvatore Turtura, genuinely of Sicilian blood and an up-and-coming nasty. Both men had paid the blood price of murder as an entry fee to the Mob, but those charges – and others – came to nothing in the past because of witness intimidation or complete disappearance.'

Hinton reined in his fury as it rose at the knowledge gangsters were daring to use the peacefulness of his patch. 'The real Westons?' he asked.

Clay shrugged his shoulders. 'They were on the plane from Toronto to New York, transferring there to Concorde for the flight to London. Both the men who arrived at Heathrow are the ones in Childswickham. My guess is the real Westons are either in concrete and in the Hudson, or were minced up in a dog food factory on New York's East Side.'

The ACC rocked the dregs in his coffee cup, staring at the movement.

'*Requiescant in pace,*' Keith said quietly, the ancient prayer heartfelt.

Hinton pushed away his cup. 'Amen to that, boy. Now let's get on. Jason, that's how we know him, in what way's he useful to Weston?' he asked Clay.

'Computers. He's good – real good. Jack's the ideas man and Jason gets the plans passed on and the money moved.'

The ACC was indignant. 'And you want me to ignore them?'

'No, sir, just leave them to us,' Clay asked of the senior man. 'We know the kind of game they play and we also know how they should be dealt with.'

'Not on my patch you don't!'

Hinton's driver rustled the sheets of his newspaper and half-turned, coughing a warning.

Clay raised a soothing hand. 'Believe me, the last thing I want to do is to have to sort them out here. When the Westons appeared in church last night they were breaking their own rules. I'd guess everything they've arranged in case of an emergency is ready to go and I want a delay.'

Hinton frowned, displeased by this turn of events, 'How long?'

'As I said, twenty-four hours – even twelve – would give us enough time to reverse their schedule.'

Keith was curious. 'How can you do that?' he asked and Hinton bent nearer to Clay, the better to hear his answer.

'A terrorist outfit, wherever it's based, is like any other business. It has overheads and it needs cash to service them. A lot of cash. At one end of the scale there are suicide bombers. They're persuadable, plentiful and come cheap because they end up dead. Forget your top terrorists as bearded fanatics. They're more likely to be ordinary men and women going to work daily in a business of some kind but what they must have is cash to buy arms and explosives, as well as a massive pile of safe currency to be squirrelled away in the Caymans or Switzerland. In return for well-planned death and destruction, there's a very nice return for the faceless middle man or woman. They're out to make life sweet for themselves, nobody else.'

Hinton and Keith were silent, thinking of festering minds and the infamy they could generate. 'What can you do in a day?' the younger man asked.

214

Clay gazed at his friend and Keith saw the beginnings of a smile. 'It's already started. We know of two cash piles originating from the main man. One is in existence to pay for terrorism and the other for buying up shares when the price is right. All the money is in the States and every cent of it traceable, eventually and with great difficulty, to Jack Weston. There's also a healthy sum in the bank here, in Broadway, and that will be untouched – for now. As for the rest,' Clay looked at his watch, 'for the last thirty minutes it's begun to disappear.'

Keith's thoughts raced. 'Transferred where?'

'Nowhere,' said Clay and smiled, chilling them. 'It's just being wiped. That includes money already transferred into the banks of suspect individuals who can deliver terror on cue. They'll come up empty and angry enough to renege on promised actions, thanks to the best hackers CIA money can buy. Believe me, on this case they've been worth every dime and dollar.'

'And where does that leave me?' a furious ACC Hinton demanded to know.

'Carrying on as usual, sir,' Clay advised him. 'Just let your teams concentrate on the Giles killing as normal.'

'Normal?' Hinton bellowed in a whisper. 'What the hell's normal any more? And what am I supposed to do about the Westons – whoever they are?'

'I'm sorry, sir.' Clay sounded genuinely contrite. 'None of this was expected to happen. Ignore the Westons, if you can. It's my guess they'll soon be gone.'

'How can I ignore them?'

Hinton ran fingers through thick curls and Keith felt sorry for the man. The ACC would never shirk responsibility and he had agreed, along with the Chief Constable, to give Clay every assistance. Turning a blind eye to anyone who masterminded killings was foreign to a man who had given the whole of his working life to policing the county.

Clay leaned forward, intent on ensuring no one else could hear him. 'Listen, sir, the Westons will be dealt with. You have my word.'

Hinton stared hard at the young American and Clay let him, bearing the scrutiny calmly, patiently, until the ACC exhaled pent-up breath in a sigh. 'I don't see I have a choice. Twenty-four hours. This time tomorrow I want Keith back working for me. Understood?'

'Yes, sir.'

'And you,' the ACC said as he glared at Keith, 'keep your nose clean and don't annoy DCI Creed. He's a touchy bastard at the best of times.'

The American was steadily working his way through a stack of paper in a folder as Keith drove away from the café on the roundabout.

'Finished?'

Clay nodded. 'Yeah. There's quite a lot of detail considering the body was found so late last night.' He settled back against the leather of Keith's car as they took their turn on the roundabout, tidying the pages of the report Hinton had left with them. 'The weather's good so at least your boss will enjoy his golf.'

'I doubt it. See that?' Keith said, pointing to a tiny cloud in an otherwise clear sky.

> 'When Bredon Hill doth wear her cap,
> Ye men of the Vale beware of that.
> When Bredon Hill doth clear appear,
> Ye men of the Vale have naught to fear,'

he quoted softly. 'We've got to hurry if we're to beat the rain.'

'Because of that cloud?'

'The legend's as old as the hills and a forerunner of wet weather.'

Clay was ready to scoff until he saw Keith was serious. 'You're not joking!'

'No, I'm not. Have another look at that report and tell me what you think. I'm heading for Buckland. Fortunately, I know the lie of the land up beyond the church and something in that file clicked.'

It was a silent journey, the only sound in the car the rustling of paper.

'The witness waiting for his girlfriend who's a waitress at the manor?' Clay was frowning as he asked the question.

'That's it. He was patient to start with but there must have been a hold-up in the hotel and the girl was late. He says he got out of his car to stretch his legs.'

'A call of nature in the bushes?'

'More than likely. Tucked away there he had no chance of seeing anything but it did mean he was on edge, listening in case he'd be caught. He says there was no sound of an engine until after the car must have passed the end of the hotel drive. He heard it rolling slowly and stop. There was a pause – he says less than a minute – after which car doors slammed, the engine started and the vehicle was driven out of the village. He came out of hiding in time to see it go past the old forge.'

'Noisy engine,' Clay read out loud. 'Small, low, probably a sports car. Why didn't he see the body?'

'That was when the girlfriend arrived. They were in the car, possibly arguing, when they drove away. His headlights would have shown up the grass verge to his left. The body was on his right, nearest the church. Megan Baverstock must have arrived soon after. When she saw Giles there was no car leaving the hotel.'

'Did the car bring in Paul Giles and his killer, this guy Cracker?'

'I doubt it. My guess is Giles had come to meet Petherbridge either in an interval in the concert or at the end.'

'Where would he have waited?'

'Again a guess. The new graveyard would have made for good cover.'

'And a suitable place to get his neck broken.'

'It would have been very private,' Keith admitted. 'All Cracker had to do was stow the body in Giles's own car, push it down the road, dump the body and then get clear.'

'He took a risk or two.'

'Did he? Or did he wait for exactly the right moment and take action?'

'Not a guy to meet on a dark night,' Clay decided, watching Keith signal and turn. 'Remind me, why are we coming here?' he asked as they began to travel along the narrow road into the heart of Buckland.

'To find signs of Cracker?'

'Huh? The expert who leaves no traces?'

'Basic law of forensics, everybody does, but we've got to find Cracker's spoor before Bredon's cap beats us to it. Can you ring Emma and get her to join us? She's damned good at noticing things.'

'You're telling me?' her husband asked with feeling. 'Not only can she tell me what I've missed, she can also tell me why.'

Keith laughed. 'That's not just being a good detective, it means she's also a woman,' he said as he parked the car.

'Why are you stopping here?'

Tyrell had pulled in his car well below where the body had been found. 'I need to see what's on the ground.'

'Won't your guys have covered every inch already?'

'Last night and this morning.'

'Then what are we looking for?'

'Oil.'

'You're kidding!'

'No. There was a sergeant in the Met who used to tell us new boys to get down on our knees and thank God if Chummy had used an old car. "These new ones are all alike as peas in a pod. Now, an old banger, it's been through a lot. Extra layers of different paints, filler where there's been rust, nothing dramatic but all giving a helping hand. Then there's oil," he used to say. "New cars have engine oil coming out matching but not a motor that's been round the block a few times. Metal scrapings, oddments of additives. Not like fingerprints but damned close."'

Buckland was quiet, no traffic at that time of day as Keith and Clay searched for droplets of oil. Eventually,

Clay thought he could see a pattern, tiny patches four or five yards apart on the tarmac near the old forge, getting closer as he walked up the village.

Keith handed him a piece of chalk. 'Circle them, please.'

Clay stared at the small white stick, then at Keith. 'Were you in the Scouts?'

'How did you guess?' The grin was reassuring. 'Actually, I learned the hard way to keep handy what I might need in a hurry.'

'That's why you just happen to have evidence bags in your trunk?'

'I could need them soon,' Keith said and continued to scrutinize the grass verge opposite the gateway to the church.

The American retraced his steps, marking each patch of oil as asked, while Tyrell stood on the gravelled way and searched carefully. Once or twice he nodded, then opened the gate into the small enclave of hallowed ground gradually filling with those more recently dead than in the plots and tombs surrounding the church. The grass between the graves was dry, and here and there were small sections bare of greenery, sometimes marked by cracks which had appeared as the soil dried.

'Ah!' Satisfied with his find, Keith pulled a large plastic bag from his pocket, labelled it and was about to cover a boot's imprint he had found when he heard a car speeding towards him. It stopped and there was the noise of doors slamming shut, voices. He relaxed. They were women's voices and he recognized them.

'Jenny!'

Keith strode to his wife. She was warmly wrapped in a navy waterproof and red scarf, her smile that of a child happy with adventure ahead. He hugged her and she kissed his cheek.

'I thought I might help – I've brought sandwiches and a flask.'

He smiled at her and squeezed her hand, bulky in its thick leather mitten. There was another smile for Emma as she waited for orders. Keith explained the footprint and the four of them surrounded it, memorizing as best they could.

'I think the man we're after waited here until he heard Giles arrive but I don't think he came by car.'

Clay was surprised. 'Walked?'

'Not up the road, that would have been too obvious. It might look deserted but, believe me, this corner of the county is very intensively farmed. Had he come in daylight he would have been seen. My guess is he came in at night.'

'Which is why he left tracks.' Emma's hair fluffed free and clean of gel. She no longer wore the clothes which draggled hippy fashion but practical jeans and a green jacket, heavy walking boots. Her eyes were bright with excitement.

Keith agreed with a nod. 'If we're in luck he's left more. Coming down this last part past the old bothy, he'd have had to stay on grass. All those holiday homes there now, he could have been heard walking on loose stones. Anyone reading the police reports might decide the killer came in the car with his victim since no odd cars were left behind but I doubt that's what happened. Cutting across country has fooled many a police force but it has to be done by someone who knows fields and hedges –'

'Or someone specially trained,' Emma added. 'Ex-SAS?'

'I think our man is more likely ex-IRA,' Keith said quietly. 'Can I ask the three of you to go up the track and see what you can find. You'll see the line of a footpath. Don't actually walk on it. Emma will show you how it's done.' Tyrell handed her a pack of evidence bags. 'Cover anything you spot as quickly as you can,' he advised, looking at the sky.

Clay glanced upwards and was startled. 'Where did all those clouds come from?'

'I did warn you,' Keith said with swift grin. 'Speed, please, Emma, before rain blurs any traces – and mind your helpers don't put their big feet all over the shop.'

'I'll have you for that,' Jenny retorted. 'What are you going to do?'

'Me? I've to wait for DCI Creed.'

Trish Paxton was the first to arrive and Tyrell smiled a welcome.

'Sergeant Paxton, good to see you again. Shall we start with the trail of oil?' he said and began to lead the way to the first spots.

'Best wait for DCI Creed,' she called.

It took only a brief glance for the inspector to see she was apprehensive. 'If you think it wise.'

She hesitated. 'He doesn't like to be pre-empted and – well, sir, he's not at all happy about your involvement.'

'That's something I can understand. Taking on a case and finding someone looking over my shoulder all the time is not my idea of good procedure.'

'But you were first on the scene and reported it in.'

'It's still not my division.'

'No, sir, but all our reports are tagged for ACC Hinton and he's the one who gave this job to DCI Creed.' DS Paxton took a deep breath. 'I'd guess, for some reason, you're kept informed of everything we know.'

'Does the thought upset DCI Creed?'

The gathering clouds had thickened, darkened, and it was almost dusk in the early afternoon.

'I'd say he's not too happy about it, sir.'

A car was accelerating after it had turned off the main road, the engine noise an expression of anger.

'Thank you for your warning, Sergeant Paxton.'

There was no time for more as a car door slammed and Creed's bulk marched towards them. 'Tyrell! What the hell are you playing at? I thought you were supposed to be on leave?'

'Technically yes, sir.'

'Don't play bloody silly games with me! You've had access to our information and taken it upon yourself to muck up a crime scene.'

221

'Partly right, sir, but I did have skilled help and witnesses to all that's been done.'

'Explain!'

'A car coming into the village during the concert and the same car leaving soon after, having probably been pushed by a very fit individual down the slope. When it was started, the engine noise was harsh enough to suggest an old vehicle and that meant the chance of oil spots. We followed them, saw where the car had slowed by the church, gone on a little and turned, parking near the new graveyard. There was plenty of light then for us to see the odd footprint of whoever waited for the driver.'

'You should've reported in and left it for us to deal with.'

'No time.' As the inspector spoke the first rain began to fall and was suddenly heavy. They ran for the cover of nearby trees. 'As you see, sir, with rain on the way we had to get all sites identified and covered as quickly as possible.'

Creed might resent Tyrell's youth, connections, ability, but he was first and foremost a good detective. 'Why were you so sure evidence could be found?'

'Not sure, sir. With my brother and cousins, I roamed the tracks above Laverton and Buckland when we were children. Long ago I'd experienced an entry to Buckland from the hill, avoiding the road altogether.'

'Yes, you're one of them, aren't you? These people,' he snapped dismissively, annoyed by Tyrell's wax jacket and rubber boots. They were practical for the job the visiting DI had been doing but to Creed they were normal wear for the type he despised.

Tyrell sensed Creed's antipathy to attitudes he would have encountered when he first arrived in this part of the county from individuals desperate to appear socially important. 'My roots are here, if that's what you mean.'

Clay swished his way to them through wet grass and was introduced to the DCI. 'Any identification, Mr Gifford?'

Clay handed over a slip of paper and his wallet opened

at the appropriate card. Creed frowned as he read the details, then again, to ensure he had grasped all the details. His eyes wary, he looked up at the American.

'It seems I have instructions to give you any help I can, Major. Whatever you're after, does it involve this case?'

'I doubt it. Giles's death is most likely only a side issue as far as we're concerned. Our targets are working from cover in this region but any crimes they're likely to commit will have results far away.'

'Should I be glad of that?'

Clay had lost his air of innocent amiability and was once more the hardened army officer. 'Very, Mr Creed.'

The DCI nodded and his mouth tightened as cars were driven slowly towards them. He was heartened, seeing his own officers arriving. 'Right, we'll get on, then. Paxton!'

His sergeant came at a run.

'Get SOCO on to the oil deposits, they've all been chalked. Primitive, but it'll do. Get 'em charted and photoed, then sampled for the lab. Make sure the footprint expert mixes his gunge pronto. You say there're prints in the graveyard, along the track and up on to the hill?'

'Yes, sir. Mrs Gifford's up there marking and covering them.'

Slowly, Creed's head turned to Tyrell, his disbelief ready to explode. 'Mrs Gifford?'

'Yes, sir. She's one of us and was DC Emma Paige until recently.'

The DCI was visibly relieved. 'I'll go and see her,' he said and strode away through rain which had turned to a steady drizzle.

Tyrell watched him go, realizing that in spite of all the effort there was no way to make a case any prosecutor could take to court. Emma and Jenny had done brilliantly to collect the cups and the fingerprints although no jury could ever hear of it. At least it was now confirmed who the Westons really were but he had serious doubts a link to Cracker Devlin could be shown to exist and said so to Clay.

'You're right again, Keith. The Westons? As Romano and

223

Turtura they were used to planning murders which leave no trace – a habit they brought with them when they settled here and became the Weston family. Incidentally, there's no record of Vincente Romano having any allergies, although both his eyes are listed as blue.'

'A contact lens too irritating for him?' Keith wondered aloud. 'It would explain why he was never seen much locally when he had to discard his dark glasses.'

'You must admit, turning up to the concert made sure you and I gave him a damned good alibi.' The idea did not please Clay.

'He's not a man to leave anything to chance,' Keith reminded his friend, 'so whatever he planned is definitely coming to a climax for him to take that risk.'

'I thought Jenny was making sandwiches for an army but I'm glad she did – I was ravenous,' Emma said as she reached for another.

'All that cold air,' Keith told her.

Jenny was indignant. 'What about our hard work?'

The interior of Keith's car was warm, its occupants free of bulky clothes. 'We should be getting back. Aunt Sophie will be concerned we've been away so long.'

Jenny shook her head. 'Not at all. She and Nanny helped us get the food ready and said it was just like old times with you and the boys. When we came away it was with "Expect you when we see you" in our ears.'

'Well, Creed hasn't any more use for us.' Keith screwed the lid tightly on a stainless steel flask and passed it back to Jenny.

Emma's giggle was gentle. 'Don't be too hard on him, Keith. Remember the creep I told you about in Cheltenham?'

'The DI you slapped in public because he had hands like an octopus?'

'Which got me transferred to Lydney and you, as I recall. A couple of months back DCI Creed apparently took him on one side and told him some home truths – very forcibly,

I heard. The men's locker room was a right mess by the time he'd finished.'

'So Creed's not all bad?'

'Unorthodox at times,' Emma said, 'but he gets the job done.'

Keith turned the key in the ignition. 'I hope he won't be too upset when he finds I've got Mickey Walsh on standby in case any of Giles's computer files survived the fire – or we get back-up disks from Giles's mother.'

Emma was curious, leaning forward to talk to Keith as he negotiated the car past police vehicles almost blocking Buckland. 'Is Mickey really looking after your house while you're away?'

'Yes, and Rose Walker.'

'Good old Rose. She's a quiet one but how can she stand the smell?'

'Mickey?' Jenny chuckled. 'He's been transformed.'

This startled Emma. 'You mean he's had a bath?'

'Showers – a dozen a week at least – and his hair's a distinct asset now,' Jenny assured her.

'Never thought I'd see the day,' Emma murmured to no one in particular.

Once through the front door of Bowman's, Keith could hear voices, laughter.

'I thought I knew the car in the drive,' he said as he went to the source of the sounds and into a happy scene. 'Ben! Where have you been? I've tried to find you but no one knew where you'd gone.'

As the others crowded into a kitchen fragrant with the start of dinner preparations, Ben Hadley stood and grinned. Keith glanced at his aunt, at Nanny Bowler. Only Nanny seemed unsurprised by events.

'You knew all along,' he accused her, and she smiled gently.

'Never tell what I shouldn't.'

'So, what have you been up to?' Keith demanded of his friend.

'London. Off my own bat this time and somewhere you'd know,' Ben told him.

Keith tried to understand the air of quiet jubilation in the kitchen. 'Somewhere . . .' he said slowly, then his puzzled frown cleared. 'Police! You did it!'

Ben was nodding happily. 'I start at Hendon in six weeks.'

In the hubbub of congratulations Aunt Sophie handed Keith an envelope. 'This came for you – a delightful young man. Said it was urgent.'

Keith saw the crest of the county constabulary in the corner, then his name written in ACC Hinton's distinctive style. Excusing himself, he turned away to read the enclosure once, twice, replacing the letter in its cover while he digested the contents.

'What's up?' Clay murmured and was answered by Keith inclining his head towards the garden.

'If you don't mind, I badly need a clean-up,' he said to everyone. 'You are staying to dinner, Ben?'

'Of course he is, darling. Nanny's already started his special pudding.' Aunt Sophie smiled fondly at the young people gathered in her home. It almost felt like old times.

Followed by Clay at a discreet interval, Keith left the room and headed for the back door. Neither said a word until they were deep in the garden and well out of earshot.

'Hinton's worried,' Keith explained, 'and I don't blame him. Devlin's perfect alibi. He has a farm on the west coast of Ireland and is in the habit of a daily walk along a cliff path. When he's away on a job a cousin who resembles him at a distance wears his clothes, takes his place and does the walk. By the time a body's been found and Cracker's in the frame for it, he's safely home. And when the Garda are alerted and check the farm, half the respectable citizens of the countryside are ready to swear it was Michael Devlin they'd seen at the appropriate time.'

'And they'd believe they were telling the truth. What power the man has over his neighbours!'

226

'It's called fear,' Keith said bitterly.

They paced the wet grass in silence, Keith aiming for the shelter of the cedar which had shared his youthful dreams and tragedies. 'Hinton's not usually given to panic.'

'Understandable, if he's had a whisper Cracker might be meting out revenge on the Westons' behalf. Don't forget, they come from a tribe keen on revenge,' Clay reminded him. 'Last night's kill outside the concert was a distinct piece of bravado, as was tossing the body to be found by the first person leaving the church.'

'You can almost hear the bastards saying "Come and get us!" knowing we'd never be able to muster a case against them.'

The branches of their refuge soughed in the wind.

'If this Cracker's on the loose, it means you and I are in the firing line, Keith,' Clay said slowly.

That cold spot was back and it had already been an accurate warning. 'It's why Hinton's concerned, but think about it. It's not just us. What about Aunt Sophie for giving us a cover story? Nanny Bowler for all the information – and remember, Romano was always aware she knew the real Jack Weston. Then there's Emma and Jenny. They helped out in the church and Emma was unquestionably in the job.' It did not take long for Keith to come to a decision. 'You and Emma are to stay here tonight. If we keep together, we should be safe.'

Nanny Bowler refused to be party to Keith's plans, however much they were for her own good.

'No one's going to keep me out of my home! I shall sleep in my own bed tonight, Master Keith,' she informed him and there was no arguing with her, although they all tried.

Only Ben's offer to occupy Nanny's spare room solved the problem and Clay accompanied Keith on the brief journey ferrying the elderly lady home, together with her lodger. Later, as Keith and Clay checked the security of the little cottage, Nanny was busy making up a spare bed for Ben.

'I'm glad of your company, lad, you know that, but I don't know why all the fuss.'

Ben had been good with his mother and his gentle firmness helped now. 'If Keith thinks it necessary, we've got to go along with it. It's only one night after all, Mrs Bowler.'

Keith and Clay drove back to Bowman's in silence. Before they got out of the car they looked around the gravelled parking area, trying to penetrate the denseness of the surrounding bushes and see if there were any intruders.

'OK,' Clay said at last. 'I'll go first.'

Keith watched him walk to the front door, casually turning and smiling as he opened it. Seconds, it took for Keith to vacate and lock the car. He walked steadily into the house, bolting the door behind him, then switching on the alarm system.

'Ben was right, it's just one night and no one's on their own,' he said. 'What could go wrong?'

Chapter Thirteen

'Keith!'

He did not stir and Jenny began to shake him awake.

'Keith! Something's wrong. The phone's been ringing and I can hear Aunt Sophie moving about.'

By now he was thoroughly aroused and raced to his aunt's room. She was tying the belt of her pink housecoat and wriggling feet into warm slippers.

'Darling, there's a fire. It's Nanny. Her neighbour, Annie Martin, rang to tell me. They're waiting for the engine but she says Nanny's out and fine, coughing a bit.'

'Ben?'

'Got Nanny out, then had to jump. Walter Martin called for an ambulance.'

Jenny was at his side and she had heard the last comment. 'I'm coming with you.'

Uppermost in her husband's mind was Hinton's warning. 'No, I need you to stay here.'

'And I don't want you to go on your own.'

Clay had been roused and was there. 'She's right, Keith.' He had dragged on a warm sweater and was pulling at the waist of his chinos. 'I'm coming too.'

'Someone has to stay here.' Keith ran back to his room and dressed in what was to hand. Jenny was already in a warm jumper and slacks, pulling on thick socks and reaching for strong shoes as Emma appeared at the door, ready to travel.

'There's no need to rush round like headless chickens,' Aunt Sophie declared from the head of the stairs. 'Keith, you and Clay go and see what you can do for Nanny. Bring her and Ben here if at all possible. The girls and I will make up beds for them – and I must remember to switch on the hot water, Nanny does so hate the smell of smoke and will need an instant bath.'

Keith saw the sense of her arrangements. 'OK, but lock up carefully when we've gone. Make sure the alarm's on and stays that way.'

'No need to worry, darling. If I'm ever disturbed at night I have your uncle's Purdeys to keep me company.'

He swung to face her, seeing calm resolution. 'Thanks.'

Outside the door, Keith waited only to hear bolts slide fast behind him, then he was on the run. Clay was waiting, checking the action of a very useful revolver.

'Purdeys? Are those the shotguns costing a small fortune?'

'They are these days. My uncle was very proud of his, they were a present from his father. One of a family of crack shots.'

'Your aunt?'

'Always hits her target.'

By now Keith had the car sweeping out of Bowman's drive along the narrow lane to Laverton.

'Would she shoot to kill?'

'Only if she decided there was no other course open to her.'

There was silence for a hundred yards or so. 'I don't get you Brits,' Clay decided. 'A nutter breaks into your home, causes utter misery, you deal with them and you're the one gets arrested.'

'That's our way. One day, with luck, it might change,' he said, seeing a redness in the night sky, billowing smoke.

He could not get near Nanny's cottage. In front of it was a fire engine, hoses snaking across her cherished flower beds. An ambulance with open doors waited, a blanket-wrapped form on one of its beds. A police car parked beside him and DS Paxton jumped out.

'Arson?' she asked Tyrell.

He wondered if she ever slept, she looked so tired. 'We

checked the house ourselves tonight, three or four hours ago,' he told her. 'There were no naked lights, no loose fuel of any kind. I'd say this was one for us and I promise you the evidence will be carefully non-existent.'

She raised an eyebrow. 'Friendly place, this village of yours?'

'Mostly. It's why they're suspicious of newcomers. Some bring their bad habits. Now, excuse me, I need to see how the casualties are faring.'

He pushed through the small crowd which had gathered until he reached the ambulance. Ben lay on a stretcher inside the vehicle, a paramedic working on his feet. Nearby, Nanny was sitting upright on a wall and wrapped in blankets, her jaw set at an angle Keith remembered well.

'Are you Inspector Tyrell?' a second paramedic asked him.

Keith had his warrant card ready.

'Glad you got here when you did. The old biddy won't budge till she's seen you.'

Hoping Nanny had not heard the comments, Keith persuaded her into the ambulance and sat with her, an arm around her shoulders. 'Ben, you OK?'

Ben reeked of burnt wood but he nodded. 'Sore, but I think it's only my ankle. I smelled smoke coming up from downstairs and went into Mrs Bowler's room to wake her up. I barricaded the door and blocked off the bottom of it – that gave me enough time to get sheets knotted and lower her out of the window. Thank God they built low ceilings in the old days!'

'How did you get out?'

'By then the door was burning something fierce and I didn't wait for anything – except Mrs Bowler's handbag. It was at the foot of the bed and I chucked that out before I lowered myself from the sill and then fell. Walter Martin was there and took over. He and Annie were great,' he said of Nanny's friends.

Keith turned his attention to the elderly woman. 'How're you feeling?'

231

'Very angry, Master Keith! It was that devil calls himself Jack Weston, wasn't it? I knew first day I saw him after he came back something was wrong. Called me Maggie. The old Jack always called me Meg, like his sister – God rest her poor soul. I'm just glad she didn't live to see all this.'

The senior paramedic was disgruntled. 'Look. I've been told there are no other casualties and I've got to get these two to hospital for check-ups.'

A few more minutes were spent negotiating, organizing, before the ambulance doors were closed and the bulky vehicle was on its way. Keith immediately went to greet and thank Annie and Walter Martin, before asking if they had seen or heard anything out of the ordinary. Walter shook his head but Annie was less positive. She thought she'd heard an engine start up somewhere at a distance but she couldn't be sure, Walter snoring so hard by then. Keith and Clay made their way back to their own car, reversing it with difficulty in the narrow lane.

'Did you expect anything like this when Weston could have felt himself cornered?'

Clay did not answer immediately.

'Surely you thought there'd be some sort of reaction?' There had been no accusatory note in Keith's question.

'Look, Keith, we knew Weston expected to live here for the foreseeable future and we were ready for that.'

'What changed?'

'Paul Giles. He's an unknown quantity.'

'You really think he's a rogue card in the pack?'

'Sure. Maybe he was dealt in by chance. A repairman who saw big bucks in Petherbridge's laptop.'

'Becoming a problem for Petherbridge and Weston – as well as for us when he ended up dead.'

'Whatever happened he was going to attract attention and that's what Weston didn't want – no crap on his doorstep while he lived here,' Clay said. 'You must admit he got it cleaned up pretty damned quick and Giles no longer a problem.'

'But "we" didn't have Giles killed, did "we"?' Keith asked, thinking of the CIA and its British counterparts.

'No way! It must have been Weston's decision to take him out in such a public manner. I guess there's no doubt now that guy's ready to run and his escape route will be well organized.'

'Where to?'

Clay shrugged his shoulders. 'Europe, somewhere. After that, who knows? The Agency will be hunting through Internet data for bookings, flights. At least the Jack Weston you knew won't have as financially comfortable a retirement as he expected. Not by a long way.'

'What about the planned terrorist attacks?'

'The Semtex ordered is still in the Czech Republic and in the Irish one, too, since no money's got through to the suppliers. As for Russian rockets which were to be used, they're in Chechnya and will stay there – till the next buyer appears. At least we've got fresh leads as to who's selling what.'

Clay was tired and lay back in his seat as Keith pulled the car on to grass just short of Bowman's gateway.

'Weston's target?'

The American counted his breaths, five before he answered. 'The guys we knew were being groomed as suicide bombers are still working as New York cabbies – for the moment.'

'That means the explosives could have been delivered and detonated anywhere in the city?'

'In theory. Our hackers have been keeping tight surveillance on those suspect companies I told you about.'

'The ones with growing funds for shares?'

'Yeah,' was a slow sigh. 'Someone in each of them's been checking prices of a particular commodity and the share cost of businesses specializing in it.'

'The commodity?'

'Oil.'

Keith was shocked into silence for a long moment. 'All this – and innumerable deaths to come so Weston could be an oil tycoon?'

'As they say, "Whatever turns you on, Buster."'

'He had money and power of a kind,' Keith said, 'was respectability that important?'

'Along with a position of authority in our country,' Clay added bitterly. 'Vincente Romano had ambition in spades.'

Keith was angry. 'No matter how many deaths paid for it? Is the security you mentioned still in place?'

The American rubbed tired eyes. 'Everywhere possible. What really mattered was cancelling the cash and I've been assured that's complete – down to the last dollar.'

'In context it makes Nanny's cottage and Ben's damaged ankle a small price to pay but there's still Paul Giles and his murder's in our territory. The killer should certainly be held accountable in a court of law.'

'Welcome to the twenty-first century.' Keith was surprised to hear such cynicism in his friend's voice. 'Weston, this Cracker guy, they consider themselves above the law. It's all a game to them and your legal men in their grubby wigs are no match for the modern men of evil.'

'No?'

'No, Keith,' Clay said with unusual firmness. 'We have to make sure there are men and women able to take on the task for us. What's the quote about evil prospering?'

' "It is necessary only for the good men to do nothing." '

'So, in this day and age, what do we need, Keith? Bad men on our side or good men who'll take action?'

No one slept for long and breakfast was a quiet spell of coffee drinking.

Aunt Sophie surveyed her guests, each one lost in their own thoughts. 'Is it too early to ring the hospital?'

'Best give it another hour,' Keith advised.

'Why Cheltenham General?' his aunt asked. 'I would have thought Evesham nearer.'

'It is but it might have taken longer to get a police guard for them. Like Broadway, Evesham's in a different county,' Keith explained to Clay. 'Neither Nanny nor Ben was in a

234

serious condition so there was no emergency. The paramedics were great and had them stable in no time but they insisted on hospitalization – said it was essential the patients were thoroughly checked out, especially because of Nanny's age and Ben needing an X-ray.'

Aunt Sophie was the only one moving briskly, everyone else slow and stiff as they began the day. Later, Clay and Emma accepted fresh clothes and the young people gathered round the kitchen table, this time to discuss tactics.

'I still can't really believe we're under threat,' Jenny said. 'I know the attempt to burn Nanny in her bed was real and she was just lucky Ben was with her.'

'And how!' Keith shook his head slowly. 'Whoever had sussed out her home must have done it much earlier when there was no sign of a man about the place.'

'And by the time the arsonist went back to start the fire, Ben was already there and asleep.' Jenny shuddered, disturbed by the possibility of tragedy.

'Annie Martin could have been right about the car.' Keith needed to alert his wife to dangers ahead without causing too much fear. 'I'll call ACC Hinton and set things in motion.'

'What things?' Aunt Sophie demanded to be told. She stood at the kitchen door, dressed for action in cord slacks, a checked wool shirt and a sleeveless fawn windcheater. There was no sign of a bandage above sturdy shoes. 'As of now, I'm fit.'

'If you are going to carry a Purdey round with you all day, I can't imagine anyone daring to argue with you,' Keith said with a wry grin. 'As for what's to happen, Nanny and Ben have to be collected sometime today. It's vital no one is ever on their own, whether they're travelling or staying put. Is that understood?'

Even Clay agreed with a Keith in his strict headmaster mode.

'I'll go and call the ACC now, if you'll excuse me?'

As soon as he rose to leave, Clay stood too. 'Where're you going? Remember, no one to be on their own? While

235

you're talking I won't listen – but I'll damned well watch out for you.'

Keith held his hands up in surrender. 'I'll have my back to the cedar tree.'

'What the hell is going on?' Hinton was impatient but Keith caught an anxious note in the senior man's voice. Clay had kept his promise and stayed alert but at a distance as Keith made his call.

'Arson. Attempted murder. Two potential victims in reasonable health and safe under a police guard in Cheltenham General.'

'On whose orders?'

'Mine. Our friends from across the sea have cleaned out Weston's cash reserves and he's livid, looking for revenge. He may still be using Cracker Devlin.'

Now the ACC was really worried and his breathing quickened. 'See here, Keith, I want you in my office ASAP.'

'Certainly, sir. When there are armed guards inside and outside my aunt's house.'

'What?' exploded in Keith's ear.

He repeated his request. 'It's an isolated house so protection can be given discreetly, but I do need a codeword, sir, so I can be assured any armed personnel who do turn up are from you.' It was necessary for Keith to hold the mobile at a distance as a string of loud expletives shattered the still, damp air and caused Clay to grin from his vantage point in the shelter of a laurel.

'All right,' Hinton said at last when his choler was under control, 'I'll send you my driver. He's qualified and good. Him, you know.'

'Thank you, sir. Major Gifford and I will be on our way as soon as we've handed over.'

'I should think so too! All this blasted cloak and dagger nonsense – it's the bloody CIA,' Keith heard him mutter before the connection was cut.

*   *   *

A shopping list was being concocted, Aunt Sophie examining fridge and cupboards while Emma dutifully took notes.

'We need to stock up, darling,' she informed Keith cheerfully. 'Extra people in the house will be great fun but not if they're starving. And wine, Emma. I leave you young things to choose what you want to drink. Fashions change, you know. At one time all anyone would pour into a glass was Mateus Rosé. Your uncle had no patience with that. "Not a bad wine," he'd say, "but better something with a solid body." He loved a good red,' she added quietly.

Keith explained about the guards.

'Then add another box of tea bags and an extra jar of coffee – and milk, Emma. Poor things, having to hang around here, they'll get desperately thirsty.'

The list complete, Aunt Sophie found them all jobs. 'Best not to sit still imagining,' she had insisted. The drawing-room grate was cleared and the fire laid ready. Dusters and polish appeared as if by magic and were handed to Emma for her to organize helpers. Clay was pointed towards the vacuum cleaner, old-fashioned by his standards and surprising him with its effectiveness. Jenny found herself directed to the flowers. 'Take Keith with you and get some greenery. The secateurs are in the scullery.'

The freedom of the garden was a bonus, the only usable colour a flaring rhododendron, its redness a defiance of the tension in them all.

'Will she mind?' Jenny asked as she held the secateurs to a branch of flower heads.

For a long moment Keith gazed at her as she stood framed by the rich green of the bush's leaves and bursts of scarlet petals. Quite when his thoughts became a prayer he never knew.

'Well?' demanded his wife.

'No, Aunt Sophie won't mind a bit. There'll be more next year.'

By the time their hostess was satisfied with all the efforts made and had insisted some of the rhododendron blooms should grace Nanny's room, two cars screeched to a halt in front of the house.

Keith checked the occupants from the study window. 'It's Hinton's men.'

His comment was not strictly true. Two of the police officers flak-jacketed in navy blue and wearing distinctive caps were women. Young, tough, superbly fit, they carried their weapons as easily as did their male colleagues and a formidable bunch assembled in the hall.

'Just thought I'd let you know we're kosher, sir,' one of the sergeants said to Keith. There was a hint of a smile in the dark eyes.

'The café at the roundabout,' Clay said.

'Thank you, Major Gifford. Mr Hinton said I'd do as a codeword. Sergeant Grant, sir.'

'I'll leave you to deploy your unit as you see fit,' Keith told him, 'but I'd better warn you, Mrs Astley may have ideas of her own.'

'Understood, Inspector. Don't worry, I'm ex-army and I worked under Colonel Astley when I was a rookie.' The smile had become a grin. 'If he trained her like he trained me . . .'

'Don't take it the wrong way, Sergeant Grant, but I hope your journey turns out to have been a wasted one.'

Grant patted the solidity his weapon. 'Don't worry, sir. When we sign these out we always aim to take 'em back unused.'

'You asked for armed support and then you refused an escort here? What the hell are you playing at, Keith?'

'There was no need, sir. Major Gifford carries a side arm.'

ACC Hinton, uniformed and furious, turned on the American. 'Yes – Major Gifford. The same man who promised me no threat on my patch. All he needed was one of my officers to paddle about in a village and the world would be saved! Now what have we got? One man already dead. A house burned out and its two occupants bloody

238

lucky to be alive! Add to that the danger Tyrell and his entire family face and I ask you, Major, what use is your word now?'

'I'm sorry, sir. May I remind you the ultimate danger, away from your patch, as you would have it, was enormous. Thanks to a great deal of work here and elsewhere the threat to thousands of lives has evaporated.'

'As easy as that, was it?'

'No, sir, not easy at all. A helluva lot of experts have been working round the clock. The man known as Weston was our target and his war chest which was to fund terrorism has gone but we do now have a clear idea where the weapons and explosives are sourced. Should other groups find the necessary cash in the future, we're watching.'

'And I must be satisfied with that?'

'I've talked this over with Inspector Tyrell and we've agreed. History tells us new crimes also mean new methods of law enforcement.'

'Bugger history! My duty is the welfare of the people of this county and all I can see ahead is some bloody shoot-out at the OK corral!'

'There is still the GCHQ problem,' Tyrell said quietly, the steadiness of his voice cooling the atmosphere.

The ACC turned to his young colleague, grateful for the interruption. 'Any thoughts on that, Keith?'

'You have said, sir, you'd alerted GCHQ as to the possible source of the leaks and that Gerald Addiscombe, his girlfriend and Petherbridge were all under twenty-four-hour surveillance.'

'Anything else you want?' Hinton asked his DI.

'Getting a tap on Petherbridge's phone would help.'

The ACC's bushy eyebrows climbed high. 'Bug his place?'

'If it can be done without his knowledge but the best bet is probably his car, sir.'

'Right, I'll see to it. Tell me, have you two had breakfast yet?'

Keith and Clay glanced at each other, coffee in the kitchen a distant memory.

'No, sir. We came straight here.'

'Then you're idiots, the pair of you.' Hinton picked up his phone. 'Let's see what the canteen can rustle up – and you'll eat it here where I can keep an eye on the pair of you. Tough day ahead, you need a good bellyful.'

'Nanny! How are you?' Aunt Sophie hurried towards a woman walking slowly, as if unsure where she was going, what she was doing.

'Very well, thank you, madam. They were very good in the hospital but I could do with a proper cup of tea.'

Aunt Sophie would have settled Nanny in the drawing room but she shook her head and made her way shakily towards the kitchen. Pulling a chair close to the Aga she put her hands on its rail, warming them. Nanny was only prepared to lean back against the generous curves of a Windsor armchair when her shivering eased.

'Was it cold in the car?'

'Not really, madam, but the way Mrs Gifford drives!'

Emma and Jenny came into the welcome of the kitchen in time to hear the comment. Jenny's laughter was a cheerful, hopeful sound as it lightened the atmosphere.

'I'm glad it's not just me who thinks so, Nanny,' she said. 'Keith tells me Emma's a fine driver – proper training for speed chases and all that.'

'All very well, I'm sure,' the old lady said, her mouth primed by disapproval, 'but I'll be glad when my stomach catches up with me.'

Emma took the raillery in good part. She had driven as was necessary to get people at risk into the safety of a house under armed protection. 'Mollie,' she called. 'Tea!'

'Come and sit by me, dear,' Nanny invited the uniformed policewoman when she came into the kitchen. 'You could do with a bit of a warm, I'm sure.'

'Oh, I'm fine, thank you, Mrs Bowler.'

'Then you've got strong nerves, my girl.'

'They've always been necessary here, Nanny,' Aunt Sophie said with a smile. 'Remember when the boys decided to be commandos?'

'That I do! Charging up behind you when you were carrying something hot and screaming like little banshees – whatever they are. Then there was the black shoe polish they smothered on themselves. Never thought we'd get it out of their hair, let alone their clothes.'

'That was one of my sons' more reasonable interludes,' Mrs Astley told the policewoman. 'When do you go back for Ben?'

'A call from the hospital will let us know when he's ready.'

'And the three of you repeat the journey?'

Mollie Armstrong nodded, keeping to herself the need to vary routes there and back. Explanations might be expected and this was not the time.

'Mrs Gifford driving?' Nanny asked.

''Fraid so, Nanny,' Emma said and grinned.

The old woman sighed. 'Thank God for seat belts!'

Looking refreshed by the break and by the food ACC Hinton had ordered for them, Keith and Clay began reading copies of reports which had been delivered. Their host answered a call on his internal phone.

'Last night's surveillance paid off,' Gifford said and Tyrell agreed as the ACC replaced the phone.

Hinton studied a sheet of paper. 'I see Addiscombe went straight from his office to a flat in a nearby block. Went up to the second floor and let himself in with his own key.'

'The flat was rented by a Ms Mavis Young,' Tyrell said, reminding the ACC of work already done, 'and we know she's a decoder at GCHQ.' Tyrell looked up from his papers. 'Any idea which section yet?'

With eyebrows raised at the silent phone, Hinton's mouth tightened. 'That's what that was all about. This Mavis Young deals with foreign trade, Middle East variety. Specifically, oil. God, what a mess!' The big man got up and prowled his office like an angry bull elephant. 'You do realize it's out of our hands now? We'll have your people crawling out of the woodwork, Major, not to mention every press secretary ever spawned by Whitehall and Downing Street. Spin doctors? The buggers'll have us in orbit!'

Clay Gifford stood and intercepted the ACC. 'I don't think you understand, sir.'

'Not understand? Of course I do! The Chief – and me – will have to account publicly for American secret agents running free over half the county in an operation every tabloid hack'll drool over as soon as he gets his teeth into it. And us.'

'No, sir.'

Gifford stood his ground. Like Keith Tyrell he was dressed in casual slacks and sweater. His hair might be longer than when Hinton first met him but there was no mistaking the Westpoint man standing resolute in the ACC's path. Hinton sensed there could be a way out of his predicament and Keith Tyrell steepled his fingers, thinking rapidly as he prepared to listen.

'Well?' The ACC waited.

'I guess last night's report also stated there was an accountant's premises on the ground floor of Mavis Young's apartment building?'

'Yes,' Hinton agreed. 'Used by Petherbridge.'

'Who's already been associated with Paul Giles and blackmail,' Clay reminded him.

The ACC groaned and closed his eyes. He thought of a bottle of smooth malt in a desk drawer, accepting that it would be a long, hard day before he could sip a few mouthfuls and relax. 'If you're right, the pair of you, I suppose it'll mean every MI branch in existence invading us – not to mention your bloody FBI – or is it CIA?' he growled at the major.

'I'll try and keep them away from you, sir,' Clay soothed. 'Let your own government people go for this woman and her boyfriend. If they also pull in Petherbridge it's still only a matter for you Brits.'

'There's also the murder of Paul Giles to be dealt with,' Keith reminded him.

Gifford shook his head. 'Have you one piece of evidence to link him to Petherbridge? Even if you could prove Giles was his personal repairman, I'd guess the same could be said of dozens of respectable men and women living in Cheltenham.'

Hinton gazed at the photo of his wife on his desk, then at a snapshot of his grandchildren. 'Bet the bastard had the black on half of them as well,' he said morosely.

'Unless there's a hard drive or two left, all proof's gone up in smoke,' Gifford reminded him.

It was not the moment to become philosophical, the ACC decided. 'So, you believe if this Addiscombe wets himself and talks, he'll implicate Petherbridge and we can get that smug bastard on a charge of blackmail?'

'Yes, sir. Once in custody, Petherbridge can be approached and offers made,' Gifford suggested.

Tyrell's features seemed carved from stone. 'Such as being removed to a comfortable billet as long as he details everything he knows about the Weston operation?'

'What's this about the Westons?' Hinton wanted to know.

'With their US money gone, they've been neutralized,' Clay assured him. 'Add to that their new life on your patch has been blown, thanks to Paul Giles's attempt at extortion. There's little doubt they'll be on the move.'

'Where to?'

'Well away from your jurisdiction, Mr Hinton. Forget them as though they've ceased to exist. As for Petherbridge, he won't want to be linked with the present fiasco involving the Westons and can be persuaded to sing.'

'But for how long?' Keith asked.

'Hey!' Hinton had caught an odd timbre in his inspector's voice. 'What d'you say, Keith? Why not?'

'I'm right, aren't I?' Keith asked Clay.

Broad shoulders lifted and dropped. 'It's the way of their world.'

The ACC watched the two young men hold each other's

243

gaze. There was a strong undercurrent of emotion, tension. 'Keith! What's this mean?'

Tyrell's attention swung back to his senior officer. 'It won't take long before there's a whisper Petherbridge is talking. A contract will be taken out on him and he'll be silenced. Permanently,' he explained, 'even if he's in a high-security prison.'

Hinton banged his fist hard on the desk and glared first at his subordinate and then at a now not so welcome guest. 'The Westons are to be "neutralized" as you call it, Major, then Petherbridge is to be set up for a contract? And that's that?'

Keith was aware of exhaustion eroding his reactions. 'Not quite, sir. There's the assassin Weston hired.'

The big man was still, his eyes suddenly shrewd, wary. 'This chap Cracker?'

'Yes, sir, Michael Devlin. I assume he's been paid part of his fee to carry out Weston's revenge on Giles. He's also had a go at Mrs Bowler and may not know yet it was unsuccessful, so he'll want the cash for that as well. Petherbridge is probably the paymaster who still has funds for unlimited revenge and Cracker Devlin needs his reputation. He'll want to be paid before Petherbridge is out of his reach.'

Hinton threw up his hands. 'That's all we need! Some gung-ho murderer on the loose and in a hurry!'

Keith was angry. 'I'm sorry, sir, but my immediate concern is my wife and Mrs Gifford. They were to collect Mrs Bowler and Ben Hadley from the hospital when they're discharged. Mrs Bowler's been released. The girls have taken her to Bowman's and they'll return for Ben.'

'They've accepted an armed escort?'

'Yes, sir. No problem.'

'Thank God for that. Now, let's have an early lunch.'

'I told you, no interruptions!'

ACC Hinton's mood had not improved as the day progressed. He had been aware of a coolness between the two younger men. Something had come between them, perhaps not an event but an attitude, a difference of opinion which could not easily be resolved. Whatever the reason the unwanted call gave them all breathing space.

'How urgent?'

Keith saw the ACC's body turn away, the head and shoulders hunch as if to hide them from the phone and its message. The man's stillness and Keith's tension alerted Clay.

Hinton replaced the phone slowly and, straightening up as if going into battle, he faced them. 'I'm sorry,' he said slowly. 'Sergeant Armstrong was with Jenny and Emma. Difficulty parking at the hospital – wrong time of day. Armstrong offered to take over the wheel and drive them to the main entrance so they only had to walk in. As she drove away . . .'

'Tell us,' Keith demanded.

'A car accelerated. All Armstrong could see was through the rear view mirror. The driver made straight for Jenny. Emma looked as if she was screaming a warning, then she threw herself at Jenny to push her out of the way.'

The muscles of Clay Gifford's face were so tense he was white. 'Are they dead?'

Hinton looked from the American to Tyrell. 'I don't know. Armstrong did what she could at the scene and hospital staff arrived immediately. Both girls were still alive when they were admitted.'

Chapter Fourteen

A young policewoman, gun at the ready, stood guard as doctors and nurses moved quickly and with quiet efficiency.

'Sergeant Armstrong!'

Mollie Armstrong straightened up, ready for a reprimand from ACC Hinton.

'Are you OK?' he asked, his eyes raking her for signs of injury or distress.

'Yes, thank you, sir.'

'So what happened?'

'I'm sorry, sir. I couldn't do anything to stop it.' Mollie was a tough young lady but she could not prevent her voice wobbling. A sniff helped.

'No one can,' Hinton assured her. 'We're mixed up with some pretty deadly characters.'

'But why Mrs Tyrell? It was certainly at her the driver aimed the car.'

'Make of vehicle?'

'BMW. Old model but it sounded supercharged. It was the noise drew my attention.'

'Driver?'

'IC1 male, forties, short dark hair. His face was partly obscured by his jacket collar.'

'When you've done an identikit and started it circulating, go back to your desk and get a statement written up. Everything, mind, starting from when you first left Laverton this morning. Any detail, however small, I want to know – and make sure you have a strong cup of tea first.'

The kindness in the last remark was Mollie's undoing and she fled to the privacy of the nearest hospital toilet to let tears flow. Hinton guessed where his young sergeant had gone but he wasted no more time on the girl, barking orders into his mobile at high speed. Communications ended, he searched for Keith Tyrell.

'Where's Gifford?'

Tyrell stood and straightened muscles aching with tension. Whatever it cost him, he presented his usual calm expression as if in full control of his emotions. 'He was in casualty, sir, but Emma's probably been taken for a CT scan before going to theatre.'

'That bad?'

''Fraid so. Cracked ribs at least. The A and E woman was worried about rib damage affecting the spleen – and then there's the head injury. No one's said subdural haematoma yet but only because they've guessed Clay and I would know what that means.'

'She's still unconscious?'

'Yes, sir. In a way it's helping Clay to know she can't be aware of pain.'

'Jenny?'

The inspector silently drew a deep, thankful breath. 'Possible fractured collar bone, damage to both wrists. She's waiting for X-rays. There might be a black eye in time so I could be needing you as an alibi, sir, in case some idiot thinks I was responsible.'

It was a faint glimmer of humour but Hinton was glad to see it. 'Where can we get a cup of something hot here?' he asked.

'There are machines but the WRVS have a canteen. Proper cups and saucers,' Tyrell said with an attempt at a grin. He allowed himself to be led away in the direction of clinking crockery, the ACC indicating a quiet corner where Tyrell was to sit.

Exerting his formidable charm on the ladies at the counter Hinton returned with a large pot, milk and a bowl of sugar, making Keith drink two cups of tea before the senior man was ready to talk. It gave Tyrell the chance to

247

collect his wits, wisps of panic, memories, information, all becoming organized as he obediently drank his hot, sweet tea under the stern gaze of the ACC.

When he and Clay had heard the grim news in Hinton's office, they had raced for the stairs, aware of a voice booming behind them. The ACC was ordering his car brought round immediately and a driver who could put his foot down. Reaching the outside of the building Tyrell had seen the gleaming limousine drawing up but Hinton was not prepared to wait for a suitably qualified driver. He had shoved a mechanic out of the way and dropped into the driving seat, taking the first corner at speed and leaving his passengers to worry about their seat belts. Once at the hospital Hinton released the younger men at the main door, going himself to find any witnesses to the accident and questioning them intensively.

'Was it Devlin?' Tyrell asked the ACC.

'Probably. The description young Armstrong gave fits and I've asked for her to see mugshots after she's completed the identikit.' Hinton saw Keith about to ask a question. 'No, I never mentioned the bastard's name. I'll not have any smarmy lawyer catch me out on that one but I did make sure Devlin's face is to be included.'

'He really does work on the spur of the moment – given half a chance,' Tyrell said quietly.

Hinton sighed and rubbed strain from his face. 'I'll bet those women were followed from Laverton on both journeys. Second time around he saw Emma couldn't find a parking space, watched Armstrong taking over, slip into the driving seat, and guessed what would happen. When she dropped the girls at the main door Armstrong thought they were safe but he was revved up and ready.'

'Yes, Devlin was ready to kill my wife.' Tyrell's words could barely be heard but there was no mistaking his cold fury.

'Come on, lad. You've got to be positive. Jenny will be back with you before you know it.'

'And Emma?' Keith had caught a glimpse of her on a trolley, a limp, beautiful, battered child.

'It was her instinctive reaction, her training, to get the intended victim out of the way. She's given you Jenny. Make the most of it when you get your wife home.'

'Is that wise? It was being with me gave Weston the idea she had to die.'

'Think, Keith. Is that strictly true?' Hinton said and waited while he endured Tyrell's angry glare. 'The others – this Mrs Bowler, for instance. I assume she was Weston's first choice?'

The DI nodded.

'It was a good attempt but it failed to kill her. Devlin needed at least one body to get paid so it's clear anyone vulnerable would be the next on his list. You made sure there was protection for Mrs Bowler and your friend –'

'Ben Hadley.'

'Both of them under guard as soon as they reached the hospital? You knew the score already. This hit man wanted any easy target, he didn't care who it was. From what I've learned from witnesses, Emma was already going up the steps when Devlin aimed for Jenny.'

'So, had it been the other way round . . .'

'Emma would have been in his sights.'

Emma was so still and small. Tyrell swallowed hard. 'And Jenny would be lying there as good as dead.'

'Which she is not,' Hinton said briskly, cuffing his DI with a friendly hand. 'Go and see Jenny. When she can get out of here, let her stay at your aunt's place. We can keep the armed squad there so they'll all be safe,' he said and put a gentler hand on the younger man's shoulder.

Tyrell shook his head. 'There's no safety for any of us as long as Weston and Devlin still breathe.'

Jenny was motionless, pale. 'Emma?'

Keith searched her face for hopeful signs. Eyes clear and alert, even if the skin round one had a tinge of purple, ready to develop into a real shiner. The lump at the side of Jenny's forehead was covered by gauze and tape, the graze on her chin had been cleansed and smelled of an antiseptic lotion. The only real damage the doctors had found was a cracked clavicle. A sling and a pillow held her collar bone immobile and he smiled at her as she managed to make her bandaged wrists look like a new fashion.

He ran a gentle finger along her free arm, hardly daring to touch her. 'I haven't seen Emma yet. The medics are doing a long list of tests.'

'Has she been conscious at all?' Jenny asked and Keith knew she was fearing the reply.

'No. I think Clay's quite relieved she can feel nothing as yet, although he's waiting for her to wake up and give him a row for something or other.' He reached for Jenny's nearest hand and squeezed it gently. Because of her training and experience with damaged brains Jenny knew only too well the lasting traumas which could be caused by a warm, living body being tossed high in the air and then sprawled head first on to concrete.

'Tell Clay to keep talking to her,' she advised. 'It's possible she'll know what he's saying, even if there's no apparent response – and ask if the hospital has a smell kit. Sometimes it works wonders.'

'Of course, darling. Now, you have to let the painkillers work and get some sleep.'

He felt pressure increase on his fingers. 'Don't leave me,' was a whisper.

Keith lifted Jenny's fingers and kissed them. 'If I get up from this chair I'll have to write an interminable report. I'm just thankful you've got me out of doing it.'

In silence they waited for the analgesic to work, disturbed at regular intervals by nurses checking pulse rate and evenness of breathing in the patient. Only when Jenny was asleep did Keith make his way to the intensive care ward and Clay sitting immobile in the waiting area. He shocked Keith by the dead greyness of his eyes as he raised his head.

'Now do you believe me? You and I, we were the ones chasing Weston but who does he try to have killed? The ones we care for. I'm sorry, Keith, but your idea of justice doesn't work with men like that evil bastard.'

Keith saw anger had livened Clay, sharpening his features into harsh determination. 'Weston's out of it, so's his son,' he told him. 'Hinton was sent a message half an hour ago. A light plane was seen to go down in the Channel about midday, on its way to France. Markings identified it as Weston's. It's taken time to trace the flight back to where it started – a private airstrip in Kent. Three people boarded the plane there this morning.'

Clay closed his eyes and leaned back against the discomfort of a plastic and metal chair. 'Good. It's taken all of them. Their driver was a qualified pilot.' There was no element of surprise in his voice or his body.

'You knew they'd go down?'

'It was an option, a laser designed to knock out the electrical system.'

'Just one way of exterminating them?' Keith asked, his antipathy adding a chill to the atmosphere.

'I prefer neutralizing them,' Clay told him. 'Don't forget, they were all killers wanted for a dozen or more murders and that's just in the past – nothing to what they planned for the future. You've got to face facts, Keith. Before Weston went he'd have known he was stripped of all his cash and I'll bet he was good and mad, looking to take it out on someone, but who could he hit? Faceless hackers in the States who'd killed his plans? No, we were all he could see. He was leaving so he put out contracts on us, with Petherbridge to settle the bills.' The American leaned forward, resting his elbows on his knees as he gazed unseeingly at the floor. 'Weston's long been one of the hard core of the Miami families and his foot soldiers don't fail and go away. They either die for it or complete the contract. Devlin'll be back.'

Keith returned to Jenny. She slept peacefully, drugs holding back recent horrors. A sympathetic nurse brought a spare pillow and a blanket, allowing Keith to doze away the hours as best he could. At four in the morning Jenny stirred a little, moved towards her damaged side and whimpered with pain. He helped the nurse ease his wife to comfort and, when she was still once more, went in search of Clay.

The police officer outside the intensive care ward was a stranger but he recognized Keith. 'Mrs Tyrell, sir?'

'Sleeping. She should be home in a day or two. Anything happening here?'

The man was not much older than the DI, slightly built for his height but case-hardened and concerned. 'I've worked with Emma – Mrs Gifford. It's terrible seeing her like she is now.'

'Has there been any change at all?'

The officer shook his head. 'Nothing. Her husband just sits there talking. I know one of the nurses and asked her what was going on. She mentioned swelling of the brain. If it is, all that can be done is wait and see. At least Emma came through the op OK – they took her spleen away around midnight. Amazing how quick it was.'

'You went down to theatre with her?'

'Of course, sir. "At all times," Mr Hinton said. No one'll get to Emma through me.'

Keith could see it was no idle boast as the man tightened his grip on the firearm he held at the ready.

The senior nurse was at first annoyed at his intrusion into her ward but Keith's warrant card and explanation placated her. She pointed to a dimly lit bed in a corner. The patient was connected by wires and tubes to machines and drips, her husband bent over her. He was speaking in a calm, cheerful voice, too low for the words to be shared with others, but there was a roughness in his throat as the hours he had endured took their toll.

Keith stood beside the bed and waited. After what seemed like an eternity Clay became aware he was there and turned. In a matter of hours the American had become aged, haggard, his eyes sunken in their sockets.

'They say Emma can hear me.' It was a man desperate for reassurance who had spoken.

'I'm sure she can. Jenny thought it would be so.'

With difficulty, Clay focused on something outside the pool of light around Emma. 'Jenny. How is she?'

'Sleeping.'

'When can she go home?'

'A couple of days, perhaps.'

'When it's safe?' Clay asked, his voice harsh, cynical. He laid his head on the bed beside Emma and despair flooded him. Keith caught hold of his friend's shoulders and made him sit upright. In time a tremor went through the American and he stiffened, became alert, then lifted his chin. 'It's all my fault.'

Keith still held him and he shook Clay firmly. 'Don't talk like that! You've only ever done what was necessary to save lives. Emma, Jenny, they're not down to you.'

'No?' Clay lifted Emma's hand, ignoring the needle tissuing out of her skin and depriving her of intravenous liquid. 'This was all set in motion when I had the bright idea of using you because you understood villagers and knew the area well. Without you we'd have persevered and taken a risk Weston was the right man.'

'Stop it, Clay. You're tired and you're wallowing. Who do you think you are to take all the blame?' Keith demanded indignantly. 'Your plan was spot on. After a few days with Aunt Sophie you'd have had from us all you needed and we'd have gone back home leaving the three villages to their dreaming. CIA hackers would have cancelled Weston's cash and stopped the terrorists. Then, far away from home one day, there'd have been a fatal accident for the so-called Westons, nothing to upset any of the villagers for long, and that corner of the county would have remained untouched.'

The American was listening, his eyes increasingly sharp, focused, as the combination of Keith's reasoning and the undertone of authority in his quiet, deep voice made inroads of reality into confusion.

'You knew nothing of Paul Giles but Weston decided he must die. Why? Because he was a blackmailer or because he was an inconvenience? So close to Weston's big day and

253

suddenly, it's all threatened. He reverts to type and calls in expert help, Giles's death to occur when he and Pether-bridge have perfect and very public alibis.'

'Yeah, us!' The brief flare of anger gave Clay more colour in his skin. 'I suppose you're right.'

'Then Nanny Bowler had to die.'

Clay frowned but Keith was not so concerned. It was the expression of a man concentrating on issues other than the damage done to Emma.

'His old way of life in New York and Miami would have been founded on revenge so the people he saw as the instruments of his defeat over here had to be killed. First Giles, then Nanny. With her gone, any of us became fair game to him.'

'We were in your HQ with Hinton. Cracker couldn't get to us,' Clay said quietly, 'which is why the hired help went after Emma and Jenny.'

'And they were well protected until hospital parking problems gave Cracker Devlin a chance.'

A nurse came to check her patient and shooed them away while she replaced the needle carrying the drip. Clay would not leave the ward, standing by the door until Keith held his elbow in a firm grip. 'Go and have a hot drink – get some rest. If you can, get a shave.'

Clay would have protested but Keith glared at him.

'Do you want to graze Emma's skin off her with your beard?'

It was nearly a smile which fought the lines newly graven in Clay's cheeks. 'I hear you but I have to keep talking to her.'

'Then I'll stay until you get back – refreshed. Go on,' he urged as his friend hesitated. 'She's used to my voice. I can give her orders and, for once, she won't be in a position to argue.'

'I wish to God she were,' Clay said with great force but he stayed at the door until he saw Keith sitting by Emma and giving her news of all her old colleagues back in

Lydney. The American was satisfied, enough for him to go in search of hot coffee and somewhere flat to lie down.

'Keith! Glad I've caught you.'

Splashing his face with cold water in a hospital bathroom had helped Keith realize it was morning but he was not ready for a session with ACC Hinton. 'Sir?'

'The Chief Constable's gone up to see Mrs Gifford. He'll spend some time with the major and then he'll be down to see you and your wife. How is she, by the way?'

'Better for a good sleep, sir.'

'And Emma Gifford?'

'Stable. It's all any of the medical staff will say. I saw no change while I was with her but she seems to have a little more colour now the transfusions have replaced blood lost by the ruptured spleen. Thank God she's no worse.'

Hinton could not hide his concern. 'It shouldn't have happened but this Cracker Devlin, if it is him, he's living up to his reputation.'

A porter hurried a trolley past them and two nurses, one large and fair, the other small and Asian, walked more slowly, comparing the advantages of two of the town's bars.

'This is no place to talk,' Hinton decided. 'My office, Keith. Soon as you can. I've the Chief's say-so for anything we need to clear up this mess. Firstly, we've kept the security tight at your aunt's house. Then, as you've seen for yourself, the guards here in the hospital for Emma Gifford and your good lady are armed and will stay that way.'

Keith watched the ACC stride away and realized there was only one person Cracker Devlin could target who was soon to leave the safety of the hospital and would no longer be under the protection of firepower.

Himself.

News of no worsening in Emma's condition had raised

Jenny's spirits. Better than most, she knew the fierce fight which could be waged by an unconscious body and mind. Time might be needed but there was always hope and there was always prayer. Jenny was a great believer in both so when she was washed and had been fed an obligatory painkiller, she was more cheerful as the breakfast trolley made its round.

'Do you know, I'm almost hungry,' she decided.

'Full English, madam?' Keith teased and was ridiculously pleased by her reaction, helping her with a bowl of porridge and a boiled egg which would have been better sliced and in a salad. She was enjoying a cup of tea when a disturbance at the ward's entrance had her smiling with delight. Keith turned and saw Jenny's parents hurrying between the beds. He welcomed them, found chairs, cajoled cups of tea and willingly acceded to their request he go and get some rest.

'I do have to go to HQ,' Keith admitted, 'but I'll be back as soon as I can.'

'Nonsense!' Jenny's mother was so like her. 'You've been up all night and there'll be a lot for you to do – catching the maniac who put our girl here, for instance. You can have her all to yourself when she's well again. Until then, let us do what we can to help. Please?'

He heard the pathos of a concerned mother and smiled at her. 'She's all yours, but don't blame me when she starts telling you what to do.'

'Mr Hinton has a visitor but you are expected,' Tyrell was told by the ACC's secretary.

He walked the short distance, becoming aware almost instantly of an almighty row.

'No, I won't have it!' was bellowed by Hinton and clearly heard through the thickness of the door. 'The risk is far too great!'

A quieter voice calmed, persuaded. Tyrell guessed the speaker's words were clipped, precise, but he could not make out what the man was saying.

'Of course it is! It's what we all want but I will not willingly sacrifice any of my officers – even if you call in God Almighty to back you up. You've bloody nearly done that already.'

The battle wore on, Tyrell waiting until there was at least a temporary lull before he knocked on the door. Eventually, he risked it and a barked 'Come in' from the ACC sounded almost relieved. Both men stood as he entered, Hinton red-faced, his curls loosened by his temper and his pounding of the desk. The DI's first impression of the other man was of a skinny farmer in a wax jacket and corduroys, the red in his cropped hair paled by grey.

'Keith, this is –' the ACC began.

'Greg Sinclair. I'm glad to meet you, Inspector. I've heard well of you.'

Almost accentless, Tyrell decided, but the Scottish highlands were there in the rolled 'r's. He received a firm handshake and a penetrating gaze from shrewd blue eyes.

'Now, Inspector Tyrell, I gather you and I share a difficult problem.'

Keith stiffened. Here it was again. 'Good work, young man, and I've come to take over.' Sinclair saw Tyrell's reaction, read his thoughts and smiled.

'No, I'm not here to ride roughshod. I was hoping you and I could work together towards a solution.'

The DI glanced at Hinton and saw a man helpless in the face of overwhelming influence.

'Your unit, sir?' he asked Sinclair.

'Of no matter at the moment – your Mr Hinton has dealt with all that. You see, when questions first began to be asked in the present investigation into the death of this man, Giles, I was alerted. Cracker Devlin has been a particular pain in the ass – and worse – for some years now. I want him, Tyrell.' The quiet countryman had hardened. 'You and yours are in his sights. Knowing Cracker as I do that will be unfair and very unpleasant since he carries death with him wherever he goes. I've been tracking him almost from the start of his career but, whatever's been

tried, the man's as slippery as an eel. It wasn't so when he
first took a life but he knew the woods and hills around
Dundalk and the people there understood they had to
keep him sweet or be added to his list.'

'So he was IRA?'

'Yes and no. He's always been his own man, lending
himself to any cause which lets him kill. Nowadays, he
waits for profitable reasons. Because of your success in
spotting the Westons, you and your friend, Major Gifford,
have potentially put money in his pocket but I think
you've also realized it doesn't have to be you, personally.
Your wives would do in helping to turn in a fat fee for
him.'

'You're giving a classic description of a psychopath.'

'Which he is, of course. Plausible, presentable – and
deadly. He can kill on a whim and he has no patience. A
young mother with three children in her car, pushed off
the road and into a swollen river because she was in his
way. That was in Scotland.' Sinclair's anger was deep,
festering, and he took a few seconds' respite. 'When he
takes on a contract he will give himself time to plan,' he
continued, 'but Cracker's always preferred to go for the
unguarded moment. He sees a family member, a child
even, as a weakness of the target and, for him, fair game.
Devlin's been thoroughly researched as well as investigated, I can assure you. By my reckoning there are at least
twenty-three murders I am one hundred per cent certain
are down to Cracker Devlin.'

'If you're so sure you have evidence, why no trials? No
convictions?'

'His alibi always holds good. Witnesses seeing him on
the cliffs when a murder is being committed hundreds of
miles away? They're good people, honest, and can't be
shaken.' Sinclair stood and stretched his neck, Tyrell seeing
a man who kept himself very fit indeed. 'I've always
hoped that one day I could make that damned alibi work
in my favour but so far I'm out of luck.' The Scotsman
leaned on Hinton's desk, concentrating his attention on the
DI. 'I have to have him, Tyrell.'

There was silence in the sprawl of the big office with its imposing furniture. Keith was remembering Jenny as he had last seen her, Emma silent and helpless. Would his parents ever be free of Cracker's shadow? Aunt Sophie? The list seemed endless.

'Will you help me, Inspector?' Sinclair asked, his question quiet, undemanding.

Tyrell thought of the need for armed guards, the constant care taken to ensure not one of his family, nor of Clay's, was left unprotected. He guessed what was being asked of him, knowing it was the only way to free Jenny.

'Let's make it soon,' he said and heard Hinton stifle a despairing groan.

The road westward from HQ was busy and passing headlights flicked at his eyes with monotonous regularity. Irritated by motorbikes roaring past and cutting in front of him, Keith concentrated by going over every detail which had been decided and rehearsed. It was essential that not the slightest possibility had been overlooked. Despite the ACC's initial objections, he had thrown himself into preparations which would help his young DI.

Joan Leggatt had been contacted in Lydney and told a little of what was happening. With Mickey and Rose she had driven to the Tyrells' home to check everything was ready for Jenny's parents to stay there. Brian Clarke had gone along with the DCI for the ride and Keith smiled as he imagined him sitting beside her as she drove, the side arm with which he had been issued easily reached but discreetly hidden. Keith guessed Brian had been the first to go into the house and check each room. As for Jenny's parents, they were safely installed at Bowman's, enjoying Aunt Sophie's company, Nanny's cooking and the safety provided by Sergeants Grant and Armstrong.

The turn off the A48 was reached and manoeuvred almost by habit, although he had to wait for another annoying motorcyclist intent on overtaking. As Keith drove slowly up the lane, then along the drive to his home, he was on edge, missing nothing the headlights illuminated. Security lights switched on automatically as he approached the house and, as far as he could see, everything was as he had left it such a short time ago, when he went with Jenny to help Clay on his hunt. Keith steadied himself, drew a deep breath, got out of the car and locked it as he gave a very good imitation of normality.

No one had been in the house. As planned, fine lines of an unobtrusive powder had been laid in an agreed pattern and none had been disturbed. Air held too long in Keith's lungs was released, and after closing all the ground-floor curtains he relaxed in the warmth of the kitchen. It was tempting to switch on the radio or play a soothing CD but he knew he needed silence.

The pine chairs around the kitchen table were the best bet, Keith decided. He had slept little in the last few days and comfort would be his undoing. An unpleasant fact to be faced was that this agonizing tension could go on indefinitely. Days, weeks, could pass before Devlin rose to Keith's bait and the idea of this tension stretching on interminably added to his exhaustion.

In spite of his apprehension, Keith's concentration was beginning to slide away and he dozed off. Waking with a start he had no idea if he had slept for a minute or an hour and sat in the silence of the kitchen, every nerve and muscle expectant as he tried to understand what had disturbed him.

There was a sound, faint at first, then louder, and he tried to identify it. The shed door was banging and Keith felt adrenalin begin to course. It was a clear, cold night and there had been no wind when he came into the house. Sinclair had talked of Devlin's nature, the assassin unwilling to waste time in a game of cat and mouse. Cracker Devlin was out there, Keith was certain, and he was relieved. The final act was to be played out, one way or another.

The banging became louder, more determined, and Keith checked again in his memory what he had been told to do. When he was ready, he hefted the long, heavy-headed torch with which he had been provided and went out, closing the front door behind him. The banging had stopped by this time but it had fulfilled its purpose. He was outside, alone and supposedly curious.

With firm strides, Keith made for the lean-to shed at the side of the garage. He had only just left the circle of light from the outside security lamp when there was a rush of sound and air and his head was in a vice of hands with steel-like fingers.

Shock lasted for a split second, then Keith immediately hunched his shoulders as he had spent the day being trained to do. He focused his efforts on the torch, holding it by the end furthest from the bulb, always aware of fingers trying to tighten in a grip which would ensure his neck fractured. Breathing was difficult but with one hand he reached for his attacker's head. His fingertips slipped over short, coarse hair. Surprise took another second from him. He had expected a crash helmet.

There was no time for more but still he waited until, as if in a fog, Keith moved with what felt like slow, robotic jerks. Both his hands met around the base of the torch. Senses were ebbing, co-ordination becoming loose, uncontrollable. Only his willpower demanded action and the weight of the torch head moved upwards in one almighty swing. Dimly, he heard it crunch on to defenceless bone and brain.

With his eyes on fire and his lungs aching for air, Keith was aware the strangling fingers had gone. There were noises and he sensed he was being carried. A ghastly sound puzzled him and he realized it was his own breathing, air being sucked in by convulsive movements. His neck was agony but the worst of the pressure had gone and as the gyrating cosmos steadied, noise became voices, quiet and purposeful.

Lights hurt his eyes. There was a different kind of movement, then comfort and a familiar smell. Keith knew he was being stretched out on the couch in his own home. He sighed with relief and heard someone groaning, realizing after a while the peculiar noises were coming from his mouth. It was quite a shock and he forced himself to sit up.

'Stay there, Inspector Tyrell,' a woman said as she pushed him back against the cushions and carried on cutting away his high-necked sweater.

'No! Present from Jenny,' he struggled to say and found it hard to speak, managing only a hoarse whisper.

'Then you can get another one and she'll never know,' the voice said calmly as the last shreds of cashmere were pulled from him.

'Much damage, Captain?' another voice asked and Keith thought he had heard it before.

'No, sir. The special vest's still intact although the neck area is twisted out of shape but it worked well. It's the extreme distortion which is causing constriction of breathing but I'll have it off in a second.'

She was as good as her word and the steel-meshed kit with which Keith had been fitted was unstrapped and lifted away. Normal air exchange was resumed and the tightness in his throat eased. Fingers prodded him but these were searching, feeling along bones and into joints, squeezing muscles and soft tissues. A shirt was wrapped around him and buttoned, then he was helped into a fleece jacket.

'A bit battered, sir, but in one piece,' the woman decided. 'He'll be functional again quite quickly but real improvement will be seen after a good rest. The inspector will need some physio to be on the safe side.'

'Thank you, Captain. You'd better go and see the cargo's ready for transit.'

'Yes, sir.' There was a quick grasp of Tyrell's shoulder. 'Well done, Inspector,' and she was gone.

Keith was left alone and he stretched carefully, twinges here and there in muscles and nerves causing him to frown. The light changed and he looked up, focusing slowly. A man stood in front of him, familiar and yet strange in a uniform Keith did not recognize.

'And you, you bloody fool,' Sinclair began, 'why did you wait so long before you hit the bastard?'

Thoughts took an age. 'I had to be sure,' he croaked at last.

'Sure? Sure of what?'

'He really meant to kill me,' emerged as a whisper as Keith found it easier that way.

Sinclair cursed, quietly, fluently, impressing Keith with his command of the English language. 'Huh! Any more sure and you'd be having this conversation with St Peter! As it is you were bloody close to being twenty-fourth on my list.'

Someone loomed close. Another uniform. 'Colonel, eight minutes to the meet and there's a wind getting up.'

'Everything squared away?'

'Yes, sir. No trouble finding the machine and helmet. They were where you predicted. Loading's complete.'

'Are the locals here yet?'

'Yes, sir, at the gate and getting restless.'

'Let them through as soon as the first transport vehicle's off site.'

'Sir.'

'I'll be there,' Sinclair said.

A door closed after the figure disappeared and Keith was aware of Sinclair's scrutiny. 'Glad to have worked with you, Keith, although you didn't obey orders as I'd have liked. Still, there was no hesitation where your wife was concerned, only when your damned principles had to be satisfied – suppose I can't fault you for that. Take it easy, now. If I were ACC Hinton I'd give you a week's leave but he's mad as hell at the pair of us.'

Keith tried a smile and his muscles almost made it. He shook the hand offered, then Sinclair was gone and Keith was alone. The stillness, the silence, were at once causes of apprehension and of peace yet he imagined he heard voices before the front door closed and then someone speaking quietly. The illusion caused beads of sweat to erupt all over his body.

'Keith?'

The voice of a friend brought with it an enormous sense of relief but he could not move easily to greet him. 'Brian!' He felt the sweat begin to cool on his forehead. 'Thank God,' he whispered.

'DCI Leggatt's with me. Your army buddies had us waiting out of sight so we haven't the faintest idea what the hell you've been up to. As they were leaving a very nice young lady stopped and said you'd need a hot drink – even told me what to get for you,' Brian said. 'Stay put and I'll bring it.'

'It's all over, Keith,' Joan Leggatt assured him.

He had tried to get to his feet when he first knew she was in the room but she had gently pushed him back against the cushions and kept her hand on his shoulder. He was not sure which of them was being reassured.

'Jenny?'

'Sleeping. I rang Mr Hinton and the hospital as soon as Colonel Sinclair had finished with you.'

'Emma?'

'I heard earlier. There's no real change but her breathing is better and one nurse thought she saw Mrs Gifford's eyelids flicker for a moment.' The DCI moved to sit near Keith and watch him but she seemed to understand his need and was silent.

He heard a cupboard door in the kitchen being opened and closed, the kettle coming to the boil and then there was vigorous stirring. Keith tried swallowing. It hurt and he decided to leave the exercise until later. Aware of Brian's return, he accepted it with relief.

'Right now, final ingredient.' From the drinks tray Brian lifted a bottle and generously splashed a measure into a steaming mug.

'That's my best malt!' Keith tried to protest, only managing a grating sound.

'So? Now's the time to enjoy it.'

The scent of lemons was in his nose and as he sipped, Keith tasted honey. A lot of honey. At first the liquid stung as he swallowed, then it began to work its magic, Brian watching him until every drop had gone.

'Another?'

'Not yet,' Keith said, surprising himself with the returning clarity of his words.

'Next job.' Brian reached into a paper bag he had brought with him, pulling out a tube. 'Analgesic gel. You're to rub it on your throat and neck, whenever it's needed.'

Puzzled, Keith took the tube, gazing at Brian as he did so. 'How much do you know?' he asked.

'Not a lot,' was Brian's cheerful reply. 'We've been sitting it out in a field somewhere for what felt like hours. Hinton's orders.' He did not reveal the end of the ACC's side of the phone call. 'Get to Keith as soon as you're allowed. If he needs to talk, let him – and then keep your mouth shut afterwards, d'ye hear?'

Brian went back to the kitchen for another steaming mug to which whisky was added. The DCI said nothing as she unobtrusively but intently followed Keith's recovery. She saw him sip the fresh toddy and realized he was swallowing more easily as over-tensed muscles relaxed. Brian chatted of small events in Lydney and the surrounding villages, giving Keith time to feel energy begin to course through him again. With this came the ability to sit upright without shaking.

'You've had a very difficult few days, Keith, and no real sleep,' Joan Leggatt told him. 'Mr Hinton's put you on immediate leave – at least until your wife is more mobile. You should have time together.'

The sonorous ticking of the grandfather clock in the hall was a background reminder of that time passing steadily and inexorably. As the seconds were marked, thoughts became ordered, logical.

'What have I done?' Keith murmured. 'Laverton was a peaceful community until I went there. All that's gone.'

His colleagues were relieved to hear his voice normal again, even if it was a little husky.

'Come on, Keith, get a grip,' was advice given cheerfully by Brian. 'You're only thinking that way because you were

265

right in the middle of events with no time to catch your breath.'

'But you don't know –'

'Keith!' The DCI's voice had a fibre of steel running through it. 'You've been working undercover and you know what that means. Only a handful of us have any information and none of it will escape. Officially, the only occurrence was that of a dead man being dumped in a village in the north of the county. A rumour has come out of HQ, I'm afraid, that a Birmingham gang had taken exception to the deceased and drove deep into the country-side to dump the body. It happens.'

Brian was nodding. 'Yes, it does. Then there was that fire near where you were staying but I gather nobody was badly hurt. I saw a couple of lines on it in the Gloucester paper.'

'That's ridiculous!'

'Is it?'

'For heaven's sake, Brian, after that there were police with guns everywhere!'

Joan Leggatt smiled bleakly. 'Were there, Keith? It's in our newsletter that an isolated country house was used for a training exercise by a couple of armed response units. Not a shot fired.'

Keith lay back and closed his eyes. If everything he had endured in the last two or three days was a nightmare, he was going mad.

'You're exhausted,' the DCI said quietly. 'Catch up on your sleep and when you and Jenny are ready, get back to work. Two or three shifts and you'll soon be convinced, along with everyone else, you've had a bit of a break in the Cotswolds – and that's all. Don't forget, when you've been undercover it's damned hard to get through each day afterwards as though nothing had happened.'

He heard the voice, the words, and was aware of what she was trying to do. In London there had been a derelict warehouse and a car park, a no-go area beneath high rise flats filled with terrified residents. Both operations had been successful but had ended in blood and mangled bodies. Covert meant exactly that. At all times.

'Jenny and Emma?'

She gazed at him, the intensity of it a strange source of strength. 'You listened to Colonel Sinclair. Devlin deserved to die and you went to your own limits to prove he was a killer. I believe you were right to do so, Keith, whatever risks you took, but you'll have to learn to live with everyone thinking the girls were involved in a parking rage incident which went wrong, miles away from your aunt's house.'

Brian frowned. 'That Sinclair, strange chap. Who was he? SO13 or MI5?'

Keith shook his head. 'Hinton never said. I only knew he was after Devlin.'

'A madman,' Joan Leggatt decided. 'Caught and convicted he'd have conned his way past half a dozen psychiatrists who'd have let him out to commit murders a damn sight faster than before he went inside.' The muscles of her face moved slowly, forming the gravest of expressions. 'We need people like Sinclair.'

Brian could see Keith was still not totally convinced. 'Would you rather be dead out there in your garden and Jenny still at risk when she comes home?' he asked and the question hung in the air.

Jenny. Keith had burned to keep her safe and had willingly offered himself. Even Sinclair had taken him to task for letting Cracker Devlin get so near to another kill. 'I suppose everything has its price,' he said at last.

The DCI's task was complete. She had kept vigil and seen Keith come back from the edge of an abyss in a way which would have ended lesser men. 'God willing, Emma will wake tomorrow and Jenny can come home. Yes, there's a price you have to pay.'

'I think you got value for money, boy,' Brian said as he stood and hauled Keith to his feet. 'Come on! We both need our beds and this time I've put a clean shirt in your spare room.'

'I'll leave you two to it,' Joan Leggatt told them and this

267

time the smile reached her eyes. 'Just remember, I don't want to see you for at least a week, Keith – but as for you, Brian, the day after tomorrow, 8 a.m. on the dot.' She sketched a brief salute towards them and was gone.

They checked the house was secure before Keith led the way upstairs. Brian was reluctant to leave him alone and they stood on the landing, saying nothing.

'Will you be all right?' Brian's question was less urgent than it had been earlier.

Keith nodded. 'Thank you, I will now,' he said and meant it.

'Then do me a favour?'

'Of course.'

'Next time half the Met comes charging down to Lydney to finish your job for you, will you let 'em? Please? I've had enough of you doing the "bitter end" malarkey.'

He was answered by a smile with no dark shadows, and Brian gripped Keith's arm before going to bed and not quite closing his door.

With slow but steady steps Keith walked into a room smelling of Jenny, listening to it echo with emptiness. His prayer was short, fervent, thanks that Jenny was safe and slept.

He did not switch on the light but leaned against the windowsill as he gazed out into the night. The weather was changing with the tide and would soon bring rain. Moonlight flickered as wind-driven clouds scudded and rolled across the sky but Keith saw nothing of the garden and the dancing branches of shrubs waiting for winter.

'We'll take him home.' Sinclair's voice had reverberated in Keith's head for what seemed like hours. In the glass of the window he imagined he could see a huge army helicopter speeding almost at water level along the Severn estuary. After the width of the Irish Sea it would avoid the Wexford coast, going south then swinging north along the shoreline until it reached the pilot's objective. Ahead would be the cliff on which so many swore Michael Devlin walked, indeed there would be some insisting they had seen him do just that earlier in the day.

In the quiet of the night Keith could almost hear the whirr of rotors, a door sliding open. Sleep was invading him fast but in his mind he saw a body falling, falling, on to surf-edged rocks below.

Cracker Devlin was home.